A PLACE OF STRANGERS

By

Geoffrey Seed

 Revel Barker
Publishing

First published 2009 by Revel Barker Publishing

Characters in this book are fictional but appear against a background of actual events. Any likeness to real people, living or dead, is unintended.

I'll never smile again (Until I smile at you...)
as sung by Anne Shelton, written by Ruth Lowe

Silver wings in the moonlight
as sung by Anne Shelton, written by Hugh Charles,
Leo Towers and Sonny Miller

He has died too often...
is from *Among The Talk And The Laughter* by Norman MacCaig,
published by Penguin 1974.

ISBN: 978-0-9563686-1-4

Revel Barker Publishing
66 Florence Road
Brighton BN2 6DJ
England

revelbarker@gmail.com

Every moral problem of the slightest interest is
a problem about who is to get hurt.
Herbert McCabe
Law, Love & Language

Dedicated to Group Captain Peter Drury-Bird
and Joan, his wife,
with gratitude and much affection

With special thanks to:
Fred Cleverley, formerly of the *Winnipeg Free Press*,
the late Michael Elkins, former BBC correspondent in Israel,
Anne Midgette of the *Washington Post*,
Anthea Morton-Saner, James Rogers, Laura Morris,
Kate, Bob and Danny Gavron,
Patrick Malahide
my wife Ann de Stratford,
the Wiener Library, London, and Yad Vashem, Jerusalem,
the late Zilla Rosenberg-Amit and all those others
who resisted in their way but are no more

Geoffrey Seed specialised in producing major TV investigations – from cocaine smuggling in Colombia and political assassination in the Balkans to bribery and corruption at Manchester United FC and the British army's covert role in terrorism in Northern Ireland. After leaving the *Daily Mail*, he worked for every leading current affairs programme – Granada's *World in Action*, BBC *Panorama* and the ITV series *Real Crime,* which critically re-examines controversial murder cases. For his Channel 4 film, *MI5's Official Secrets*, inside sources risked jail to expose the true extent of State spying on trades unionists and political opponents. The late Paul Foot described it as one of the seminal programmes of the 1980s. *A Place of Strangers* is Seed's first work of fiction. It was inspired by an intriguing tale a retired diplomat once told him over supper but which no amount of air miles or meticulous research could fully stand up. Seed has written about crime, terrorism and policing for the *Sunday Telegraph.* He is married with three children and lives in the Welsh borders.

Prologue

It will take Ella Virbalis an hour and forty minutes to get home from downtown Winnipeg where the skies are greyer than stone and there is ice in the air. One hundred minutes. Not long. But time enough for a man to die an ugly death.

At 4 pm, Ella pulls on the green felt hat and thick woollen coat she bought last week and takes Mr Wilson's letters – stamped with the Queen of England's head – to Josie in the mail office then rides the clanking wire cage elevator to the showroom three floors below.

She leaves by the store's front entrance, waving goodbye to the salesmen amid their walnut bedroom suites and plush chesterfields, and walks head down against a keening prairie wind to the coach terminal on Graham Avenue.

There is still a moment to ring Yanis from the phone booth outside and tell him she is on her way. Yanis sounds happy enough, maybe a little tired after his shift at the railroad depot, but he tells her he is OK. *See you soon.* That is what he says. Those are his words.

Ella joins a queue of shoppers, all wrapped tight against the weather. The Grey Goose coach draws to the sidewalk. Ella hands her ticket to the driver. She sits on her own towards the back, counting her blessings. When all is said and done, they are not doing badly. Immigrants expect to work harder than most. But getting a job as a filing clerk, even for three days a week, means they can now afford little luxuries they had done without before. They are even having a vacation after New Year, heading south across the border to Phoenix and all that glorious desert sunshine.

Six passengers leave at the Brunkild stop then the coach heads out along Highway 3, cutting through the unrelieved plain of wheat that bends and sways to the ends of the curving earth. Ella gets off in Main Street, Carman – a woman of fifty five winters with the blotched pudding face of a kulak on the make and running to fat. She passes working men coming home in heavy check shirts, parking their Buicks and Plymouths on asphalt drives where kids play ball and jays argue in the elms.

Yanis will be reading his *Free Press* by now… or making her coffee or digging over his vegetable plot in the back yard. Rosa should be home from school, too.

Ella walks up the wooden steps to her front porch, unlocks the white door, newly painted, and shouts to Yanis from the hall. He does not reply. There is no aroma of coffee brewing. And Rosa's coat is not on her peg either, though it is coming six.

She fills the kettle and switches on the electric stove. There is no need to but she re-arranges the plates on the shelf above then peers over the blue gingham curtains into the yard. Yanis is nowhere to be seen. His newspaper lies folded on the kitchen table. *Angry Khrushchev Warns The West.* The picture of his pig's snout of a face fills her with all the horror she prayed they had escaped for ever.

Ella goes back into the hall and the connecting door to the garage. That is where Yanis must be – messing underneath the car, covered in oil, unable to hear her.

The garage door is slightly open. The air comes cool to her face and smells... smells of gasoline, maple logs, paint. There is something else, too. Something unpleasant. Drains maybe. She is not sure.

It is his slippers she sees first... her present to him last Christmas. Plaid slippers bought from Eatons. Imported all the way from England. Not cheap. That is what she sees now – those same slippers, lying untidy on the floor by an overturned crate with empty bottles of Whitehorse beer half falling out.

Ella looks up as she knows she must. And there he is – Yanis in his socks and dirty overalls, turning slowly from a rope looped round a rafter and biting into the flesh of his red raw neck. His eyes are open but blank. Urine drips from his turn-ups. He has fouled himself, too... like a terrified child expecting to be beaten.

Ella's stomach heaves. Her hand goes to her mouth. She lurches back to the kitchen. The kettle hisses steam into the room. She pulls open a drawer and snatches the bread knife. She hurries back to the garage and forces herself to stand on the beer crate gallows. Yanis's body sways into her, heavy like a punch bag. His stiffening hand touches the inside of her leg with grotesque intimacy. He stinks of death and shit and she wants to vomit but has to stab and saw at the rope above his head till it frays and gives way and he crumples to the concrete like a puppet.

And in the unnatural silence of that moment, Ella Virbalis begins to shake uncontrollably. This was a day she always feared might come but she is consumed by another dread truth which she must try to keep to herself like so much else in their lives.

Never in a hundred years would Yanis Virbalis have slipped a noose around his own neck. This was no suicide.

Never... never... never.

6

Chapter One

'Three minutes to air, studio. Three minutes.'

Even from the gallery above, McCall sensed everyone's edginess that night – the floor manager counting down to transmission, the tech crew, the vision mixers in the director's box. A chill of unspoken menace had blown in from the slicked black streets outside with the men now watching from the wings, jackets unbuttoned and lumpy with guns.

Only one person seemed unaffected – the Prime Minister herself. Margaret Thatcher commanded the still, calm centre, waiting amid a serpent's nest of camera cables for her cue to address the nation. Barely a day before, she had stepped defiant from the ruins of the hotel where she and her cabinet were meant to die by terrorist bomb. Here was Boudicca and Joan of Arc made flesh, gazing into her place in history, a glorious imperatrix ranged between her people and the murdering enemies within.

'Two minutes, everyone. Two minutes.'

McCall saw the Director General and two fawning BBC governors have their passes checked by the same unsmiling Special Branch cop he had tried schmoozing earlier.

'All you need to know chum is I'm the guy who shoots the guy who shoots her. Now piss off, I'm working.'

The studio sparks glanced at the gallery clock then quickly adjusted his lighting rig. Sound wanted a last check on Thatcher's mic for level.

'Prime Minister, would you care to say what you'll be having for supper?'

'A very large Scotch.'

'Anything else?'

'Another one, I expect.'

'That's excellent, Prime Minister. Thank you.'

McCall moved back to the control box. All the monitors displayed the same unforgiving close-up of Thatcher's avian features... the raptor's eyes, the turkey neck.

'Quiet, studio. Going in thirty seconds...'

McCall knew serious Westminster watchers who thought Margaret Thatcher alluringly sexy. He didn't get it. But then, McCall had no mother to become Oedipal about.

His confusions were not put to bed so readily.

'…and cue Prime Minister.'

Bea was always uneasy about going into the attics of Garth Hall. The poorly lit rooms didn't bother her any more than the steep stairs, though the frailties of age were taking their toll. It was more the feeling of entering a crypt, a chill reliquary where the paper remains of those long gone were slowly disintegrating into the dust of a past waiting to claim her, too. The buckets beneath the leaking roof had to be checked regularly or they would overflow and ruin the bedroom ceilings beneath. But the weather was turning dry and cold so she had nothing to empty. The gardener said they might be in for a white Christmas.

Bea paused before leaving. There was no sound save for the sigh of timbers shifting one against another under the imperceptible weight of time. Her eyes took in the silt of abandoned possessions and all the pieces of furniture neither she nor Francis had wanted downstairs when they had married. She opened a drawer of an ugly sideboard and a hundred years and more of their family histories lay before her – copperplate letters of love and war, mutiny and trade, each full of hopes and plans and the scuttlebutt of daily existence. There were photographs too, curled into tight little tubes. Bea flattened a few out, pictures of soldiers and sailors and those who would grieve when they did not come back.

But who these people were, what their lives had been, she had no notion any more. Even for her, they were just memories in the minds of those who had joined them since. Only Bea and Francis survived from their ancient lineages of warriors and adventurers and people who had done their duty, whatever the cost.

After them – what? The days of their years, their passions and secrets… all this would slip from recall and there would be no trace of their passage to eternity.

She picked up one of the letters and its fibres fell to pieces as soft as snow. What had these ghosts left behind? Maybe a fingerprint of whoever had licked the pale red stamps in Bombay or Benares and posted their dreams across the world to the house where they were born and their spirits would return.

She thought of how little time was given, what little mark we make. Then she heard her husband shouting from downstairs.

'Bea… Bea? Where are you? Someone's stolen my keys.'

'I won't be long. Give me a moment.'

'We must lock up or else someone'll be breaking in.'

'No, Francis. No one's going to break in.'

The Prime Minister swept out from the Lime Grove studios in a black Jaguar followed by a Range Rover with tinted windows to hide the weaponry and field dressings within.

A researcher suggested a drink. McCall said he was whacked. It had been a long day. They all were. But for reasons he could not fully explain he felt an almost agoraphobic paranoia about being in a public place that evening. It had struck him before, working in the tribal enclaves of Northern Ireland where all was tear gas and hatred and no one knew when the next car bomb would fill the gutters with blood and glass and waste. He wanted only to feel safe this night. And to lie with Evie.

He drove across London to the garden flat in Highgate he had not visited for weeks. Never phone, never ask, never tell – that was their arrangement.

They had met in a bar, strangers adrift and remaindered for reasons the other had not needed to know. He was not required to send flowers or give presents and Evie didn't question whether he had other such comfort women or not. Neither felt bad about using the other.

All life becomes a convenience eventually... something warm, something sweet, something to take away the bitterness of what happens. Everyone needs that. But how to keep it? That was a trick McCall had not yet learnt.

He parked the Morgan and crossed the street. Evie's light was on. He pictured her dresser and its blue and white plates, the antique sycamore table scrubbed till the grain stood proud. Her bed was brass and iron with a hard mattress and soft pillows. She answered his knock in her dressing gown. Her eyes took a moment to smile.

'Well, well, well – '

'Hello, Evie.'

'– and there's you fresh from consorting with the Prime Minister. I *am* honoured.'

'You watched it, then?'

'Of course. Thatcher's a baleful old witch but she's still a class act.'

McCall followed her indoors. She nodded to a campaign chair. He sat down as she went into the kitchen. A tape deck clicked on. Goldberg Variations. That brought back their first time together. She had sat across him, hands clasped behind her head, baring breasts like bee stings and moaning till she came. He had left before dawn next day, fading from her life like they'd never met, leaving no proof they ever had.

Evie returned with two heavy cut glass tumblers and a bottle of rare Bruichladdich. She poured the malt then folded herself into the corner of a low sofa.

'So, McCall... looking for a bed for the night, are we?'

Both grinned across the bare expanse of varnished floorboards between them. Nothing more needed saying. It was possible McCall could get to love Evie's smile – slightly asymmetrical but true and honest. Not all those who had smiled on him were that. But this was risky territory. It was safer to talk of terrorism.

'Your lot must be on high alert.'

'No more than usual.'

'Come off it, Evie. The IRA just nearly murdered Thatcher and all her cabinet.'

'Don't start on one of your fishing trips, McCall.'

'And what about all this industrial unrest – the miners fighting it out with the police on the streets. The country's at war with itself.'

'Maybe it is.'

'So the spooks can't just be twiddling their thumbs.'

'You know better than to ask.'

'Just this once.'

'You're crossing our line, McCall.'

'Thatcher says we're under attack. You must be hearing something.'

'Yes, I am – the sound of lots of people praying.'

Bea sat profiled at her dressing table, brushing out her hair for the night. She tilted her head in the mirror, making the best of what remained and pouting the lips so many men once craved to kiss... and some had succeeded in doing.

In a silver-framed photograph by her pots of lotions and creams was a bitter sweet reminder of all that had gone. She had been arriving at some society reception, glittering in diamonds and fur like a movie star with Francis on her arm in all the pomp of his military attaché's uniform. How glamorous and young they looked, how they shone in those dull days of post war austerity. Even the spies of their opponents were mesmerised. Such times they were... all bluff and double cross and combat to the death back then but lost in unwritten history now.

Francis came into her bedroom searching for a collar stud box he'd misplaced – like much else recently.

'We are going to see him, aren't we?'

'Who, dear?'

'The boy... for Christmas.'

'Mac? Of course we are. I've told you already.'

'Is he bringing Helen?'

'No, Francis. Do try to remember these things. That's all over long since.'

'Oh, right. Such a pity. She was jolly good fun, was Helen.'

10

She might have been – yet she had still betrayed them all. But Helen wasn't the only one guilty of that.

Chapter Two

Garth Hall, half-timbered Tudor with a Georgian wing of soft red brick, rested in weak winter sunlight, the ribs of its sagging roof shading through like the carcass of an exhausted animal. McCall had never thought of Garth as anything but unassailably permanent, rather like Bea and Francis themselves. But that morning he saw the house for what it had become – hauteur all gone and as impoverished by age as an ex lover met by chance. Yet the remembered pull of this place on McCall would never slacken. This was where his life began and all his journeying would end.

Bea was pegging out washing on the orchard lawn as McCall drew into the stable yard. He had thought her a princess once, someone conjured from the pages of a picture book. Even now, silvery-haired and buttoned into the pelage of Francis's old gardening coat, she had kept all her allure if not her elegance.

'Mac – you lovely boy. Come here.'

It had been almost a year since his last visit. They embraced then each smiled into the face of the other with wordless affection. Bea seemed hale enough but, close-to, McCall detected a slight yellowy greyness about her face. They went indoors, arm in arm. Margaret Thatcher had all but broken the bitter miners' strike yet Bea's kitchen was still full of candles in wine bottles in case of more power cuts.

'That damned woman, Mac. Working people deserve a decent wage.'

'Sure, but she thinks the strike's all been a plot by the hard Left –'

'Typical.'

'– and the miners just pawns used to break a democratic government.'

'Because the workers won't bend the knee, it's all a communist conspiracy.'

Bea shooed her ginger cat off the table and served leek and potato soup. Politics were put aside then. The talk was only of all their yesterdays. It felt to McCall as if he'd never been away. Garth always took back its own eventually, made them feel at ease and safe so they never wanted to leave again.

'Where's Francis?'

'Can't you guess?

'He's gone to Russia, hasn't he?'

'Where else?'

The eastern boundary of Garth's ten acres was Pigs' Brook, haunt of kingfishers and grass snakes and fat little fish. In summer it eased off to a trickle but with the rains of winter it became a swell of fallen branches and debris washed down from the Shropshire hills. It had gradually elbowed its way into Garth Woods, nibbling at the banks where oaks, beech and ash held sway. This was where Francis built his shed, his *dacha*, like those he had seen in the Soviet Union during missions in the iciest days of the Cold War.

On weekends home, he would shout 'Off to Russia!' then be away in Garth Woods till supper, writing official reports to the accompaniment of a gramophone. But often, he would just sit and listen to the wind in the trees and the wash of water over pebbles, for Francis had much to forget.

The dacha was constructed of timber and sheeted in corrugated iron, painted red oxide. Inside were two rooms with shelves of books and files, a pot-bellied stove and a pair of soft leather armchairs. Power came from an overhead line beyond Pigs' Brook so it had electric light and sockets for a kettle and toaster. Here was Francis's demesne.

McCall's earliest memories were in this private brambled place, overgrown with rhododendrons and trees that shielded the dacha from those who would steal its secrets. When it snowed and the light faded, Garth Woods became quiet. Creatures that hunted, creatures that cowered, none moved in a landscape sewn into a winding sheet of its own making, tired and needing to rest.

McCall, the urchin child, would stand with his backside to the hot stove like Francis the man, Francis his hero. There would be stories then, tales of battles and bravery and the way the world had been before God's British Empire was blown to bits.

McCall saw Francis through the dacha's side window, setting up the Eumig projector he had bought during a posting to Vienna. Francis was rarely without his little amateur movie camera. Much of McCall's childhood was preserved in the square yellow boxes of mute Kodak stock that lined the dacha shelves.

Francis laced in one of the black spools, unaware of McCall by the door. He closed the curtains and switched on.

The Eumig's worn cogs squeaked and a beam of light cut through the twinkling specks of airborne dust and onto the little silver screen.

Suddenly, they were in the past.

Somewhere on an empty beach when sunshine splintered on the crest of every wave, a man and a woman run barefoot across gleaming wet sands. They stop short of the camera, put their arms around each other and dance a can-can, breathlessly hoofing their legs in the air till they collapse in a heap, happy and giggling. The picture changes and there is Francis again, an Englishman-on-holiday – trousers rolled to the knees, bowling a ball to a kid in a vest and flappy white shorts, slogging away with a new cricket bat and running like the wind.

Bea, her long black hair untidy in the sea breeze, smiles as she returns from the Alvis with their basket lunch. Francis chases the boy across the hummocky sand dunes then carries him, kicking and bucking, through the spiky long grass, back to Bea at their beach towel camp.

The child blinks against the sun then smiles at the camera and is gone.

For McCall, it was as if some escape hatch had opened from all the hideous and bloody complexities of the day and he had slipped back to life as it once was but could never be again. He had no recollection of that trip to the sea, only of what was lost.

The footage tailed out. Everything in the dacha went dark. Francis switched on the light and saw McCall. Both were trapped between then and now and it took a moment for them to shake hands, almost formally.

McCall lit a fire to get the panelled drawing room warm for supper. Bea wore a sheer silk dress stitched with beads of French jet and in the half light of evening looked like a dangerously alluring Deborah Kerr cast against Francis's ageing David Niven.

McCall told them about Evie and asked if she might come for Christmas. Bea could hardly contain her delight. Francis remained quiet as he had for most of the meal. Then he left, saying he had matters to attend to.

Bea and McCall moved to the wingbacks either side of the sooty brick inglenook. She rested her feet on a small embroidered stool. The table candles died one by one and the pious whiff of wax drifted in the silence between them.

'I'm overjoyed that you've got a new girl, Mac –'

He nodded and fixed his gaze on the child's alphabet sampler behind her, sewn in the days of smocks and fealty.

'– because you have to start afresh. Never forget that one gets over absolutely *anything* in the end.'

'Is that what you believe, Bea?'

'It's what I *know,* dear. Love's a cruel emotion. Hard to heal when it goes sour.'

The wind was getting up. It tore through Garth Woods and bits of twig shot against the drawing room's leaded windows as they talked. The weather forecast was for rain turning to snow. Bea asked McCall to check the buckets for her.

'What buckets?'

'In the attics. The roof's leaking all over the place.'

'Then why don't you get the builders in?'

'Have you any idea what that roof would cost to repair?'

The six attic rooms were reached by a narrow wooden stairway winding up from the back landing that servants once used to get to their beds.

McCall unlatched the wide plank door and felt at once the draught of childhood unease that had frightened him the first time he had dared walk up. The treads were gritty underfoot with peeling lime-wash and grains of fallen plaster. Here and there were the folded husks of dead bats amid the frass and fume of decay.

A moment later, he stood where once he had played, in a magical land of his own imaginings – a kingdom only he could see, only he could rule.

He saw again the forgotten soldier's helmet from the Great War, the guts of old wireless sets, broken tinplate trains, brown boots and white pumps, sepia portraits in wormy frames and drawers full of gossipy letters from the Empire's outposts, slowly being torn to bedding by the generations of mice that ran in the dancing dust.

Here were ghosts and treasures caught in the cobwebs and slanting sunshine where he would hide and seek that which could not be found or properly explained.

All was as it had been and it transfixed him now as much as then.

Who am I...who am I?

A jump cut newsreel of memories flickered through his head – rope swings, secret hide-outs in the woods, a cowboy outfit and a silver six-shooter firing caps in a cornfield gouted with poppies... always a confusion of poppies, soaking into the bloodied earth.

Bang! Bang! You're dead.

And they all fell down and didn't get up again but it was only playing, wasn't it?

Alone in her bedroom, Bea was conscious of not feeling entirely well. An odd, almost out-of-body, sensation came over her, as if she was drifting away from her reflection to somewhere between this world and the next. She was an intruder in a house she knew intimately and wanted to cry out but the mouth in the mirror refused to form any words. Then, without

14

warning, Bea dropped to the floor. Her face pressed into the rough carpet pile, yet she couldn't move – not her hands or her legs, not even her eyelids to blink.

All that was familiar became remote and unreal. It felt like dying, afraid and alone, her confession unheard, her sins unforgiven. She could see the first flakes of snow sweeping across the window. And Bea was drawn back into a past she never left.

It is dawn, pitilessly cold but the sunrise sky is clear. The puddles in the narrow street of worn cobbles glisten gold like pools of smelted metal. They catch Bea's reflection. There is fear in her eyes. Something is happening, something dreadful. Dark figures flee through the wire-drawn alleys below the virdigris cupolas of great baroque churches and across the ancient bridge above the sly waters of the Vltava. Its carved stone saints look down upon them, powerless in the face of the coming enemy. The town hall's clock face moon and sun spin in their orbits and a clashing of metal hammers signals the end of time. All colour drains from Bea's world. A column of troop carriers grinds over the granite setts of the sepia streets, guns snouting for prey. The hot breath of cavalry horses condenses in the chill air and soldiers in greatcoats, rifles raised, march where only trams once rumbled by.

Still the invaders come, drilling across the martyred square until, in one final balletic movement, their weapons all point at her head and her eyes are drawn into the infinite blackness of their barrels. As this image dissolves, so Bea hears the droning of bombers and fire begins to fall to earth from a molten sky. Then she is running through empty medieval cloisters, past campaniles ringing with muffled death... running so hard her lungs feel full of powdered glass.

A door opens before her leading into a big walled yard with tall iron gates. And in the icy street beyond stands a human tide of shadow men, each sewn with a yellow star, eyes wet with weeping, wide with terror, soft with pleading.

Help us... save us... help our children.

Who are these people? What is she to do... what *can* she do? She sees one man, alone... one among so many. His beautiful agonised face implores her like Christ's on the cross. Bea goes to him, takes his supplicating hand and leads him away as she knows in her heart only she can do.

And as she does, so the engines of destruction start up and black gas begins to seep through every street and house, over the green fields and silvered trees and into all of God's holy places for there is nowhere this poison cannot reach.

15

Chapter Three

McCall woke. He thought someone was crying but with the gale outside he could not be sure. It was a wild night. He needed a pee and crept along the landing to the loo. As he passed Bea's bedroom, he heard her muttering. He opened the door quietly. Bea was slumped by the bed in her favourite dressing gown, the one patterned with irises. She had no idea who he was.

'Get out, get out. They're up at the castle.'

'Who's up at the castle, Bea?'

'The Nazis – Hitler, all of them.'

He tried to lift her but she resisted, suddenly made strong by fear.

'No! Leave me. Can't you see their guns?'

'There's no one here, Bea. It's a nightmare. Come on, you'll be catching cold like this.'

'They'll torture me.'

'No you won't. Why would anyone want to torture you?'

'To find *him*, of course'

'Find who?'

'The man they want to kill, that's who.'

Francis was not around so McCall struggled to manoeuvre Bea back into bed on his own. He pulled the covers up to her chin and she lay rigid until whatever was in her head passed and she lapsed into an uneasy sleep. She looked as pale as her pillows, so vulnerable without the artifice of cosmetics and deathly still, too. It was a strangely transfixing moment – an affecting image of her mortality he had never had to confront before. The very ground that had once been solid beneath him was giving away and he'd hardly noticed. He could only stare at what she had become and remember how she had been. McCall held her hand and thought what a terrifying place the subconscious could be.

Some frames get frozen, others fade to black. But what if all that had been lost could not be found and cut together again? Who will ever make sense of the story and what has happened?

Show us the pictures in your head, little boy.

16

What pictures?

The ones you've turned to the wall.

McCall was always haunted by a vision of his childhood self, crawling like an insect across a sleeping face. But who was this person – a Sir or a Miss? And why wouldn't they wake?

He remembered a street of shops opening onto a village square where markets and fairs were held. But all were closed, windows hidden under canvas awnings and untroubled by trade. There was a blue-brick house and a woman getting him dressed, preparing him for a journey. Then some strangers came.

Say hello to the lady and gentleman –

But he couldn't. He stiffened and backed away but he and his cardboard suitcase were carried outside to a car. And so began a long ride into the unknown, down an endless tarred road shimmering wet with heat haze and cutting as straight as a lay line across the flat black earth until at last he reached Garth Hall. Here, they gave him porridge with golden syrup because they seemed to know he liked the sleeping lion on the tin. The new people sat and watched their stray eat every spoonful, fearful he might escape should they turn round for a minute.

And when evening came, they took his reluctant hands and led him upstairs to the bathroom at the far end of the landing and helped him to brush his teeth. In his bedroom, freshly decorated, his red leather sandals were unbuckled and he was helped off with the once white shirt and the wide flannel shorts that made his legs look like sticks. He got into the striped pyjamas they had bought and the lady counted his ribs as she fastened the buttons. They gave him a teddy bear to hug and he held it by the paws. Next month, he'd have other presents. He was going to be four.

Bea told him years later she had leant against the open window, bare arms folded, and stared at the stars of the satin black night as Francis read a story about a magician who made wrong things come right. His words carried on the evening air, still heavy with the heat of the day. Bea shivered and did not know why. She drew the curtains and knelt beside the bed. Mac's closely clipped hair smelled of disinfectant.

In all that time, he had not uttered a single word. They made sure he was asleep before creeping away to the drawing room. Francis poured them each a whisky and they had sat in their own chairs either side of the big brick inglenook, dusty with wind-blown ash from a long dead fire. The hall clock marked the passage of their thoughts which they did not share. Bea put a match to the table candles and sat in their shifting yellow shadows. She had got what she wished for and there was an old saying about that.

Here was the stepchild who would be their arrow to the future – but not if the world's new warmongers dropped the atomic bomb on Korea. They were living in dangerous days.

Doctor Preshous examined Bea later that morning. He did not think she had suffered a stroke as McCall feared and advised only bed rest. Francis was not as concerned as McCall thought he should be. But ever since McCall arrived back at Garth, Francis had been cool towards him, almost as if his presence was unwanted.

After the doctor left, McCall sat by the hall phone, unsure if he should cancel Evie's visit. Bea might not feel like entertaining. Yet without Evie to lighten the mood Christmas would be a miserable affair. It was beginning to feel right to let Evie see behind his curtain a little, to ask questions so she might understand. But he had let his guard down before. For now, he stalled and went to check on Bea instead.

She was asleep. One of the attic letters she had been reading had fallen under the bed. McCall laid it with the others in her bureau. It was not locked as normal – and neither were its two hidden compartments behind the alcove's carved pillars.

In a house of so many unknowns, McCall the child had always been drawn to this most secret of grown-up places.

'Show me, Bea. Go on. Let me see.'
'No. These are my treasures in here.'
'Can I play with them?'
'No, Mac. They're too precious for little boys to play with. And if I find you've been snooping, I'll cut off your fingers with my scissors.'

But now, thirty years and more on, he could look. The left side compartment was full of sealed envelopes, some rings and pieces of costume jewellery. The other contained only more letters and personal papers – and something soft and folded, made out of dark material. Even as he took hold of it, Bea stirred. She could wake in a moment. McCall stared at what he had pulled from its hiding place. It was an armband, old and frayed and bearing the inscription *Schutzmann* sewn in silvered Gothic lettering. He had no idea what it meant or whether it was simply someone's name.

But stitched alongside was something far more familiar... a white circle of cloth containing a Nazi swastika, blacker than sin.

Chapter Four

McCall stoked the drawing room fire with split cherry logs that cracked and spat beneath the Jacobean overmantle. Beyond the french windows, rooks and crows blew about the frosted trees of Garth Woods as smuts from a chimney. The sandstone tower of St Mary and All Angels was just visible and its bells, cast by Abraham Rudhall three centuries before, tolled for good people to come and worship.

Bea was improving but not enough to attend the service. Francis would go alone. McCall had an urge to pray, too – but to whom, he was never sure.

He picked up Francis's footsteps in the snow, going from the dacha through the stillness of the woods to the bridge over Pigs' Brook. From there, the field rose steeply towards the church. The sun was low in an intensely blue sky. McCall threw a long shadow but felt very small. He passed between the graveyard's screen of yews and thought again of Bea's worries about Francis.

'He treats me like a stranger sometimes, as if he hardly knows me any more.'

'What's his general health like?'

'He'll be seventy-five next birthday, Mac. I'm afraid we all wear out one day.'

McCall heaved open the iron-banded door from the porch into the church. It smelled of tallow and polish and stones laid on damp earth. He saw Francis kneeling alone in the Wrenn family pew where his ancestors had always sat. Their regimental flags, once so proudly followed by the *gallus* lads of villages thereabouts, hung beneath the hammerbeam roof, threadbare and gone the colour of dried blood.

Francis was religious in an odd, English, sort of way. Throughout his life he had believed in God but would not have been remotely surprised if, at the comedic end of it all, it wasn't one huge wheeze and he had wasted a lot of Sundays for nothing.

On this day, Francis displayed a humility McCall had never seen before. He simply looked defeated. McCall stood puzzled by the baptismal font. Exactly when had his hero yielded to this impostor?

The service ended and the faithful few departed their hard seats. Just Francis and McCall were left, alone in a timeless silence at either ends of

19

the church. Then the old warrior buttoned his long check overcoat and shuffled down an aisle worn smooth by brides and biers and those who had passed that way before. He ignored McCall's warm greeting and was strangely aggressive.

'Have you started spying on me, too?'

'No, Francis. Of course I'm not spying on you.'

'She does, all the time.'

'You mean Bea?'

'I've seen her. She knows I'm on to her.'

'I don't understand, Francis.'

'No, you won't. There's no reason you should.'

They emerged from the porch and stood by the fissured memorials to ancient parishioners. All around, the trees were full of clacking jackdaws. In the distance, a sexton in brown cords and patched tweed jacket inspected the grave he'd dug in the rusty Shropshire soil and which would be filled in the morning.

Perhaps Francis saw this being done for him one day then he, too, would be at peace in the earth of England.

'My mother lies somewhere about here, Mac.'

His voice became softer, gentle like the Francis of memory. He moved away to read the inscription on a leaning slab of plain stone covered in bird lime and rashes of yellow green lichen.

> Death, like an overflowing stream
> Sweeps us away, our life's a dream
> An empty tale, a morning flower
> Out, down and withered in an hour.

'No, this isn't the one. I thought it was near here.'

'Let's come back tomorrow, Francis. Have a proper look, then.'

'No, I want to find it today. It's got to be close by.'

McCall knew better than to argue. But it was only then he noticed Francis was not wearing boots or wellingtons but tennis pumps, soaked through to his socks.

McCall wanted to fetch the Morgan and drive him home. But Francis, six feet tall and wilful, suddenly forgot all about his mother and tramped off through the snow towards Garth Woods. McCall could only follow.

They reached the dacha and Francis's mood changed again. He let McCall kneel and dry his feet with a towel then refill the stove with more wood. Francis's walking boots were by the door. He just hadn't bothered putting them on. In a moment more, he had fallen asleep in his scuffed leather armchair.

McCall saw Francis had not put in his small dental plate, nor had he shaved properly. Tufts of whiskers sprang from the cleft in his chin and on

20

his cheek-bones, made pink by the wind and patches of broken veins. His thick white hair, once so neatly trimmed, was over his grubby shirt collar.

Something disturbing was happening to Francis. This most cultured and particular of men was letting himself go. Worse than that, he seemed to be losing his mind.

The hall clock was silent. It had always been Francis's job to re-wind it each night but he no longer bothered. Francis forgot so much these days. Bea, still weak and unsure about why she had collapsed, pulled on its ropes and reset the ornate hands to chime the hours. She thought of Christmas to come and those that had gone. They must really enjoy themselves this year, be happy and make Mac's new lady friend feel at home, then who knows…

She went back upstairs to her attic letters. Some had envelopes, others didn't and many bore the teeth marks of mice. Bea handled each with infinite care, as if these were the mortal remains of a loved one. In a way, they were, and that must have brought comfort to those with nothing else to hold.

It began snowing again. Bea watched from her window as it fell, softly, like time itself, slowly blurring her memory of whatever had been there before. Nothing stirred outside. Hard days were coming… cold, hard days when the earth could not be dug for the dead.

She saw again the walled yard and its iron gate through which the black sleeves of those outside fluttered like the wings of birds trapped in a cage.

Bea asks the name of the only one she can set free.
'I am called Arie.'
'Where are you from?'
'I live in the city of Vilna.'
'Then what are you doing here?'
'I was trying to leave.'
'What is happening in this place?'
'Our world is coming to an end, that is what is happening.'
'But why?'
'Please. There is no time to talk. I am a Jew. Help me. Please.'
And the wireless announcer's words drip like acid in her ears.
'…the slightest resistance to the occupation will lead to the most brutal reprisals.'
Long into the night, Bea hears the ceaseless movement of displaced people and the grating iron wheels of their handcarts, loaded with possessions and being pulled across the cobbles outside. And in the underground sluice rooms of Pankrac Prison the torturers hone the

21

guillotine's blade and oil the runners of their meat hook gallows. Far in the distance, great black locomotives coal up in the snow-blown marshalling yards and shunt their wooden freight wagons into place for the one-way journeys eastwards yet to come.

McCall saw in Francis's sleeping face what he had so recently seen in Bea's. This is how the end would look, both dead to the world. He had little notion of life *after* Bea and Francis. They had always been there – the constellations by which his uncertain life had been navigated. They alone had never betrayed him.

He crossed to the table, spread with a disorganised jumble of Francis's wartime papers and intelligence reports about Allied bombing raids for the book he had always threatened to write but never did.

An aerial reconnaissance photograph showed the catastrophic damage to the German port of Emden in spring 1941. The caption said a new bomb had caused people's houses 'to take to the air'. Nearby was an Air Ministry assessment of Bomber Command's fighting men that Francis had underlined in green pen.

'...triumph and disaster are met and vanquished together. If the first be their lot, the thankfulness, the exaltation, are shared equally by the crew; but if the "whirligig of time brings its revenges", they have mounted it together. They are of necessity subjected to strain but are men in the prime of youth. For them, the shapes of life and death are very real. Each man's life may depend at any moment on the skill and courage of his comrades.'

Francis began to move in his chair. McCall hurriedly put the papers back then caught sight of Francis's handwriting in his log book.

'Detail of work carried out. 4/3/40. Aircraft: Wellington. Duty: Attack German submarine off Heligoland. Remarks : Duty successful, submarine hit from 1,400 ft. Crew: Captain Fl Lt Francis Wrenn; Navigator P/O Thomas Eaton; 2nd Pilot F/O Paul Moore; Wireless Operator Sgt Peter Plowden; Rear Gunner Sgt Edward McCall.'

McCall ran his finger over the words like a slow reader and spoke his father's designation and name. 'Rear Gunner, Sergeant Edward McCall.'

He felt a tug on his line, far away, in the deepest waters of memory.

'Good Lord, Mac – you shouldn't have let me nod off like that.'

'Well, you looked too content to wake.'

'Decent walk, wasn't it?'

'Certainly was. I've made us some tea.'

'Good. I've got some biscuits somewhere.'

Francis rooted among his tins and found half a pack of digestives. He was back to his jovial self again, as if nothing abnormal had disturbed the regard between them. Here was the Francis of old, stretched out in his torn leather armchair, feet towards the open doors of the stove, every inch the pilot waiting to be called to combat.

The light outside was dying.

'So you still go to church regularly, Francis?'

'Oh, yes. I've got to meet my Maker one day.'

'But not for many years, I hope.'

'I don't know about that but I still need to understand my life and what it's been for.'

'You've led a good life, Francis... an honourable life.'

'That's what you think, old son. There's much you don't know about.'

'What don't I know about?'

'Most of it, I'm afraid.'

McCall looked closely at Francis and saw a hint of distress cross his face.

'Tell me, Francis. I'd like to hear.'

'You know, these days I can't always remember but I know there's something.'

'Something to do with the war?'

'Of course, everything's to do with the war.'

'But what about it worries you?'

'Everything, Mac. Every bloody thing I did.'

'You had to, Francis. The Nazis would've overwhelmed the world.'

'But I was up there, up there in my aeroplane looking down.'

'And so?'

'So I saw exactly what we did, what hell we created.'

'But British cities were bombed first, Francis... people died in their thousands.'

'Yes, I know all about that. But I saw what *I* did, Mac – me.'

Then, without warning, Francis's head went down on his chest. His shoulders began to shake, slowly, remorsefully. McCall put his arms around him as he would a tearful child.

'Francis, Francis... come on, what is it?'

'All those bombs, Mac... those poor, poor people.'

'You must try to forget those days.'

'How can I forget? Whenever I close my eyes I'm down there in that furnace and it's *my* skin on fire, *my* lungs full of flames and I'm responsible. *I* did it.'

In all the years and in all his stories, Francis had never spoken like this.

'You did your duty, Francis. You're not a murderer.'

'No, not a murderer... a mass murderer.'

Chapter Five

Evie's train journey from London took eight hours – yet another IRA bomb scare at Paddington then a landslip near Ludlow, caused by heavy snow. When McCall met her she was tired and cold and regretting the ordeal.

'If there's a next Christmas McCall, you come to *me*.'

Bea was well enough to oversee Garth Hall's preparations. An aroma of spices spread through the house from a juniper and port marinade for the Christmas day Parson's Venison. Every bauble, streamer, plait of holly and ivy, was positioned just right. Her cleaner, Mrs Craven, polished each piece of the drawing room's darkly glowing furniture and even shampooed the carpets.

McCall seemed restless and distracted. Bea wanted to believe this new girl was special, that he was anxious to make a good impression. She had never understood why he was still unmarried at nearly forty. He was no matinee idol but he'd had enough women. They fell for his eyes, soft and brown like his long twisty hair, but sad, too. Yet his relationships never lasted. No female could ever be content with him away at wars and far off places. They never were when he was on newspapers and they hadn't been since he became a television producer.

Bea longed for him to find someone and return home then maybe a child might run about the old place. Only the sound of its laughter and tears could buy the promise of tomorrow.

McCall arrived back with Evie shortly before supper.

'You're most welcome, my dear, most welcome indeed.'

They touched cheeks and smiled.

'Thank you, Mrs Wrenn. What a magical house you have.'

Bea guessed she was younger than Mac, self-assured and pretty enough. But her most striking feature was the hair – billows of it, gloriously pre-Raphaelite gingery red... exactly like Helen's. Evie wasn't some random selection. This girl had been chosen for a reason.

Bea instinctively listened for an accent, an assuring clue to class and origin, but detected only received pronunciation. She gave their guest her 'half-crown tour', showing her rare pieces of porcelain on the

24

Montgomeryshire dresser, explaining who was who in the line of ancestral portraits hanging from the pastel blue panelling.

'The house must be terribly old.'

'It is, very old. I doubt that Shakespeare had learned his ABC before it was built.'

'Goodness. So was this your family home?'

'No, Francis's... but we've lived here since the war.'

The door opened and Francis came in with snow on his gardening cap and carrying a heavy wicker basket of logs from the shed outside.

'This is Evie, dear... Mac's friend.'

Evie smiled and offered a hand that Francis didn't take. He stared at her instead, as if trying to recall her face.

'Brought a toothbrush? Could be stranded here for days. Bloody unions.'

Supper was onion soup, paté and smoked salmon but they had hardly sat to the table when the electricity flickered off. They were left in candlelight that could've made for more intimacy but only worsened Francis's temper. He picked at his food and drank too much. Then he turned to their guest.

'Who did you say you were, again?'

'I'm Evie, Mr Wrenn... a friend of Mac's.'

'And what work do you do?'

'I'm a civil servant.'

'Yes, but what do you *do*?'

'I analyse information for the government.'

'What sort of information?'

'Pretty routine stuff, really.'

'Yes, yes, but I want to know exactly. Tell me.'

'No, I'm sorry but I don't think –'

'What department are you in?'

'We work closely with the Home Office and the Ministry of Defence.'

'Is that right? So I shall conclude you're engaged in some sort of covert activity...'

'Mr Wrenn, please –'

'...what we used to call 'spying' in my day. Don't worry, missy. I've met plenty in your trade.'

Bea shut her eyes in embarrassment. McCall intervened.

'Francis was in the diplomatic service once, Evie.'

'Oh, really. Where did he serve?'

'Eastern Europe then Scandinavia, along the Soviet border... so he knows a bit about Intelligence work.'

Francis stared at Evie over his glasses.

'But only from a desk, you understand.'

25

McCall tried to say this wasn't the whole story but Francis cut across him.

'There's an old Russian proverb, missy... the less you know, the better you sleep.'

McCall lay with Evie in the bedroom he'd had since childhood. The wallpaper was plain yellow, the wide-chamfered beams plastered and painted cooking-apple green. Christmas Eve gradually became Christmas Day. The toys and presents of earlier times still sat on his shelves – Dinky cars, a clockwork engine, Just William books, a wooden fort and plastic planes to replay Francis's war.

The room was like the rest of the house, a kind of museum, kept just as McCall had left it... a shelter, should life go wrong. Here was security, an absence of threat. Evie was intrigued by it all, just as McCall had meant her to be, subconsciously or not.

'What's the story here, McCall?'

'Depends which one you mean.'

'OK, why don't we start with yours?'

'Isn't Francis more professionally interesting to you?'

'I don't sleep with Francis.'

'So what do you want me to tell you?'

'Why you're a bit of a mess, I suppose.'

'That's nice. Thanks.'

'Come on, Mac. You know what I'm saying. Tell me about your real parents, how you came to live with Bea and Francis.'

McCall took a moment to reflect. To answer was to embark on a journey with no clear destination. That's why he had never set out on it before. Yet why did it feel safe to submit to Evie's questions now?

'My parents are both dead.'

'I'm sorry. What happened?'

'Car crash. I wasn't with them. I was only very young.'

'So how did the Wrenns get involved?'

McCall went to his wardrobe and retrieved a shoebox – *Boys Size 4, Oxford-style Allweathers*. He took out a black and white photograph and handed it to her. It showed five young men with short, Brylcremed hair, togged up in fur-lined flying suits and leather gloves, checking a map beneath the four propellers of a huge bomber. Evie recognised Francis immediately.

'Wow, how handsome was *he*? Like one of those leading men in the black and white movies.'

'Wasn't he just? Francis was the captain and the guy standing next to him, the fair-haired one... that was my father.'

'Ah, so that's why the Wrenns took you in.'

'My father was Francis's rear gunner.'

'God, it's unimaginable now, isn't it? Every mission could be your last…'

'Yeah, thousands of young men… shot to bits, blown out of the sky.'

McCall took a second photograph from inside an envelope addressed to him. Evie saw the same fair-haired airman but a while later, posing in a grey striped de-mob suit and proudly cradling a baby. A slim, dark-eyed woman in a light skirt and buttoned cardigan leaned against a sunlit picket fence. On the back, someone had pencilled '*Lizzie, Edward and baby Francis, Somerset 1946.*'

'So this is you with your mother and father?'

'Happy families, yes.'

'And they even named you after Francis.'

'My father hero-worshipped him.'

'Comrades in arms, I suppose.'

'Yeah, skippers were more trusted than God. Skippers got you home while the other guy was otherwise engaged.'

They lay back on their pillows. Evie held McCall's hand. Her gentle interrogation continued for she sensed this was what he wanted.

'Do you have any memories in your head about your parents?'

'No… nothing at all.'

'Which means you could never mourn.'

'How could I? I was too young even to know them.'

'You'll think this is psycho-babble, McCall, but not mourning isn't healthy. Grief shouldn't be left to fester in your head, you know. It needs dealing with.'

'Maybe but all I've got to deal with is an old photograph.'

'You must build a picture of them as real people, talk to Bea and Francis about them. They'll have information, maybe more photographs like this.'

'It wasn't them who gave me it.'

'No?'

'It was just sent to my boarding school.'

'But not by them?'

'No, they were overseas and it was posted in Ludlow.'

'And it didn't come with a letter or a note?'

'No, nothing.'

'But why would anyone think it important enough for you to have, yet not say who they were?'

McCall shrugged and reached inside his cardboard box. He handed Evie a torn piece of yellow newsprint, flaking like leaf tobacco.

A couple were killed on Monday when their Austin Ruby collided with a wall near their home at Mendip Cottage, Churchill. Elizabeth and Edward McCall died instantly. Mr McCall had a distinguished war record, flying on numerous bombing raids as an RAF gunner. Their 3 year old son is now being cared for by friends.

Evie shook her head.

'How tragic… that lovely family picture then this miserable little paragraph.'

'Doesn't amount to much, does it?'

McCall's memory box was almost empty now. A thin gold wedding ring and a cheap emerald brooch lay at the bottom. Before McCall closed the lid, Evie made out a few childhood birthday cards, some letters – and a colour photograph of a slightly younger McCall, his arm around a smiling girl with striking ginger hair remarkably like her own.

'Who's that?'

'No one who's around any more.'

Chapter Six

Bea couldn't sleep that night. To close her eyes was to see only a kaleidoscope of faces – of Arie, of the Francis she had loved, of Helen and her reflection three doors down the landing who, please God, might yet be Mac's salvation, and of her long-dead mother and despicable father. But most of all at this time of Christmas, it was the memory of a child that kept her awake – the girl she was tutoring in Prague when Hitler's troops stole in with winter and all was lost.

That face, colder than marble, lived forever behind Bea's eyes for, even in the innocence of her nine years, she knew what was to happen when few about her understood. Bea still grieved at the wickedness of it all and damned herself for not doing more. In the bureau was a letter she had written to her father on March 18 1939.

I suppose the London papers will have reported the Germans occupying Bohemia and Moravia and now their troops are everywhere here in Prague. Those I've been unfortunate enough to meet have been civil once they established I was English. Mr Malindine at the embassy has been marvellous and you must not worry on my account. He is arranging my documentation and I will soon be home. I am told that Herr Hitler has installed himself up at the castle, horrid little man. There is a lot of confusion in the city and people are trying to leave for the countryside, as no one feels very secure. The family I am with are Jewish and they and their little girl are trying to get to safety in Poland.

On Bea's last day, she had knelt and kissed the child and wept at having to be parted for there was love between them. The girl took both Bea's hands and said she should go in life and peace for nothing else could be done. Bea ran down the steps and looked back at the house, though she had promised herself she wouldn't. And there at the window was that austere little face, old beyond its years and framed forever in Bea's time of fear.

Now, in the dark before dawn, Bea thought she heard the music of Holst. Mars, Mercury, Saturn... the bringers of war and messages and old age.

She is in Celetna Street with Arie once more, hurrying through the Old Town Square where Hitler's pennants ripple in the whip-crack wind. Arie's hands are trembling. He reads and re-reads the documents in disbelief. They commute his sentence of death.

'Why have you done this for me?'

Bea smiles. She touches his hunted face with the backs of her fingers and knows Christ lives, for she has saved him from Golgotha.

'Because I can.'

Her Jew will survive. The others, those lost souls trying to get exit visas like his at the embassy, she cannot help. No one can. They will be moved, maybe not next week or next month but whenever the factories of destruction are ready.

'We must leave before curfew.'

Bea surprises herself with the authority in her voice. The occupiers patrol the muted town in bricks of six with rifles and dogs. Arie knows Bea is right. Only spies stalk this place. He must take his chance for the talons of the Nazi eagle are at the throats of all. Bea and Arie hurry away like lovers eloping. Men in dark drab suits queue on the frozen pavement outside the Municipal House for their ration packs of 'Memfis' cigarettes. There will be other queues later... for food, soap, coal, work, registration and the last queue of all – for the final journey of the *untermenschen,* north to Theresienstadt and later, the bathhouses of Auschwitz-Birkenau. But that is for the future, after Adolf Eichmann arrives.

Bea and Arie board the tram to Wilsonovo Station. They pay and stare down at the slatted wooden floor. Nothing is said between them and the other strap-hangers. Silence is safer. They get off at the road junction where the signs point to Wien and Brno and Kutna Hora. And everywhere around them the beetle-black Tatra cars of the SS hunt the deserted streets. Bea and Arie walk quickly, hugging walls all billboarded with announcements of the Fuhrer's total power.

It's getting late. The art nouveau beauty of Wilsonovo's architecture is lost on them. A policeman with a silver-buttoned tunic and holstered gun checks their passports. He stares into their alien faces. A British passport. A French passport. Gestapo-stamped passes and British visas. Everything is in order – so why in the name of God is he not letting them go?

The fireboxes of the simmering locomotives glow crimson. They bellow and gasp, wanting to be off. Families and friends mill along the platform through breakers of rising steam, weeping and touching and passing oranges through open carriage windows to the lucky ones escaping to Warsaw. *Lucky?*

God help them.

Bea and Arie watch the policeman pick up the black telephone in his sentry box. Their knuckles grip pale around the handles of their suitcases. He talks quietly into the mouthpiece. His slit-trench eyes never leave theirs.

Lying on the bed where her mother in law both conceived and delivered Francis, Bea was confronted yet again by the near molecular intricacies of those random decisions and events that shape any one life. To turn left or right, to take a bus or walk, accept an invitation or turn it down – each option capable of creating a different future and within that, so other decisions will be made causing it, too, to be endlessly reshaped till death intervenes.

An entry in her little diary for that March read:

> *Caught the Prague-Nürnberg train and travelled via Cologne, Aachen and Dunkirk for the ferry home.*

But by then she had already made a choice and her life would change forever.

Bea and Arie look from one to the other. The policeman's superior arrives and examines their papers. The station is in chaos behind him, awash with humanity. He has no time to waste on this. Everything seems to be in order. He rebukes the officer and waves them onto the platform to be engulfed by clouds of engine smoke.

They find a carriage and sit close together. The train shrieks and lurches forward, slowly grinding out of the suburbs. Their hands touch, just for a moment. Bea twines her fingers in his. They are on their way. They look straight ahead. The engine picks up speed. The heads of other passengers fall on their chests, lulled to sleep by the clattering monotony of the wheels on the rails.

At Nürnberg, people come, people go, then the train leaves the half-timbered town behind. Bea wipes condensation from the window with the sleeve of her coat. Out in the black night factories and furnaces blaze in full production for the war everyone is afraid must come.

Great sheets of light and flame are thrown across the shadowed landscape. It is like staring into hell. Bea shivers and Arie puts an arm around her and she is glad. She looks into his sallow face, into the unfathomable eyes of her Jesus. How little she knows of him yet how unimportant that seems. It won't always be like this. When they get to England, they will become very close.

Bea has never been more certain of anything in her life.

Chapter Seven

Christmas lunch saw Francis in spirited form, if eccentric dress. He had matched a dinner jacket to cavalry twill trousers and his tennis pumps then harangued Evie about British unions marching to the beat of Moscow's drum.

'Stalin's useful idiots, that's what they are. Don't they see the threat?'

'Mrs Thatcher says she does.'

'And well she might. I hope you're doing your bit to help her?'

'I don't understand.'

'Come, come, missy. If people like you aren't spying on all these communist infiltrators and terrorists, I want my money back.'

Bea could barely hide her discomfort. She cut distractedly at the Parson's Venison – lamb done up above its station – and served it with potatoes and parsnips from Garth's own kitchen garden. After lunch they moved to the easy chairs round the inglenook and she was glad when Francis dozed off.

McCall attended to the fire. Bea thought him rather dark-eyed and pale. He could be sickening for something. She always worried about Mac. He had too much nervous energy ever to put on any weight. She had a photograph of him covering some African tragedy or other and looking like a famine victim himself.

Bea allowed herself a sideways glance at Evie. Her mind went back to a different conflict and the day of her own wedding, happily walking through Garth Woods to the church in that endless autumn sunshine with all those laughing boys who went away, never to return. How unreal those far off times seemed now, such a conjunction of gaiety and death they came to accept as normal. Evie caught Bea looking at her.

'Mac's been telling me how his father and Mr Wrenn fought in the war together.'

'Yes, but Francis doesn't like talking about all that any more.'

'No, it must have been a terrifying ordeal for them all.'

'It was... more than you will ever know.'

Then Francis sat up suddenly and fixed Evie with an almost angry stare.

'Aren't you the one who ran off with somebody?'

'I'm sorry, Mr Wrenn. What did you say?'

'Now you've come back.'

'I don't –'

'– Look, everyone... Helen's come to her senses.'

McCall took Evie for a walk in Garth Woods during the hour before sunset. He apologised again for Francis's rude and erratic behaviour.

'He's hardly the same person from one hour to the next.'

'Spooks get like that.'

'No, I'm serious. He's never behaved like this before. I'm going to have to talk to Bea about him.'

They leaned over the wooden bridge across Pigs' Brook. Water rushed under a thin skim of ice as a full moon emerged from behind the tower of St Mary and All Angels. Night was closing in.

'So Helen was your big love?'

'I suppose she was, yes.'

'The girl in your memory box –'

'– You saw her, then?'

'Couldn't miss her, could I?'

'No, not really.'

'Was Francis right... did she run off with someone?'

'With a friend of mine, yes.'

'That's hard.'

'I'd no idea. Not a clue – and there's me supposed to be a savvy hack.'

'I don't think anyone ever sees the signs... not till it's too late.'

'We should've been going up the hill there... to the church.'

'So Bea and Francis approved of Helen?'

'Adored her, yes.'

'They must have taken what happened badly.'

'They did, very badly. They'd built up on our getting married... it broke their hearts.'

'Didn't do much for yours either, did it?'

They headed home through the silent trees on paths McCall roamed as a boy and might have walked with a bride. Evie wasn't sure whether hearing his back story made matters better or worse. Sometimes, the past was often best left to lie where it had fallen, not disinterred to offend the senses again.

'I think this is another line you've got to draw, McCall.'

'I try, believe me.'

'But you haven't succeeded... why's that?'

'They had a child, you see... Helen and my friend.'

'Ah, I understand. When did this happen?'

'About seven months after we split up.'

'So you think it might have been yours?'

'I don't know and that's the bugger of it. I don't know if I ever will.'

When they arrived back, Francis's mood had changed yet again though not for the better. Bea helped him to bed. McCall said he wanted to speak to her alone. Evie stayed reading by the drawing room fire. Bea set some mousetrap cheese and half a pack of water biscuits on the kitchen table and McCall uncorked a bottle of Tanner's Claret.

'Come on Bea, what's wrong with Francis? Why's he like this?'

She started talking, slowly at first, as if to herself.

'I've known something wasn't right for a while now but I've just worked round it, put it down to him getting older, being under-occupied but I've been covering up for him so no one ever knows the daft things he does, but it can be so maddening, getting something so fixed in his head I can't shift it no matter how hard I try, and then he just laughs and says *it's a so-and-so, old girl* and I give him a kiss and we start again but blow me if he doesn't go and do something like putting the kettle down the loo because he thinks it's the cooker. I tell you Mac, it's awful. Sometimes, he gives me these murderous looks like he did to Evie when he woke up this afternoon, evil almost.

'There've been times when he's waved his walking stick at me as if he's going to hit me with it and he calls me all sorts of names, really wicked. Next minute, it's as if nothing's happened and he's the same old Francis again. I just don't know what's going on but I shall have to do something, get Doctor Preshous to call and see what he thinks because it's all so dreadful, Mac... so bloody, bloody –'

33

The tears began then, smudging her careful make-up into a sad, creased mask. McCall shushed her gently. She heaved and sobbed and pulled so hard on the little golden crucifix at her neck that the chain broke.

McCall let all this happen till at last she grew quiet and a sort of calm gathered around her. Bea poured the last of the claret.

'Never forget, Mac – life can be a shit. An absolute S, H, one, T.'

Chapter Eight

Bea knew time distorts and memory deceives, leaving only perception to endure as truth, for that was all there was. She hovered over the past like her own ghost, unable to exit the drama she herself had authored.

A storm rages as their train steams into the railhead at Dunkirk from Aachen. Bea peers through the blue beads of rain on the carriage window. The ferry they want pitches in the swell of the English Channel by a line of shallow-draught barges. Arie takes her hand and they run through the downpour, clutching their suitcases. Bea's coat is torn open in the gale and she tries not to catch her heels in the slippy steel tracks that lace across the quay. They buy tickets and board the boat. Freedom is but one more ordeal away, somewhere beyond the spuming waves.

Other passengers shelter in stairwells and cabins or draw courage in bars reeking of spilt beer and tobacco smoke. The salt-spray air is filled with the cries of children and those being sick. Arie and Bea go up on deck and find space beneath a swaying lifeboat. They hold on to each other and defy nature as they had defied the Nazis. And, in time, the sea quietens itself and through the drifting grey mist Bea sees a whitened strip of land dividing sea from sky.

'I told you I'd get you to England.'

They disembark and Bea makes a two shilling trunk call to Daddy at the Air Ministry. She waits to be connected by the operator then presses Button A and hears his fault-finding voice.

'What the hell do you think you've been playing at?'

'I've not been playing at anything, Daddy, just trying to get home.'

'You're just like your mother was, never listening to a word I say.'

'I'm getting a train up to London in the morning.'

'You'll need to buck up your ideas, young lady. There's a war coming.'

'You don't need to tell me. I've just escaped from the enemy.'

Outside the telephone box Arie realises all is not well. He watches her from beneath his wild black hair, falling in rings over the collar of his mourner's coat.

They find rooms in a small hotel in a side street, exhausted and needing to sleep. Next day, both are pre-occupied with the new realities of their different worlds. They sit opposite each other on the carriage's moquette seats, heading for London. Bea looks out at gently wooded hills and red-tiled villages. History will soon be written here, in trails of vapour and smoke from burning planes, high above the Weald. For now, every turn of the train's wheels brings her closer to Daddy's recriminations.

How can she ever tell him about Arie? *You'll never guess what, but I've bagged a refugee.* Or her feelings for him? *I'm really rather fond of him.*

Daddy won't salute any of that nonsense. What seemed decent and honourable – and thrilling – in the medieval maze of Prague's occupied streets will be scorned as yet another example of the self centred wilful ways she'd certainly not inherited from him. She could already hear the derision in his voice.

You do realise he's a Jew boy, don't you?

Put a knife in Daddy's hand and he would always twist it. Mummy discovered that to her cost.

Arie holds her with his messianic, poet's gaze.

'I owe my life to you.'

'You mustn't exaggerate.'

'I do not exaggerate, Beatrice.'

'Lots of people were getting out of Prague somehow.'

'But to what, Beatrice... only to that crucible of suffering to come.'

Arie believes the Nazis have begun the ultimate pogrom. This burden is carried in the depths of his seer's eyes. The Nazis hold Jews like him to be a plague bacillus, the disease in the blood of pure Aryans that is responsible for all their ills. Arie thinks it will only get worse. Not everyone accepts this. Mr Malindine at the British Embassy didn't.

'Prague has some thirty thousand homeless Jews at present but they're not truly political refugees, just people who've panicked and come here.'

Arie's disbelief isn't checked by Bea's hand on his arm.

'Haven't you heard of Dachau, then?'

'It's a holding camp, isn't it?'

'A *holding* camp? It's where Jews are being murdered for being Jews.'

'I grant you things are difficult but it doesn't do to overstate matters.'

'How can the legalised destruction of people be overstated?'

'Forgive me but that isn't quite happening.'

'Then why are Jews being hung and shot and burned out of their homes every day?'

'These are indeed trying times but let me assure you, everyone's doing their best.'

Bea took the diplomat to one side.

'Please, please, Mr Malindine... can't you help just a little bit?'

'I'm sorry but I have my instructions.'

'But matters of national security are involved here.'

'I don't know about that but I do know even people with papers are being turned back when they land in England.'

'This man won't be. He's different, you see.'

'But, Miss Bowen –'

'Mr Malindine... you do remember who father is, don't you?'

He did. And now, she is nearly home – with Arie. But the closer the train gets to London, the more remote he seems. She fears her part in his plan, whatever it might be, is almost over. A worm of doubt crawls through her mind. Did she misread that *frisson* between them in the embassy yard? Bea couldn't bear to think that. Arie attracted her like no other man she had ever met – so foreign. Dangerous, almost. She couldn't believe he would walk away from her now... not after all she had done for him.

He leans back with his head against the carriage window, eyes closed. She looks at him, worn down by concerns she cannot even imagine.

But what does she truly know about this man?

He told her he was born in Paris in 1902. His family name is Minsky and his parents moved to Vilna to start a timber business. They are clever, educated people, wealthy and influential. Arie speaks five languages and could have been a rabbi but is not religious. He studied philosophy and writes poetry and was visiting friends in Prague when the Nazis marched in. That was when Bea saw him queuing in the icy street outside the British Embassy. He has never mentioned his profession so she's no idea what he actually does for a living.

So on that morning in April 1939, clattering by the dirty back sculleries of south London, this is all she knows about the man opposite. It isn't very much.

If Arie Minsky is good at anything, it is keeping himself to himself.

They take a taxi to Bea's flat just off Great Titchfield Street. The city bustles and jostles as it ever did. But there is tension and uncertainty on the faces of those around them. Bea buys an *Evening News* from a cripple whose legs were blown off at Passchendaele. It reports the Prime Minister saying conscription into the army is being introduced now Germany is threatening Poland. Arie reads this and retreats deeper into himself.

There is no food in the flat. Bea takes him to a Lyons' Corner House near a toyshop selling tin helmets for children to play games of war. They sit in colonnaded gentility. A black-frocked Nippy attends their table. She wears a white cotton coronet in her neatly bobbed hair and has two rows of tiny pearl buttons trimming the front of her dress. They order mushroom soup, poached eggs and toast.

'For one so young to have such an elegant apartment suggests you are not without social standing, Beatrice.'

'No, not really. It was my mother's but she died two years ago.'

'I am sorry for that – but why do you not live with your father?'

'Well, he and my mother separated when I was a child and I chose to live with her.'

'Did that make some difficulties between you and him?'

'It has never been easy. I took my mother's side, you see.'

'What does he do, this father of yours?'

'He's in the RAF, an Air Marshal.'

They finish eating and as they leave Arie asks her something faintly unsettling.

'Will you show me how to use the telephone kiosk outside?'

'Of course. You never said you knew anyone in England.'

'They may have moved away but I need to find out.'

'You could call them from my flat. I have a telephone.'

'That is kind but the public telephone will be just as good.'

So Bea explains and waits on the pavement close by. Arie takes a small diary from his pocket. His back is turned but he is obviously talking. The call takes only half a minute then they return to Bea's flat. Nothing more is said about the person he rang. Bea makes up a bed for him on the sofa. She sees inside his case. He has two white shirts, some socks and several folders with papers inside. She cannot read what is written because it is in a foreign language. That night, as Arie sleeps, Bea makes a telephone call of her own.

Fog settles across Hyde Park and Westminster. Buses and taxis appear and disappear in a great conjuring trick of theatrical mist. Hazy figures scurry by, then vanish. Bea and Arie walk quickly through the damp murk towards Caxton Street. They find a café and Bea buys him coffee.

'I'll be an hour, maybe less. Wait here. Whatever you do, don't leave this place.'

She moves along the rank of cabs by St Ermine's Hotel and steps inside its marbled lobby. The place has been turned over to anonymous men in army uniforms busy about their business, which is preparing for war. Bea tells the receptionist she has an appointment with Major Peter Casserley. She waits by a spiky palm in a brass jardinière. Bea has met Peter several times before. Daddy would like them to see more of each other.

Peter approaches down the hotel's sweeping staircase. He's got his trademark red carnation in the lapel of a well-tailored suit of grey worsted.

'Beatrice – how lovely. Let's go up to my office.'

Bea is wearing a wine-coloured afternoon gown with embroidered reveres which her mother sent away for just before she died. It came from *Good Housekeeping* and cost seventeen shillings and sixpence but she had long since left Daddy so could spend as she liked.

'So you've only just got back?'

'Yes, I'm still quite tired.'

'And you actually saw the Nazis march into Prague?'

'It was utterly awful, Peter. Those Germans are unspeakably wicked.'

'Is that what you want to talk to me about?'

'Partly, but I rang for another reason.'

Casserley's office is at the end of a long carpeted corridor on the third floor. It is quite small and poorly lit. He has a desk with a sit-up-and-beg typewriter, a black telephone and a map of Europe on a plain white wall. He bids Bea take the spare chair.

He smiles into her face and gives her his full attention. He is a strikingly good-looking man, the right side of forty with receding dark hair. Bea accepts his offer of a cigarette. He lights hers and puts his own in a holder. It would be a mistake to think Casserley effete. He is setting up a secret army of saboteurs to fight the Nazis behind their own lines when the time comes. Bea knows this because Daddy told her.

'I've met this man in Prague who could be useful to you.'

'Go on.'

'He's got a French passport, speaks French like a native – and other languages, too.'

'Not too much use to me in Prague, Beatrice.'

'No, that's it, you see. He came back with me.'

'Did he, by God?'

'Yes, he's here in London.'

Casserley fills his fountain pen from a small bottle of blue-black ink and writes the date at the top of a lined pad. He waits for Bea to continue.

'He's convinced that Herr Hitler plans to wipe out all the Jews.'

'Is he a Jew?'

'Yes, from Vilna but he was visiting friends in Prague when the Nazis invaded so he couldn't get back.'

Casserley stops writing. He looks at Beatrice as if wondering how far to trust her.

'There's been a lot of clandestine activity in Prague of late.'

'What do you mean?'

'The Jews are smuggling their brethren out of Europe through there to Palestine. God's chosen people are nothing if not resourceful.'

'All I know is he says he'll do anything to help the British against the Nazis.'

'How do you think I could best use him?'

'For intelligence, Peter. He's got connections, all across Europe.'

'Not a communist, is he?'

'What if he is?'

'It's just as well to know these things, that's all. Maybe I should take a look at him.'

He stops writing and stands with his back to her, looking out of the window into the sunless quad behind the hotel.

'Does your father know about this chap?'

'No, nothing.'

'Or that you brought him back with you?'

'Certainly not.'

'Where's he actually staying in London?'

'He knows someone who's got a place here.'

Casserley sits down again. He removes the cigarette end from his holder and inserts a fresh one then leans back, legs outstretched and crossed, black brogues gleaming from spit and polish.

'I can't tell you how glad I am you're home, Beatrice. I've really missed you. Why don't we go out for supper tonight?'

Bea opened the ivory-coloured musical box on her dressing table. Arie had bought it for her in a shop near Dover railway station. Its little pink ballerina turned as she was ordained to do and the room filled with the tinny notes of *Goodnight, go to sleep*. Bea watched till the porcelain figure could dance no more for in all its tawdry innocence was the story of her life and the memory of a lover's first kiss, summoned back by the tune of a cheap clockwork toy.

Chapter Nine

McCall fell ill with bacterial pneumonia on New Year's Day. His forehead was hot and damp, the right side of his chest in spasms of pain. The white sheets were speckled with a fine spray of blood he had coughed up during the restless night. A locum drove out to Garth Hall and prescribed antibiotics.

Francis was nowhere to be found as Bea and Evie prepared lunch.

'You must think us a family of old crocks, Evie.'

'No, it's Mac working too hard that's the fault – and him not looking after himself properly.'

'I'm afraid you're right. I worry about that boy. Always have.'

Evie was due to catch a late afternoon train back to London. Part of her did not want to go. For someone who had read maths at Somerville and was an empiricist if nothing else, the indefinable *presence* she experienced in the stillness of Garth's brooding time-shifted rooms defied rational explanation. It was as if she was being called by those who had once dwelt there and now awaited her. She could just about describe the *how* of what she felt, but not *why*.

Less ethereally, Evie also knew she was being tested, auditioned to complete Bea's mission in life. But could she ever measure up to Helen's broken promise? Or did the entrancingly painted scenery of Garth Hall hide a stage door through which it would be wiser to disappear before the audience whistled her off?

McCall was asleep when Evie went to kiss him goodbye. Bea drove her to Ludlow Station but the London connection was delayed two hours by more bad weather. Bea suggested coffee and cake at De Grey's.

Flurries of snow danced around the spangled Christmas decorations still strung between the busy narrow streets. Clee Hill loomed in the distance, pure white against a slate blue sky.

'What of your people, Evie… your parents?'

'There's only my father.'

'Oh, I'm sorry to hear that. Your mother's passed on, has she?'

'In a way, yes.'

Evie knew she was not obliged to reply in these terms. But as McCall always said, everyone has need of a priest some day.

'How do you mean, Evie?'

'She left us… I was only little.'

'How awful. But you and your father must be very close.'

'Yes… we were, once.'

Again, there was a pause, a silence Evie deliberately left in the air.

40

'But not any more? You've had a falling out?'

'Something like that, yes.'

'Do you want to tell me about it?'

Bea smiled in sympathy across the table. Evie was suddenly close to tears and looked away.

'He says he never wants to see me again.'

'No, surely not. Why should he say such a thing?'

'It's my work, you see... he's never approved of what I do.'

'What's he got against it?'

'He says I'm a traitor.'

'A traitor? In what way?'

'A traitor to him, to my class... everything he's ever worked for.'

'And what's his job?'

'He's a miner... or he was till this damned strike began and his pit closed down.'

'I see... and your work, Evie – what is it you *really* do?'

'Can't you guess? Francis did.'

In his fever, McCall wandered through time and space. Garth had 24 rooms with attics and cellars and pokey places where maids once curled up after each long day. Some were shut off like graves from where the dead had risen.

Aunt Lavinia's was one such room, a little bed-sit mured at the end of a passageway, chilly and unlit and frightening for a child. Lavinia was Francis's aunt, a widow from the Great War who could go from happy to sad in a moment. But she had disappeared from his life one day and they would not tell him why.

McCall remembered her dressing table-cum-desk and red plush armchair set by a tiny hob grate. The rug by her single bed was worn through to the threads. Behind the curtains, bleached patternless by the sun, the bodies of emptied flies spun slowly from broken webs of gossamer. Her sensible skirts and dresses still lay in the chest of drawers where she left them, smelling of talc and camphor. And in the oval photograph on the wall above, there she was... Lavinia, forever 20, standing in front of Garth Hall in a pale cotton shift, bashfully happy, shortly before her wedding – and the telegram that would bring the worst of news from France.

McCall could still see her damp old eyes. In his early, bewildered, days he thought her a magician – an inventor of games, a teller of stories, the keeper of all the secrets of Garth Woods.

'Am I staying here forever?'

'Would you like to?'

'Can I?'

'Of course you can. This is your home now. We're your new family.'

'Are you my Mummy?'

'No, not quite.'

'So is Bea my Mummy?'

'More than me, yes. But you're very lucky – you've got both of us.'

'Who is my Daddy, now?'

'Well, that's Francis, isn't it? He's your special new Daddy.'

'And where's my other Mummy, the one I used to have?'

'She's gone away, my lovely.'

'Is she coming back one day?'

'I don't think she is, no.'

'Where is she, then?'

'A long way away so it's best you forget her. You're Bea and Francis's, now.'

So he does… and he is. They possess him, body and soul, and mould the surrogate son they want. But McCall lacks their warrior streak. He is made of a lesser clay – easily broken, hard to mend. Why didn't Helen realise that?

'I need to get away from all of this, Mac.'

'All what? What do you mean?'

'From London, all these wedding plans. It's getting too much for me.'

'Why don't we go up to Garth for a long weekend?'

'No, Mac. I want some time for me. A bit of peace and quiet on my own.'

'Something's wrong. What is it?'

'No, nothing's wrong, honestly.'

'Where will you go?'

'Haven't decided yet… but somewhere wild, somewhere by the sea.'

'On your own?'

'Of course on my own, silly.'

She holds his gaze for a moment longer than needed. Does he know then? Is this the moment he realises? She touches his cheek and smiles so he cannot see behind her soft green eyes. A taxi arrives. Her bag is already packed. Everything is planned. No words are spoken. So what remains fixed in amber from that day? Her marmalade hair, back-lit by the sun, new jeans, stone-washed, long legs wherein he would never lie again. Then she is gone with the life growing inside her.

Later, he would sit in St Marys and All Angels. Here, they would have wed, have had *their* children baptised. McCall imagined all the revenant faces of those whose imbricated lives of farce and tragedy had been played

out in Garth, staring down the centuries at him, waiting for the next act…
or the last call. After McCall, there might be nothing. Then he would have
failed everyone.

Wintry farmland blurred by the carriage window as Evie made herself
small in a corner seat with a book she couldn't concentrate to read. Her
mind was taken up with McCall, the lost boy, Francis going senile, Bea –
clever, shrewd, wicked old Bea. Bea asked and never told. What a spy she
would have made. Only the vetters knew something of Evie's background
and now this old lady. How interesting. It was a question of trust, of
unburdening oneself. And feeling the better for it.

The train came to an unscheduled halt between bare tractor-rutted fields
and long ditches of icy melt water draining from the dirty snow. Evie
shivered. It all reminded her of home, of Rixton Moss and the peaty brown
earth that heaved and shifted and could swallow a house. Gales would cut
clean across the flat land from the Irish Sea, tearing the sedge-fringed
birch woods and forcing smoke back down their chimney. She would sit
with Dad, still grime-eyed from his shift at Astley Green but with nothing
to get washed for anymore. She had gone back to Dublin… his wife, her
mother. *Gone to whoring where she came from.* Evie hadn't understood.
Not then.

Mum had unruly red hair, too. Sometimes, father would look at daughter
and she would not be sure if he loved or hated what he saw. They said
bodies could rise from the peat, sacrificed centuries before with the fear
still set in the face. Evie would dream of this, of finding her mother
floating in one of the long, dark dykes on the Moss, her hair trailing behind
like a wake of blood.

McCall had his chest X-rayed at hospital and was told he still was not fit to
go back to work. That morning he saw Mrs Craven, who had taken over
the job of Garth's cleaner and occasional cook from her mother, Winnie
Bishop. He asked after Mrs Bishop's health.

'Doing her best but showing her years, like the rest of us.'

'I could do with a walk. Maybe I'll go and see her.'

McCall's affection for Winnie Bishop ran deep. It was to her he went
during Bea's long trips abroad with Francis. If Bea represented the
manorial, Mrs Bishop was the village, for Winnie had her own reasons to
covet McCall.

Garth Woods were eerily still that morning, dripping damp with fog. He
crossed Pigs' Brook and walked up the church field to the old people's
bungalows that backed onto the cemetery. Mrs Bishop greeted him in a
clean white pinny, freshly ironed.

'I've seen you look better, young Francis. Pneumonia isn't to be sneezed at so you take care not to do too much too soon.'

Her kitchen table never lacked for cakes she had just *bakered*. As she went to boil a kettle for tea, the church bell began a single funereal toll. Through the bungalow's patio doors, McCall could just make out the black-caped vicar and a string of elderly mourners on a slow march through the mist. Mrs Bishop stood beside him.

'There's another who's got the secret.'

She was full of folk sayings and bits of country lore – couldn't abide knives left crossed on a plate, wouldn't ever pass another person on the stairs. Misfortune needed no encouragement. Hers was slate and chalk wisdom. Book learning counted for little but she knew right from wrong.

Mrs Bishop clucked over McCall as she always had, making sure his plate was full and he was warm before the gas fire, shelved with the Toby jugs and pot dogs he remembered on her cottage mantelpiece above the Coalbrookdale range where she had cooked and he had felt safe. She handed him a fold of paper.

'I've been clearing out. You have this… isn't much.'

It was a crudely printed coloured map of the world at war in 1916, draped with Union Jacks and patriotic servicemen.

'Got this for knitting a jumper for Empire Day.'

'To Winnie Gwilt, who has helped to send comfort to the brave Sailors and Soldiers of the British Empire who are fighting to uphold Honour, Freedom and Justice.'

'It's lovely, Mrs B, but wouldn't your daughter want it?'

'Doesn't like history things, her. You have it, young Francis.'

Few people ever used his proper name. Mrs Bishop always had from those first bleak times when she had fed him beef tea and boiled eggs and let him play in the Garth Hall scullery with anything he liked. She knew about the car crash and told Alf, her husband, she just wanted to take the poor little mite home because he didn't weigh more than a ha'porth of copper and couldn't speak a word from shock.

McCall smiled at her fondly – smaller than memory allowed, the colour gone from her pot doll's cheeks and her hair no more than a winter frost.

'It's really kind, Mrs B. A lovely present.'

'I've writ some words on the back.'

He read them, knowing she meant every one. Then she produced an envelope of photographs and spread them across the table like Tarot cards. McCall had not seen these before – little Box Brownie prints of Alf, tie-less and tipsy outside The Plough, leaning on the handlebars of his Rudge; Mrs Bishop looking self-conscious on a day out, wearing other people's cast offs and hoping it didn't show.

And there was a picture of McCall, no more than seven, laughing on Mrs Bishop's back step with David, the boy she would lose to leukaemia and who now lay on the other side of her garden wall. McCall smiled to himself and shook his head.

'God fits the back for the burden, Francis –'

Both boys were in short pants, sandals, home made pullovers and happy. David was a late baby and all the more loved for that. But in the picture, his dark eyes were already hollowing out. She must have known, even then. She would have to give him back.

'– but Alf was never the same after. Killed him in the end, it did.'

'I can just about remember David's funeral.'

'I can never forget it.'

'What a heartbreak for you.'

'If you'd not been there to look after, Francis, I think I'd have done myself in.'

McCall thought he should go. But Mrs B kept ruching the edge of her pinny and clearing her throat. She had more to impart, something bottled up and corked with age.

'Never seemed right to me, not fair at all.'

'You mean about David?'

'Not just that, though the Lord knows it hurt enough.'

'What, then, Mrs B?'

She picked at the tablecloth, biding her time. When her words came, they were as bitter as only the old can make them, dried in a heart shrivelled by hurt.

'Them at Garth… didn't always want you, you know… not as much as me.'

'Bea and Francis? But they took me in when I had no one.'

'Not your own flesh and blood, they wasn't.'

'No, but they were the next best thing –'

'– As I could've been. I prided in you. I was as close to you as them, wasn't I?'

'Of course – as good as any mother to me, you were.'

'Well, there's some that forgot that in all their goings-on.'

He walked home through the graveyard where David lay. The village children had filed into the dark church from the sunshine of their playground to sing *All Things Bright And Beautiful* for a friend who would not be coming back. Of the ceremony itself, McCall's only memory was of all the flapping black-winged birds that fell about his head from the bell tower.

David had been a brother substitute. But he became someone else who vanished from his life for a reason McCall never understood. Maybe he

45

had done something wrong or they hadn't liked him. Until now, he had never thought of Bea and Francis feeling that way.

McCall was tired after his walk and went to his bedroom. He re-read the words Mrs Bishop had written on the back of the map she had given him.

'To my boy Francis, to remember me by. Affectionately yours, Mrs B.'

He opened his memory box and took out the envelope he had received at school many years before with the photograph of him as a baby with his parents. Give or take a bit of arthritis and failing sight, they had been written by the same person – no scholar but neat and tidy and legible. He had always suspected Mrs Bishop sent the picture. What he could not work out was why – or how she had got it.

Chapter Ten

So Evie's father had disowned her. Snap.

Bea leaves St Ermine's Hotel and collects Arie from the café. They disappear into the discreet London smog, arms linked, safe from those who would not approve. Bea tells Arie that Casserley is interested in him.

'He said they're planning something special.'

'What sort of thing?'

'Casserley wouldn't say but his people will contact you.'

They hurry along pavements lacquered by harsh electric light that spills from little shops and restaurants. There is something of Prague's dark menace about the streets and the strangers passing by, eyes watchful from beneath the brims of their hats. Bea, eight years younger than Arie, intelligent but self-centred and mercurial, feels an aphrodisiac sense of power flowing from being privy to secrets. Matters of life and death are in her hands. She is taking part in history. But Arie says nothing will prepare her – or the world – for what is to come.

'How can you know this?'

'How does a poet know anything?'

'But why would the Germans kill all the Jews? It doesn't make sense.'

'Didn't you know? We and the Bolsheviks are in a conspiracy to dominate the world.'

'No one can possibly believe that.'

'Hitler says it so the Germans believe it.'

'But they're such cultured people. Everyone knows.'

'Yet they will hunt us down like vermin until we are no more.'

Bea has no reference points – no folk memory of pogroms or burning ghettoes or a thousand years of Jew-baiting and blood letting. Arie says even those who have will not understand, either.

They reach Bea's apartment where Arie will stay until the future is decided. Her father, the Air Marshal, won't be informed. Bea plans to see him in his rooms in Bentinck Street at the weekend. She had telephoned him and told him more of her escape from Czechoslovakia and the peril she had been in.

'We're all in peril, Beatrice. That's why there's going to be a war.'

Days pass. Arie goes out most mornings. He does not say where he has been or what he has done. Bea knows better than to ask but feels excluded and does not like that at all. He never returns before supper, sometimes even later.

Now he stands leaning against the sink. The trousers of his dark suit shine with wear. He looks through the net curtains at a group of children playing outside, swinging on a rope tied to the arm of a gas lamp. Their shouts and laughter come through the slightly sulphurous air. Bea wonders about Arie's family. Where are they this night? She daren't ask – and he never talks of them.

Arie boils a kettle of water for tea. She notices how noiselessly he moves. He pours. His fingers are taperingly long, like a musician's. He sips his tea which he takes with lemon, not milk, and with one spoonful of white sugar.

Then Bea's telephone rings out. The unexpectedness of the bell startles her. She rises to answer it but Arie is up from his chair first. He motions her to stay still and quiet then goes into the hallway and lifts the receiver. Bea hears him talking in a low voice but not in English. Arie returns and finishes his drink. He offers no explanation. His eyes are hooded and black. He is not sleeping properly.

'Arie... look, you must tell me. I will be able to help you, won't I?'

'In what way do you mean?'

'With whatever Casserley gives you to do.'

Arie pours more tea for them, taking time to find the right words.

'Beatrice, what is to come will not be like Prague.'

'No, I realise that.'

'This war started for some of us a long time ago and you will come to see that what happened in Prague was just a game... a little game like those children outside might play.'

47

'It didn't feel like a game. It just made me want to fight the Nazis even more.'

'And so you will but you must not hope for something Major Casserley cannot allow. The war that is coming will be fought in many different ways and places. Do you understand?'

Bea understands all right. She is not to have another starring role like that in Prague. She feels cheated and angry like a child denied its own way.

'Who was that on my telephone?'

'Someone you would not know.'

'Maybe not, but who was it?'

'Beatrice, please... I am humbled by all your kindnesses but I cannot answer.'

'It was a woman, wasn't it?'

'No, not a woman – a comrade.'

Why should she believe him? She gets up and washes their cups at the sink so he doesn't see the tears she cannot stop. If it was not another woman then he is going to his death with Casserley and she will have brought it about and will suffer like all those widows after the Great War. Suddenly, she is aware of time passing.

'How long before Casserley's ready?'

'Soon, very soon.'

'And then?'

'I'll be sent for special training.'

'How do you know all this?'

'We're not without friends, Beatrice.'

'They couldn't help you in Prague, could they?'

'No, then there was only you.'

'So why can't it be me again... both of us – working here for Casserley?'

'Understand this, Beatrice. There is a gun to our heads wherever we fight.'

'Might you be sent abroad?'

'I will be sent to wherever I'm of most use. Those will be my orders.'

Bea is unable not to cry openly now. Arie comes to her and holds her. He has not done this before, not in this way. There is a new tenderness about him... a compassion for her and maybe for himself, too. Arie knows they are trapped in this hour glass together, helpless against the gravity of events.

They kiss, gently at first. She is aware of the roughness of his chin and the tight, tensile feel of his shirted back. It excites her like nothing she has ever experienced before. Bea knows what is to happen next. It is as if she was created for this moment, this sweet meeting of destinies, pre-ordained like their first had been.

She prays he needs her as much as she wants him. Whatever she had been given in her indulged life was as nothing when set against her longing to possess this Christ-faced man.

She leads him to the bed where none but her has ever slept. The light outside is failing. The children have finished their game. Bea unbuttons her dress and allows it to fall to the floor. Arie watches but does not move. She takes off her remaining clothes, indifferent to modesty or convention and stands before him like an offering to the gods who cast them together.

'Come, Arie… for me. Please.'

In a moment more, they are in bed. She takes him unto herself, takes the life which is hers and sustains her own, caressing, biting, loving the whip-cord body that writhes in spasm in her arms till he is spent and wordless in the dark by her side.

They lie covered by a white sheet like the newly dead.

Night passes. Bea stirs. She hugs Arie who hasn't slept. He is warmed by the closeness but afraid of the breaking dawn. She makes tea and brings it to him. They sit, backs against the bedhead, still naked. Bea is vibrantly alive, initiated at last into womanhood and all its power. But Arie's face is grey with guilt. Bea fears he will now talk of the wife he must surely have and the children he has lost in the east. She kneels astride him and takes his face in her hands.

'What is it, Arie… what's wrong?'

'Why did you choose me?'

'I didn't choose you. It was written, it was meant to be.'

'I do not believe in predestination, Beatrice. We all have free will.'

'Yes, but in that queue, in the embassy yard… I saw you and I knew.'

'You knew what?'

'That our lives were somehow meant to join together.'

'And because of a stranger coming to that place, I should live while others die?'

Arie is confronting an idea far outside political theory and rationality.

'That you should come from your country, Beatrice… should be there at that exact moment and feel this way about me, a stranger. Explain this to me, please.'

'I can't but it was like I'd always known you'd be there, waiting for me to arrive.'

'No, this I cannot understand. It is beyond all calculation.'

'But that's what I felt. That's what happened.'

His face betrays confusion and helplessness. Somewhere, hidden within him, there is also a terrible fury, blown from the desert of grief he has been forced to leave. For the moment, it is controlled but its day will come.

49

Before anything else can be said, the apartment door is banged. Arie gets out of bed quickly. He pulls on his clothes, unwashed in a heap on the floor, and orders her to answer. Bea wraps herself in a dressing gown. Standing on the step is Peter Casserley and another man in civvies. Casserley tips his trilby to her.

'Beatrice, good morning. Your guest decent enough to receive visitors?'

He pushes passed her unbidden and enters the flat. Arie emerges from the bedroom, fully dressed and holding the cheap leather suitcase he had carried from Prague.

'Minsky – glad you're ready. Say your adieus, there's a good man.'

Bea knows from Arie's eyes what has been done behind her back. She can think of nothing to say, not in sorrow or anger or supplication. Events she herself contrived are in spate. The urge to kiss him, to cling to him or demand of Casserley his safe return – all this must be suppressed. She can do nothing but hold his poet's hands in hers and grieve. Arie is marched from the flat as if he is being arrested and taken into custody. Casserley leads the way. Arie gets into the back of a waiting saloon.

Bea, alone and cold on the pavement, tries to glimpse a final image of the unmoving face she adores. Then, all that is precious and all that is rightfully hers is driven away. It is followed by a second car, a black Humber with a uniformed chauffeur and a limp RAF pennant on its polished wing.

As it passes, so Bea sees her father staring out at her with contempt and distaste.

Chapter Eleven

McCall took a welfare call from a freelance cameraman he had once shared a ditch with during a forgotten little African war.

'You need a holiday, chum. Somewhere warm. Pneumonia isn't funny.'

'I'm not laughing.'

'Did you hear Ricky Benson's died?'

'The stills guy? But he's younger than me.'

'That's my point. But it was him in the coffin, believe me. I said to his wife "Ricky's looking a bit peeky" and she says "Well, he's not had a drink for three days".'

'We all need the love of a good woman.'

'Listen, McCall – do yourself a favour and get on a plane and get some sunshine.'

'Yeah, but where's the buzz lying on a beach?'

'There isn't one but it's a fucking sight safer than getting a tan in Bongo-Bongoland.'

It took all morning for the results of McCall's second hospital X-ray to come back. The inflammation in his lungs had not reduced enough to sign him off. He drove back to Garth and found Bea's note propped against the sugar bowl on the kitchen table. With it was a photograph of his father he had known nothing about.

Thought you might like this, Mac. Forgotten we still had it, somehow lost in the bureau. Am shopping with Mrs Craven. Try to keep an eye on Francis.

Here was only the third picture of Edward McCall he had ever seen... this stranger who'd given him life. It was black and white like the others and showed the same intense young man at the controls of a Wellington bomber's tail gun as he prepared to leave on another mission. His pale ascetic face looked so unsuited to the utilitarian mechanics of aerial warfare. But it was the eyes that riveted McCall, big with dread and seeming to draw his son into that claustrophobic bubble from which there was no escape. Kill or be killed. On the back, he had written:

'All tail gunners must surely all go mad. It is like being suspended in space, looking into a void with no sense of being part of the aeroplane or the crew. I feel so detached, just me, running my own little war against the enemy, waiting and watching.'

Francis always said Edward had nerves of steel and they brought each other luck. That was how they survived.

McCall held to this as he put the picture in his memory box and closed the lid. But something nagged at him, some little pinch of guilt he had first registered at Evie's questioning. Why had he shown so little curiosity about this unlikely warrior, still less about the woman he had married and borne him a son? Who were these people, *what* were they?

He forced himself to imagine his father taking off that late afternoon, the blood, guts and fragile bones of the man, so aware that a single burst from an enemy gun could cast him down to earth, screaming at the stars as he fell. Only a fool wouldn't be petrified.

McCall, weaker than he would admit, became nauseous at the thought. He went to the bathroom and sank his face in a bowl of cold water. For a brief second in the mirror before him, McCall fancied he recognised this man he never knew. He went to touch his reflection but there was nothing... just silvered glass and a memory of terror not properly understood.

Evie gazed towards Piccadilly from behind the long net curtains of her office in Leconfield House. Distant figures came and went through the drizzling January day, each unaware of the plots and conspiracies fomenting on her desk. Here were transcripts of phone intercepts, tape recordings from MI5 listening devices in office walls and Special Branch memos written by cops who had got their press and trade union snouts pissed in Gordon's wine bar by Charing Cross Station or the pub off Fleet Street they called the Stab In The Back. The miners were now a broken force, down on their knees, never to rise again. Mrs Thatcher had slain the enemy within as surely as she had seen off the Argentinean generals without.

Dancing on graves could now begin in the Carlton or Travellers clubs or wherever power took money to bed and fucked the rest of us. God alone knew she had tried to warn her father without showing out too much.

'You're being led to defeat, Dad... why don't you start thinking for yourself?'

'Like you, you mean – spying for the bloody bosses?'

In the slanging match that followed, he accused Evie of unforgivable treachery and disowned her. He had never understood the females in his life. He made only one visit to Oxford, when she went up in '68. They had tea along The High. He asked where her accent had gone and why her friends were so la-di-dah. In such a place of silly gowns and funny hats, it was her father being laughed at. He was soon headed north again, back to a world he knew and she had left for ever. It was for the best she never invited him again.

He was not a wicked or stupid man nor did the Realm need much defending against him. But it was still a shock to see him in some covert police footage of a baton charge they had made on horseback outside his colliery. Miner linked arms with miner in a single, fluid mass like starlings yawing from a hawk. The camera zoomed in to the main troublemakers. Each contorted face was an image of alarm and hate, hands raised for protection against the stamping hooves. Evie knew some of these men – fathers of kids she had played with, husbands of women her mother had known. And there was Dad...

but no one needed to know that. Something Bea said when they had parted reminded her of all this.

'Never forget that laws are man-made, Evie. Some are so morally wrong, it can be one's duty to break them.'

She had really taken to Bea but the old lady's Leftist sympathies seemed so out of character. Then again, communistic traits often ran in the duplicitous ruling classes of England. That much she had observed.

Doctor Preshous had ordered McCall to exercise. He had taken to walking Garth Woods each afternoon, barrowing back fallen branches to saw for logs. He needed to rest every so often and would sit listening to the stream just as Francis had. Nearby was the great crown of an ash tree and its play dacha Francis had built for McCall. Here was childhood in a box of planks with a make-believe chimney and doll's house windows, all slowly rotting in the seasons, no longer a place of safety.

Garth Woods were overcast. But its dun earth would soon lighten with snowdrops and yellow aconites then daffodils, anemones and bluebells. The woods were all about life, death and renewal.

He turned towards the bridge over Pigs' Brook then saw something that made no sense – bits of paper the size of playing cards, impaled in the trees along the path. McCall reached one down – a page ripped from a hymn book with a verse underlined in green pen.

O Lord, turn not Thy Face from me,
Who lie in woeful state
Lamenting all my sinful life,
Before Thy mercy gate.

Others were highlighted with a verse from the same hymn.

And call me not to strict account
How I have sojourn'd here;
For then my guilty conscience knows
How vile I shall appear.

Some mad ritual was being carried out. Even as McCall retrieved the last one, the young rector came across the bridge carrying all the hymn books that had been vandalised then strewn across the church field. He seemed distressed but relieved to see McCall.

'I'm terribly afraid this is Mr Wrenn's doing. One of the ladies in the bungalows saw him and rang me.'

McCall hardly knew what to say beyond promising to pay for the damage. He turned back towards the dacha where smoke rose from its metal stovepipe. He heard raised voices coming from inside. Bea and Francis were having a row.

'You're spying on me again… spying, spying, spying –'

'Don't start all this again, Francis.'

'You shouldn't be in here. Get out. You're not allowed in here.'

'Please, Francis. Stop this. I just want you to come home and have something to eat.'

'You think I don't know about your game, don't you?'

'What game, Francis?'

'I'm on to your secrets and don't think I'm not.'

'I haven't got any secrets.'

'Oh, no?'

'No, I haven't. Now are you coming to eat or not?'

'Just clear off, you witch. Leave me alone – do you hear?'

Bea emerged in her long gardening coat and green boots. It looked like she was sobbing. McCall caught up with her and asked what was going on.

'I'm not a doctor, Mac, but I know I can't take much more of this.'

He found Francis staring into the wood burner which roared with flames. He looked up at McCall as if he were a complete stranger. On the floor were more ripped pages from *Hymns Ancient and Modern* and a slew of aerial reconnaissance photographs of German cities he had bombed. Francis threw one at him without preamble.

'See? What can't speak can't lie.'

'It was dreadful, Francis. All war is dreadful.'

'You know nothing, boy.'

'No, I wasn't there.'

'Well, I was. I saw it all from my aeroplane.'

'But it's all over, now.'

'Not for me, it isn't.'

'Tell me why, Francis.'

Francis started rocking in his chair in great distress, back and forth, back and forth, fingers gripped around his knees.

'Firestorms… firestorms. Bombs and incendiaries… thousands of tons of them. Everything destroyed, all the people. All destroyed. A wind of fire so terrible...'

'You were doing your duty, Francis.'

'My duty, was it? My duty to turn my fellow beings into living torches?'

'It was all a wicked waste.'

'Not wicked, boy – pornographic.'

McCall saw other photographs under Francis's chair – close-ups of German civilians Francis had helped to incinerate. Men, women, children, like seared logs, reduced to a third of their size in pools of their own liquidised fat.

'Come on, Francis. It's getting late. We should go back to Garth.'

'No. She's there. Thinks I'm not on to her, you know.'

'Bea's concerned about you, Francis. She loves you.'

'Strange sort of love, boy… still, she's covered her tracks pretty well.'

'What tracks are you talking about?'

'You'll find out one day.'

'Why not tell me now?'

'Because information shared is an advantage lost, that's why.'

'But Bea's your wife –'

'She's much more than that, little friend… much, much more.'

Chapter Twelve

This morning, the British Ambassador in Berlin handed the German Government a final note, stating that unless we heard from them by eleven o'clock that they were prepared to withdraw their troops from Poland, a state of war would exist between us...

The prime minister's voice comes as sombre as an undertaker from the wireless in Bea's lounge. She is standing in the bath, drying herself with a soft white towel. The room is full of steam condensing on the checker board tiles. Her face is shroud grey in the mirror. It will be lunchtime soon. But she doesn't feel like eating. Not today.

She pulls the plug chain and makes to step out onto the square yellow mat she bought last week at Liberty.

Her eye is caught by something in the eddying water – a thin brush stroke of dilute crimson being drawn through the swirling bubbles towards the drain. It seems to have no connection to her. Yet she feels something is wrong. It makes her afraid and she does not know why.

Almost at once, a fierce pain detonates deep within her, sudden and shocking like the blast of a bomb.

...I have to tell you now that no such undertaking has been received and that consequently, this country is at war with Germany...

She stares down at her treacherous body. Blood drips from her, exploding against the virgin enamel as the water empties away. Bea presses the towel into herself. A vivid scarlet stain, wet and warm, spreads behind her fingers.

She is overtaken by panic and runs naked from the bathroom. A trail of bright red spatters marks her uncertain passage over the new mat, down the woodblock hallway and across the green and white linoleum in the kitchen.

Bea sinks to her haunches in the middle of the floor and wraps her arms tight around her folded knees so she is small again, like a child, moaning between the cycle of contractions ripping at her stomach.

Then it happens... a spasm so violent that she screams until at last it ends. Maybe her neighbours will think murder is being committed here but she does not care for she knows something is being done to death in this place. On the floor, in the sticky pool between her feet, she sees the tiny creature her body refuses to nourish any longer.

She picks it up with such tenderness, as if it might break, and holds it in her votive hands, pink and precious in its translucent sac with fingers and toes, little arms and legs and a face that looks like a boy's. And in that head, what wisdom there would have been and in those sightless eyes, what love might have shone.

It rests now, this child with no name, still and starved of life so Bea will never know what it could have become, what it would have achieved.

Fatigue overwhelms her and she crawls across the bloody floor on hands and knees to her bed where she returns to the womb and everything goes dark. When she wakes, Bea boils water and every trace of the son she would have worshipped is scrubbed away so that he never happened... he never *was*.

Just like his father must be.

Outside in the street, with eyes so full of tears it is like walking under water, the faces of people and the noise of traffic distort and bend, and all the time the parcel in her pocket weighs heavy though it's only small, no bigger than a kitten and just as soft, wrapped in sheets of tissue paper.

She passes through a narrow back entry behind a restaurant where they throw their waste in bins. No one sees her. It takes only a second or two. Then it is over. But it will never be over. It will callous her heart for ever.

Even now, all these years later, those wormwood days were with Bea still. Such loss she suffered, such pain at the duplicity of men. She remembered Casserley's clipped charm at besting a rival, her father's glowering face. Of Arie, there was to be no news, neither letter nor message. An unbridgeable gulf had opened up between their lives. What happened in Bea's apartment was suffered alone, endured in secret.

Casserley's team moved out of St Ermine's. Someone said they had gone to train under arms in Scotland. Maybe that was where Arie went to learn the business of heroic death. Bea would not have dared ask her father.

They did not speak for months – not until after war broke out and he ordered her to join the Women's Auxiliary Air Force.

'We must all do our duty, Beatrice. Our personal feelings count for nothing at times like these.'

For the Air Marshal, the disgrace of *that Jew boy* was a family scandal beyond forgiveness, mitigated only by her meeting Francis the following year.

Bea parks the Hillman Minx opposite the officers' mess. Across the airfield, a dozen trainee pilots practise take-offs and landings in flimsy Avro Tutors, all string and canvas like the flying coffins of the Great War.

Bea, smart in the pressed blue uniform of an Aircraft Woman First Class, walks to the canteen. Her black hair is short now, cropped to regulation length. She is in regulation service knickers, too – grey like the thick lisle stockings the girls all hate but have to wear.

She rooms with another ACW1 called Joan who is waiting for her with a mug of tea. Four Harvard trainers just delivered from America roar over the canteen's tin roof. They duck instinctively but the new recruits crowd to the windows to watch them turn into the sun and wheel over the placid Wiltshire countryside.

'There's a dance tonight, Bea. You are coming, aren't you?'

'Probably not.'

'But it'll cheer you up. Come on, be a sport.'

Bea checks the time. She has to drive the Group Captain to Andover Station soon. She feels herself being stripped naked by the would-be airmen. The mature ones, those who have started shaving, call her the *Ice Maiden*. She is not deliberately aloof but they are just boys who have never done anything and probably won't now… not with the way the war is going.

That evening, Joan drags Bea to the mess. Orderlies in white waistcoats serve schooners of sherry on trays. A raw-boned Flight Officer called Maureen puts Jack Jackson's big band records on the gramophone. It is romantic dance music but that is all anyone wants. Joan says Bea should find herself a nice young man.

'Why should I?'

'Because we might be at war but life's for living, Bea. We've got to carry on.'

Joan accepts an offer to dance from a gauche trainee pilot, barely out of school. They join a circle of officers and wives and invited local worthies, all done up in Sunday suits and party frocks. Bea watches from a corner table, alone. A slushy Anne Shelton record is put on.

I'll never smile again

Until I smile at you
I'll never laugh again
What good would it do?

Bea wants to leave now. The tobacco smoke is getting to her. She steps outside to breathe clean air. A full moon illuminates the expanse of Salisbury Plain, empty and desolate. Bea thinks only of Arie, what he is doing at this precise moment under the stars of the vast, unknowable sky.

For tears would fill my eyes
My heart would realise
That our romance is through.
I'll never fall in love again,
I'm so in love with you.

The blackout curtains cannot shut out the noise of people laughing. The bar is doing great trade. Everyone is wearing a brave face, not wanting to think about what might be in store. Bea should not have come. She begins to walk back to her billet.

'Not leaving, are you?'

Bea turns and tries to locate whoever had spoken to her from between a row of poplars, silver against the inky blue night. It is a warm, confident voice, full of authority and familiar with command. A man steps from the shadows. He is an officer, a flight lieutenant, tall, open-faced and smiling.

'Stuffy in there, isn't it?'

'Yes, Sir. It is rather.'

'I was watching you. I was going to buy you a drink, then you left.'

'I'm afraid it's a little too crowded for me.'

'And I bet you wanted to be on your own.'

'Well, it's such a beautiful night.'

'Missing him, are you?'

'What do you mean, Sir?'

'Come on, we're all in the same boat.'

He offers a cigarette and lights it for her. They sit on a slatted metal bench within earshot of the forced gaiety they had left behind. Bea steals a glance at her admirer. He is older than the rest. There is a look of battle about him... eyes never still, always waiting for the next enemy.

'You're Beatrice Bowen, aren't you?'

'How do you know my name?'

'Your father's a brass hat.'

'What if he is?'

'That puts the wind up some people round here.'

'Well, it shouldn't. And what's your name, Sir?'

'Francis Wrenn. I'm teaching these oiks how to fly. But not for much longer.'

58

'Why's that? Where are you going?'

'Back to bombers, thank God. Get some action.'

They return to the mess. Francis Wrenn dances embarrassingly close. Joan gives Bea a leering thumbs-up behind his back. The boy pilots look on over their pint pots. They keep their mouths shut. That much they have learnt.

> *Please don't bring your lips so close to my cheek,*
> *Don't smile or I'll be lost beyond recall,*
> *The kiss in your eyes – the touch of your hand makes me weak,*
> *And my heart may go dizzy and fall.'*

Bea asks Francis why he was watching her.

'Isn't it obvious?'

'I never saw you.'

'You've never seen me for weeks.'

Bea senses something happening within her – a feeling of being released from a kind of widowhood. She is suddenly young again. And wanted. Most extraordinary of all, she is sure Arie would not mind.

The music fades. The evening ends. Francis walks her back to her room. He doesn't kiss her that night. But from then on, they spend every available minute together.

They get weekend leave and drive to the Wrenn family home in Shropshire in Francis's little brown and cream Austin 10. He asks if she is happy.

'You know I am.'

That's the truth. He's not Arie... but who could be?

It is a long journey. Cows sway drowsy with heat in the shadows of orchards grown heavy with fruit. The fields have burnt yellow under the parching sun and the beds of rivers run dry.

Francis turns off the road at last and onto a grassy track between stands of beeches, thick with olive-green leaves hanging motionless in the warm evening air. They bump along by hedges of hawthorn then cross a cattle grid to a gravelled drive.

And there is Bea's first sight of Garth Hall, washed in the golden light of the dying day. Soft pink roses climb on wires strung across its great oak frame and a wisteria, with a trunk thicker than a man's thigh, twists out of the earth by the front porch door. A piano is being played. Bats fall and flit from under the eaves and all the windows are open to catch whatever breeze night may bring.

Bea can only gaze and smile. For her, nothing about Garth is new or unexpected. It all feels so familiar... just as the embassy courtyard in Prague had done. This is a place she was born to find on a path only she could tread. A calm comes over her. To Bea, the spirits of this house are real but intangible, like the scents of flowers. She feels herself being welcomed by those who had gone before. They bid her to stay awhile, as they had done in their time.

'Bea? Where are you? Come and meet my family.'

They are greeted by Lavinia, his father's widowed sister, prematurely grey and in a beige stockinette frock showing a neck reddened by the day's sun.

'You are most welcome. Francis wrote to say how wonderful you were.'

Bea feigns embarrassment. His father, the old judge, approaches and bows a white head that had been darkened by a black cap at many an assize. He shakes Bea's hand with judicial formality and examines her with unblinking eyes. Bea knows she is already on trial. Later, at supper in the drawing room lit by oil lamps and candles in polished brass sconces, the talk is of war. Nothing else is on anyone's mind.

Francis Wrenn is the family's last hope of continuity, a young life that will be wagered again and again on the roll of a dice. His father wants to know if Hitler will invade.

'Looks like it. The French ports are solid with German barges all stuffed with military equipment.'

Lavinia says the Germans have already started bombing England.

'Somewhere in Surrey was hit only last week and they say there are German planes flying over us to spy out the docks in Liverpool.'

The judge knows Bea's father is high up in the Air Ministry.

'What is his opinion of what's happening?'

'I've never known him this worried. The situation must be very bad.'

It has been a tiring day. Bea is excused with a slight headache. Lavinia shows her to a guest room off a long landing. Bea lies naked in an iron bed. The drapes hang limp by the open window. The night is lit by the moon and the stars. She cannot sleep. She thinks of Prague and guns and planes with bellies full of bombs. Most of all, she sees the face of a child whose blood was on her hands.

Francis is walking across the lawn with his father. Their words carry like cigar smoke.

'Have you asked her, my boy?'

'No, not yet.'

'Don't you think you'd better get a move on?'

Do they talk of her? Is it her life being mapped out? Does she mind… does she care? No one has a future anymore. There is only now.

After breakfast next day, Francis walks Bea through the shaded rides of Garth Woods. The birds are silent and the black pebbles in Pigs' Brook are scarcely damp. Francis leads her up to St Mary and All Angels, through grass turned to straw in the relentless heat. It is cool and quiet inside the church. His warrior forebears lie in vaults beneath their feet. Those who did not come back from the Crimea or France are remembered in white marble tablets on the unadorned walls.

Bea sits in the Wrenn family pew. Light filters through the stained glass window above her and spills across the aisle like colours from a paint box.

'If the Nazis invade, we're finished, Francis. I've seen what they do.'

'We may only have a short time.'

'Does that make you afraid?'

'I could lie and say it didn't.'

'I feel quite hopeless… as if nothing we could do would be enough.'

'Well, I'm damned if I'm giving in.'

'No, we don't have any choice.'

'Look, Bea… you must know by now what I feel about you. It's as if I've known you all my life… from that very moment I first saw you.'

'That doesn't make much sense.'

'No, what doesn't make any sense is me, maybe dead in a few weeks.'

They walk into the churchyard, shielding their eyes from the glaring sun. Bea is in a sleeveless cotton dress, navy blue with small white dots. She is fair skinned and burns easily so Lavinia has lent her a boater. They wander between the ivied tombstones, set under spreads of sycamores and yews that darken the day.

Bea finds the stone of *Mary,* laid to rest in 1811, aged three or thirty – it is crumbling to dust to they cannot be sure. But her inscription can just be finger traced.

> *Death, like an overflowing stream,*
> *Sweeps us away, our life's a dream,*
> *An empty tale, a morning flower,*
> *Out, down and withered in an hour.*

They are kneeling, face to face, by Mary's grave. They kiss by silent mutual agreement. Then his hands move down her shoulders and around her waist. Bea lies back and draws him closer to her and feels how much he wants her. She unbuttons her dress and parts it. Francis, made infant again, takes her breasts and dares touch the inside of her leg which is silkier than swansdown. In a moment more she frees him to come into her and his body bucks as if electrified. He moves urgently and crudely and it is over quite quickly. She smiles and kisses him and they lie together on that airless, windless, day, as still as those around them, holding hands under the mourning trees.

It was then Bea agreed to marry him for she could not turn the corners ahead on her own.

Chapter Thirteen

McCall was crossing the rehearsal studio when a sudden pain like a boxer's jab to the kidneys collapsed him to the floor. His head hit the concrete and he lost consciousness for several seconds. He came to, bleeding badly and confused enough to think he had been caught in an explosion. The duty nurse dressed his wound in the first aid room and said he was showing symptoms of pleurisy, maybe worse.

'You should never have started work this soon after pneumonia.'

She drove him to casualty where they gave him intravenous antibiotics and drained his chest.

Evie found McCall in the flat he rented near Shepherd's Bush Green, alternately shivering and sweating, still coughing up blood. She was on leave and had rung Bea who said McCall had ignored all medical advice and returned to London. Evie surprised herself by how worried she was.

'You look dreadful, McCall. I'm taking you back to Shropshire.'

Evie stayed at Garth for two nights, making sure Bea did not have to cope alone. For this, Bea was grateful. They were getting closer.

Francis had decamped to the dacha and was sleeping there. His irrational behaviour and mood swings alarmed Bea more each day. Yet she put off making the call she knew to be inevitable. But with McCall, she stood over him while he rang his programme editor to say he had been ordered to convalesce for at least six weeks.

Bea desperately wanted Francis coaxed back to the house. McCall, still weak and anaemic, set off after breakfast. A sharp wind cut through Garth Woods and the yellowing lakes of new daffodils beneath the beeches and oaks that always seemed so constant but which would crash to earth in their time like all else.

Francis was huddled by the dacha's open stove in his overcoat. He glanced up as McCall entered but showed no sign of recognition.

'Hello, Francis.'

'I'm cold.'

'Let me stoke up the fire, then.'

'I don't think we've met, have we?'

'Of course we have, Francis. I'm Mac… you remember me, don't you?'

'Have you brought any biscuits?'

'Yes, and I can make us some tea, if you want.'

Francis appeared slightly afraid. He had lost weight, too. The food cupboard was open and McCall saw mouse droppings by a slab of ginger cake Bea must have brought. He stacked the wood burner with dry logs and put extra sugar in Francis's mug. Francis took it without a word of thanks and stared into the flames. The Eumig had been set up on the table and several boxes of film left opened alongside more aerial photographs of German cities he had helped to destroy.

'How do you manage to sleep on these chairs, Francis?'

'Sleep? I can't sleep any more.'

'You could, if you moved back up to Garth.'

Francis ignored him and went stiffly towards the projector. He tried to lace in a reel of film but his fingers refused to co-ordinate. McCall helped him. The box was marked *Hamburg, July 1943: Onboard camera, Operation Gomorrah.* The screen remained black for the first few frames then blazed into a thousand silver starbursts as cascades of high explosives and incendiaries fell from their bomb bays and erupted far below.

McCall noticed Francis's hands tensing and jerking involuntarily as if he was back in his cockpit, incontinently afraid his aircraft would be shot down into the hell he himself had ignited. Fires beyond counting raged out of control. From the camera position nineteen thousand feet up, they seemed to spread like runnels of boiling milk, bubbling into a devastating tidal wave of destruction.

This was a biblical revenge, an inferno of awesome intensity, fed by oxygen sucked from the atmosphere and converted into yet more hurricanes of flame. And so it went on. In such a burning sea of stones, nothing could have survived... no house, no person. No hope.

'People just melted... sank into the tar of the streets where they lived.'

'It must have been a nightmare.'

'I could feel the heat in my aeroplane.'

McCall switched off the Eumig and led Francis back to his chair by the stove. The once indefatigable Francis, the gallant *Boy's Own* hero of McCall's childhood, appeared exhausted by remorse. Here was a reckoning from the other side of history.

'Try to think of happier times, Francis... all the good you've done in your life.'

'I adored her, you know.'

'You mean Bea?'

'Do you know how beautiful she was?'

'Of course – I've seen the photographs.'

'And she was mine. I'd have given her anything she ever wanted. Denied her nothing.'

'She knows you love her, Francis. Why don't we go and tell her again?'

Francis's gaunt, unshaven face shed its weariness. He became as happy and trusting as a child. In a moment more, he and McCall walked through Garth Woods, hand in hand, as they had so long ago.

They got Francis undressed with a deceitful promise of chocolate. McCall had never seen him without clothes before, never seen him so reduced, so vulnerable. The flesh on his flanks and arms was withered and pale, his genitals shrunk to those of a boy.

Bea managed to slip his pyjamas on and persuade him into bed. Doctor Preshous arrived and asked him some insultingly simple questions – where was he, who else was in the room, what date was it? Francis struggled to answer and to witness his confusion was unbearable.

Bea followed McCall downstairs and they sat in silence either side of the kitchen table till the doctor joined them.

'I've given him an injection. He needs to sleep.'

'What do you think is wrong with him?'

'A sort of dementia, I'm sad to say.'

McCall said Francis had just described some wartime experiences in great detail so he couldn't be that bad.

'What happened years ago will be clearer than the events of this morning.'

Bea said they should have given him a bath.

'They'll do that at the hospital, Mrs Wrenn.'

'Hospital? Why's he got to go to hospital?'

'For everyone's sake, not least yours.'

'But I've managed with him here so far.'

'The good days are going to get fewer, I'm afraid.'

'Why? What's going to happen?'

'He'll decline quite rapidly to the point he won't even know who anyone is.'

The doctor left and McCall put his arm around Bea's shoulder.

Bea wanted McCall to take her into Garth Woods to pick the daffodils with which she filled the house each early spring. There was comfort in normality. Neither spoke much. Great mounds of dark clouds threatened a downpour and the wind carried the mewling cat-cries of buzzards hunting the church field beyond the trees.

When the storm struck, they had gathered armfuls of flowers. They took shelter in the dacha. McCall rekindled the stove with a few sticks and tidied away Francis's papers and photographs. Bea made coffee. The rain drummed against the dacha's tin roof, beating a retreat from all they hoped would never end.

'I can't put him in a home, Mac.'

'But he's going to need proper professional care.'

'It seems so utterly... disloyal.'

'You heard what the doctor said.'

'I'll have Mrs Craven to help.'

'She's not a nurse, Bea, and you're not as young as you were.'

'After all these years... what a dreadful way for everything to finish.'

Life, as they had always known it, was close to the end.

'If it's any comfort, he told me this morning how much he loved you.'

'I know he does but it's like there's someone else inside him – some awful stranger.'

'That's not the real Francis.'

'It's the names he calls me, Mac.'

'He said you were a spy, didn't he? Why should he say that?'

'I've no idea. That was his world, not mine.'

'So it was just his paranoia coming through?'

'Francis has much to be paranoid about.'

McCall refilled her cup and put the coffee pot back on the wood burner to keep warm.

'Tell me about him, Bea... about how you first met.'

She looked into the far distance, through the curtains of rain at the misted-up window.

'It was at a dance... such a hot night, early summer. He was *so* handsome... so dashing. But he was an officer, you see, and I was just a driver and it wasn't the done thing for officers to start affairs with junior ranks. They could sleep *up* but not sleep *down* so the camp commander had him in but Francis just told him to go to hell because he was going to marry me whatever anyone said. Francis was like that, very buccaneering... could get away with murder but all the men adored him and he'd already flown a lot of raids so I suppose a blind eye was turned to us, especially because my father was an Air Marshal and no one dared upset him. Anyway, we got married later that same year... 1940. But they were cruel days, Mac... so many never came back. We lived near the base... a little cottage we found... and he'd fly off on these night missions and I'd wait in the garden at dawn and look for him landing because his plane had *KMS* on the side which Francis said stood for *Kiss Me Sweetheart* but I knew if I didn't see it, I'd probably be a widow.'

The cloying, honey-butter scent of the daffodils, part bouquet, part wreath, saturated the air they breathed. The rain didn't relent.

'And the wedding itself… was that a splendid affair?'

'It was up at the church here. All the village turned out.'

'What a glamorous couple you must have made.'

'We did, rather. We must have shown you the film of it.'

'What film? I never knew it'd been filmed.'

'You know Francis. He filmed anything that moved. He got one of his crew to do it, not very well as it turned out but we're all recognisable.'

'I must see it. Where will it be?'

'About here, I suppose. All his films are in here, somewhere.'

It took twenty minutes to locate a Kodak box marked *Big Day,* lost behind a row of ring binders. McCall wound it into the Eumig. Bea waited, suspended between joy and anguish at what she was about to re-live. Then the sandstone porch of St Mary and All Angels appeared on screen and Bea and Francis walked into the bright sunshine of a September day long ago.

McCall's earliest recollections of her were not wrong. She was truly a radiant princess, casting her cinematic smile at the laughing well-wishers who would throw their confetti for ever more.

Francis looked every inch the sardonic immortal McCall remembered – the man who gambled his life against the Nazi hordes and won. He stood proud in the Number One uniform of a flight lieutenant with patch pockets and two braids on his cuff. They gazed lovingly at each other before Francis took Bea in his arms and kissed her for the camera.

The shot changed to show Garth Hall's front lawn set with trestle tables under the shading trees and laid for a feast of country food not available on ration coupons. There were bottles of wine from the old judge's cellar, chickens and beef and a keg of beer to toast the joyous couple. Bea passed happily between the guests in a woollen shirt dress, slightly waisted, with bell sleeves and a corsage of creamy white lilies pinned at the left shoulder.

'I pressed those flowers later. They must still be in the attics, I think.'

'Is that Mrs Bishop waiting on?'

'Yes… she'd not long married herself.'

Some of the lost faces at the feast danced across the grass to a wind-up gramophone with a polished metal horn and in her head, Bea could still hear the song.

> *'Silver wings in the moonlight*
> *Flying high above*
> *While I'm patiently waiting*
> *Please take care of my love.'*

The camera position moved again, this time from the other side of the tables to reveal the old house and the entire pastoral wedding scene in a last, elegiac composition in the setting sun.

Just before the footage tailed out one of the airmen – rather serious-looking and little more than twenty – walked across the picture, turned and looked into the camera then made towards the open porch door of Garth Hall. McCall shivered. He knew that face... knew it so well. But why wouldn't he?

The rain stopped and McCall took Bea home. Mrs Craven said Francis had not moved. The doctor had rung to say an ambulance would collect Francis at nine next morning.

Bea looked upset by the speed of events. McCall went to check on Francis. He lay foetally in the bed where he had been born and McCall feared for the visions tormenting his subconscious. Was he up in his bomber sweating with terror, or down below in the smouldering wasteland with the corpse rats or the fattening maggots and putrefying remains of those whose unknown lives he'd blown out? Who wouldn't lose their mind at such thoughts? But McCall had to get back to Garth Woods.

The wind still carried through the trees, water polished the smooth black pebbles in Pigs' Brook and fire burned in the dacha's pot-bellied stove. Yet to McCall, everything seemed suddenly different. It took only a minute to re-lace the wedding footage into the Eumig and for it to clack through the cogs and gates. And there again was his father in life, not an image frozen in a photograph, but young and real and moving about this place – Garth Hall. Here was the man who had put McCall into his allotment of time and space yet had left little or no evidence linking one to another. McCall ran the silent footage over and over again. He had to *know* his father, to see into that nervous, uncertain face, the close cut of his fair hair, the uniform that clothed his slight frame, even how he walked in the seven seconds it took for him to get from the wedding breakfast to the porch. Seven seconds of light and shade and shadows on a tiny strip of emulsified film. It wasn't much. Not to make up for a lifetime of not knowing.

Chapter Fourteen

Two paramedics arrived with the ambulance and led Francis through Garth's red and black tiled hallway.

'Come on, Mr Wrenn. You be a good boy for us.'

Francis looked bewildered. Eyes that once danced with brilliance had gone lifeless and dull. It was as if the sun had set on his soul. Again, McCall could not square this man with the memories in his head.

'Are we going to the embassy?'

McCall hadn't the words to reply. Drops of overnight dew fell on Francis from the wisteria above the porch and ran down his cheeks. McCall watched him shuffle across the slab-stone threshold of Garth Hall... one father passing the ghost of another. His captors manoeuvred him into the ambulance. They wrapped an orange blanket around his shoulders and fastened a safety belt across his middle. Bea climbed in and sat beside him. They held hands then the ambulance doors closed like curtains at a crematorium and they were gone.

McCall followed an hour later. The hospital had been a Victorian asylum, planted with flowers and cedars to soften its hard brick face. But the windows remained barred. McCall walked down a long narrow corridor, painted cream and green. Ludford Ward was overheated and smelled of urine and institutional food. Thin arms waved at him from seas of white sheets, drowning with the faint voices of the nearly dead.

'Come to your Daddy.'

'When can I go home?'

'Are you the doctor?'

McCall tried to look straight ahead, not wanting to see what Francis would become. He found him sitting on a plastic-covered chair in the ward's communal area in a hospital gown of faded blue cotton. Bea stood next to him. McCall had to force himself tread those final steps... to stand in plain sight, complicit in having Francis put the wrong side of Bedlam's iron gratings. Somewhere, deep within his disordered mind, Francis might remember what he had lost – and who had stolen it from him.

'Where am I?'

'You've not been very well, dear. The doctors are going to make you better again.'

'Has the ambassador arrived yet?'

Bea and McCall looked at each other. The pace of Francis's decline had thrown them both. McCall still had so much to ask him, more so now he had watched film of his father.

Till then, Edward McCall had seemed just a small figure lost in the landscape of the past, defined only by those who had been there. But seven seconds of mute footage changed everything... that half smile then the short walk into Garth Hall where his son, yet to be born, would live and be brought up. Here at last was something tangible, some coincidentally shared ground on which he might create a father to mourn. This wasn't to deny the affection he felt for Bea and Francis, simply to affirm his debt to those who had put him on the earth. What was harder to confront was the guilt of not doing so long before.

Bea always enjoyed riding in the Morgan. She would want the roof down and a breeze in her face. It made her feel young again, brought back those happy-sad war days, spinning down country lanes with the laughing boys who had flown off into the night and were no more. McCall drove her from the hospital up to Long Mynd where kestrels hovered above the purple heather on the mountain's steep valley slopes.

'I hated seeing you get in the ambulance with him... those doors closing.'

'Old age is like that, Mac – doors closing, one by one.'

McCall parked and they got out to look west towards the poet's blue remembered hills. He wondered if Bea might cry but was not surprised when she didn't. Like Francis, Bea had warrior blood, too. The drive back to Garth took them by a carved fertility figure on a Norman church. It was supposed to ensure better harvests and fill the wombs of barren women so they might also be prized.

McCall mentioned watching the wedding footage again.

'Why did you never show it to me before?'

'I'm sure we did, years ago.'

'No. I'd have remembered.'

'You'd only have been little.'

'My father was in it, wasn't he?'

'That's why we'd have shown you.'

'Well, I've no memory of it.'

'How did it make you feel, seeing him in life?'

'I used to think that what you never had, you never missed.'

'And now?'

'I've changed my mind. Is there any film of my mother?'

'No, nothing. We never had any contact with her, I'm afraid.'

It could have been the debilitating consequence of illness or the unravelling of all he held dear but McCall felt physically and spiritually empty, needing to hold tight to someone or something that wouldn't give way. They arrived back at Garth and he found himself wanting space and air and time to reflect. He left Bea phoning Mr Fewtrell, the Wrenns' family solicitor in Ludlow. Francis's complicated affairs would require much sorting out. McCall went instead to Garth Woods to pay a last homage.

He sat on the wooden bench Francis had built by Pigs' Brook. He closed his eyes as Francis would and let the sound of water and wind carry his elemental, wordless prayer to whatever force directed men's lives. Francis had died in all but the final diagnosis. For those left in this suspended grief, what was there to do but hope it would end soon – and that there might be forgiveness for ever admitting such a vile thought into their heads.

The pot-bellied stove in the dacha was cold. McCall brushed out the ashes then filed away all the old RAF pictures and reports Francis had left lying about. He stowed the Eumig in its case and put the reels of film back in their boxes on the shelf. When all this was done, he took a last look round. Never again would he stand here with Francis, never sit in the battered armchairs talking about the war or listening to those coded stories of his unreportable skirmishes with the Soviets.

McCall wept then, wept for all that had gone and all that he had never known.

Chapter Fifteen

Some of the attic letters lay unread on Bea's bureau. Their echoes of Empire, who had done well at polo or badly at bridge, were of little interest now... not with Francis so tortured. One of Bea's old uncles had suffered the same way after the Great War. He survived physically but, in his head, remained trapped in that continent of mud and corpses from which no man ever truly escaped.

Mac had told her of Francis's remorse for bombing German cities. He must have forgotten their honeymoon in London. She never would... those Nazi bombers laying waste to all the tenements along the Thames. So many thousands of people were to die in fires that made the sun grow pale. Her mind archived the alien drone of Hitler's air force. It could still wake her... that and the nightmarish vision of his doll-like troops, marching in perfect unison through Prague without a soul between them. Memory stores fragments of experience like these, keeps them safe for when they'll be needed.

The war years of Bea's marriage were book-ended by such atrocities.

She remembered a newsreel... a steel-bladed bulldozer pushing a hill of human remains towards a mass grave in a liberated concentration camp. Naked, emaciated bodies slicked with watery excrement, people without names or dignity or gender, flopping into a pit – offal from a butcher's block. Others, not yet dead, lay in their own diseased waste on shelves in verminous unlit barracks and stared into the unblinking camera, living skulls hanging like lanterns in hell.

History had never recorded sights like this before.

When the cinema's house lights came up, Bea didn't move – couldn't move. Arie had not exaggerated. This had been Hitler's plan for every Jew in every *shtetl*, town and city where they could be whipped into trains of cattle wagons for transportation to these abattoirs at the edge of the universe.

For Bea, the cultured German people were responsible for all this. The inheritors of Beethoven and Bach, Nietzsche and Goethe, transmuted into a nation of baying executioners. Jurists legalised murder, engineers designed the machinery of mass killing, doctors supervised barbarous experiments. And all the common people joined in to man the guns and gates against those marked down for extermination.

Bea was overwhelmed by a powerless rage at what she had seen. For her, this nation had anointed itself with the essence of wickedness, distilled it from the human tar pouring from their crematoria chimneys. Francis should feel no guilt.

Her hatred mouldered within her like grief at the loss of a child.

The ward sister rang Bea to say Francis had spent a restful night. Bea never trusted hospitals. Her father hadn't lasted five minutes in one – not that she had grieved much for him. He never forgave her for siding with her mother, still less for Prague and *the Jew boy*. How fitting that when Daddy departed this life, so Arie returned to it.

Bea never expected to meet her lover again. It was less painful to believe Arie killed in the war, easier to make a life with one who'd survived. She drew comfort from her mental picture of the child they would have had. It was possible for her to hear the sound of his laughter, feel his arms around her neck. She had even given him a name – Liad. It meant 'eternal' in Hebrew.

For her, Liad was real. Sometimes, walking in sunshine, Bea fancied she saw his shadow at her side, holding onto her. Liad would never leave Bea... but then, neither would her guilt.

...the parcel in her pocket weighs heavy in her hand though it's only small, no bigger than a kitten and just as soft, wrapped in sheets of tissue paper...

Where was the absolution for that?

St Clement Dane is packed with bottle-nosed dignitaries and politicians for the Air Marshal's memorial service, all wanting their names in *The Times*. Francis departs early for a meeting in Victoria he cannot miss. The choir finishes *Lead Us Heavenly Father*. The padre blesses the congregation. Bea walks to the marble-floored vestibule. She dutifully glad-hands the uniformed buffers who loathed the man whose praises they had just sang. Then she has had enough.

Outside, a September wind gusts off the Thames and lifts the black veil of her hat. She could cross left to Essex Street where Daddy's solicitor waits with forms to sign. Or she could go right, between the buses and cabs crawling along Fleet Street where there are coffee shops and time to think. A world can turn on such an inconsequential moment.

She goes right and edges through the traffic towards the plane trees outside the High Court. The pavement is a swim of jostling office workers, barristers, reporters and clerks. Here and there are rival newspaper vendors shouting their invocations like cripples at a shrine. Bea looks back along Aldwych. And in the human tide approaching, her gaze is drawn to a life that is hers and a face that is back from the dead. Arie is walking towards her... Arie, her persecuted Christ, greyer now, leaner too. Yet to see him is to doubt the evidence of her own eyes. How can this be explained, this second coming? Are the orbits of their worlds always destined to pass so dangerously close?

Bea feels again that first electric tremor of excitement. But she is nervous, afraid almost. She breathes more deeply. Arie gets closer. He walks not two yards from the tree that conceals her. He limps slightly, appears more tormented than she remembered, brutalised even. But who wouldn't after what has happened?

She buttons her long angora coat for warmth and follows him... as she knows she always will. The ring on her finger looks gold but is turning to pinchbeck with every moment.

Arie folds up the collar on his brown jacket. It makes him look like a black marketer with something to hide. A flat-bed truck loaded with huge rolls of newsprint reverses between them and into a delivery bay. She loses sight of him for a second and panics. But he is only across the street. She

72

steps into the road. A taxi swerves. A car horn sounds. She makes it to the other side and sees Arie approach a blue-chinned man in a trilby on the corner of Bouverie Street. Bea holds back.

Arie pauses by the man and says something discreetly. As he turns to leave, an envelope or small package passes between them. Bea only sees this because she is looking. No one else would notice as their coat sleeves brush together. The man disappears into the crowd. Arie carries on towards Ludgate Hill.

In the distance is St Paul's where all the brick-heaped bomb sites have been colonised by rose bay willow herb and buddleia that soften the devastation and make it appear natural, like ancient ruins. Bea starts to run. She shouts Arie's name.

He seems not to hear. They are by a bar called Mooney's Irish House when Bea catches up with him. She tugs his coat and he spins round, his face somewhere between anger and guilt.

'Arie? Arie, it's me.'

'Beatrice?'

'I couldn't believe it when I saw you.'

Arie gives no smile of pleasure at their re-union. He quickly checks up and down Fleet Street. Then he takes her arm and guides her firmly into the pub. The air is layered with yellowish tobacco smoke, the bar lined with men in demob suits drinking pints. Arie finds an empty corner stall. Bea sits and waits, still trying to take in this coincidence of time and place. He returns with two glasses of bitter.

'This is all they sell.'

'Water would've done… it's just so wonderful to see you.'

'What are you doing around here?'

'Oh, you know, some family matters to sort out.'

And all the while Arie fixes his gaze on the door as if he is expecting someone he does not want to meet. There is always uncertainty about Arie, a hint of static in the air.

'So what brings you to London?'

'This and that. A bit of journalism.'

'How interesting. Who are you writing for?'

'Only a small periodical. You wouldn't have heard of it.'

'But how long have you been back in England?'

'Not long… a couple of months, I suppose.'

Arie's eyes never settle. He examines every face coming into the bar as if to calculate risk and threat.

'I never thought we'd see each other again, Arie. Of all the things to happen –'

'Did you think I was dead?'

'Yes, sometimes I did. That last day… it was so awful.'

'I'm sorry it was like that… but I killed a few Nazis for you.'

His voice could not have been calmer or more measured.

'You and Casserley's men must've been in Europe, then?

'Yes… with the resistance people.'

'I saw those dreadful newsreels, Arie… those camps.'

'Belsen?'

'Yes… I haven't the words to say how I felt.'

'Neither had I.'

'You saw it, too?'

'Not the newsreel…'

'God, Arie… No!'

Bea wants to hug him but can only gently stroke his hand instead.

'It was only one of the camps, Beatrice. There were others.'

His eyes are black and stone hard.

'What of your family? What happened to them?'

'The Vilna ghetto was liquidated.'

'So…?'

'…So no one is left.'

'Arie, how can you bear it? I'm so dreadfully sorry.'

'Yes, but I am not alone in this. Millions have died. Millions.'

She takes a sip of beer and sees him looking at her left hand.

'Are you a mother yet, Beatrice?'

Bea shakes her head and looks away. She fights the urge to tell him about Liad, the child who must always be denied, the son whose blood ran between her fingers seven years before. How could her tears be measured in the grief that drowned his world?

'Tell me about this lucky man, your husband.'

'He's called Francis. He was a bomber pilot.'

'So, a lucky man and a brave one, too.'

'He's had to go to a meeting or he'd be with me.'

'Is he still in the RAF?'

'No, not any more. He's something in the Foreign Office.'

'Is he, now? Which department, do you know?'

'No, he never talks shop. He's very British like that.'

'Well, he should mind his step.'

'In what way, Arie?'

'Because your Foreign Office is run by Arab lackeys.'

'That sounds very heartfelt.'

'If it is, it's because some of us have every reason to think this way.'

74

She notes Arie's accent has become almost officer-English, clipped and dismissive. He keeps looking at his watch. He's anxious to be going. But Bea isn't.

'What are you *really* doing in London, Arie?'

'I've told you. I'm just here to do a bit of writing.'

'I'm no longer a child, you know. Tell me the truth.'

Arie half smiles and finishes his drink.

'I'll tell you something, Beatrice… something that might interest your husband.'

'What sort of thing?'

'The British mandate to rule in Palestine will not last much longer and when your people go, there will be conflict, maybe even another war.'

'Must that be so, Arie… after all we've just been through?'

'It is precisely because of all we've just been through that it will be so.'

'The newspapers say the Jews aren't being allowed back.'

'They're not. The Arabs don't want us and the British won't upset their Arab friends.'

'So what's happening to the Jews who can't get to Palestine?'

'You might not credit this but some of them are still in the death camps. There's nowhere else for them to go.'

'That's appalling –'

'Then you should tell that to your Foreign Secretary.'

'Mr Bevin?'

'Yes, that bloody Jew-hater… and you should tell your husband that we Jews will have our independence. We won't go quietly to the slaughter… never again.'

Arie stands up, ready to leave.

'Arie, I want to see you again. I really do…'

'It is better you don't.'

'Why? You mean the world to me, you must know that.'

'No, it wouldn't be wise.'

'But I want to help you.'

'You did already, remember?'

'Yes, but I mean now – with whatever it is you're doing in London.'

'But what would your important husband say?'

'Francis? He doesn't need to know.'

Bea hears her words fractionally later than the mental impulse to utter them. She is aware of what might follow. So is Arie. Bea looks at him, trying to see the poet behind the warrior, the Messiah who had clung to the bars of the embassy yard in Prague. It was still there like an imprint on a shroud.

Then, as if against all judgement, Arie takes a card from his inside pocket. Their fingers touch as he passes it.

Arie Minsky, Freelance Journalist & Consultant: Telephone MUSeum 2843.

'I have an apartment in Gower Street. Now, we really must leave – separately.'

'But why like this?'

'Beatrice, please... this is not a game. You must do as I say.'

Bea goes first. They do not kiss. Arie does not smile or turn around and is gone into the crowd leaving her alone on the pavement.

A surge of energy runs through Bea's body. It is like Prague all over again. There is danger and risk to her existence again. God had plaited Arie into her life once more. She would not give him up so easily this time. There was Liad, too. The ghost of their child. He needed his father. Francis would understand. Just as Arie had understood about her marrying Francis.

Chapter Sixteen

McCall locked the dacha door and made for Francis's other refuge, the church of St Mary and All Angels. He reached the porch to a drum roll of thunder from a bruised sky. McCall sat in the Wrenn family pew and stared up at the cross and its tortured man, skewered through the bones of his wrists and praying for the end to come. McCall feared he would not be equal to Francis's impending death, not up to the job of coping with this parental loss. Those who remain must look deep into themselves, at who and what they are and where they have come from. McCall couldn't know... not for sure. He was suffering a kind of double vision, confusing the outlines of two fathers, two mothers... two lives.

A volley of hail hit the stained glass windows and a litter of unswept autumn leaves scratched across the draughty nave. Someone touched his shoulder and McCall started back in alarm. But it was only Mrs Bishop, a finger to her lips.

'Putting flowers on David, I was. Come in to shelter.'

McCall motioned her to sit by him. Mrs Bishop was not conventionally religious. God had sinned most foul against her and that she could not forgive. But village always bent the knee to church. That was the way of it so she attended on her terms, prayed in her way. She looked closely at McCall's darkly drawn face and knew he was still sick – but whether in body alone, she couldn't be sure.

'You're upset about poor Mr Wrenn.'

'Yes... it's harder than I ever thought.'

The rain gradually moved west into Wales. They went outside and stood amid the graves. Flowers that had been left in jam jars were beaten down and lay across their little handwritten cards, rinsed of all love and memory now.

'You must look after yourself better, Francis.'

'I'm trying.'

'Come over to me. I'll feed you up.'

'I'd like that.'

'Then we can have a talk, like we used to in the old days.'

'What would we talk about, Mrs B?'

'Anything what's bothering you, of course.'

They paused. The sound of thunder came again, but distantly, like a fading migraine. McCall did have a question which only Mrs Bishop could answer.

'It was you, wasn't it, Mrs B?'

'It was me *what*?'

'...that sent that photograph of me to school, me as a baby with my parents?'

'Don't know what you're saying.'

'Come on, Mrs B. It's your writing on the envelope.'

'That a fact, is it?'

'I think so, yes. But where did you get the picture, Mrs B?'

'I'm not saying I did.'

'I can keep a secret. I just want to know more about them, that's all.'

Winnie Bishop took time buttoning up her shapeless coat and adjusting her hat. But she was reared to tell the truth and shame the devil.

'I found it.'

'Where did you find it?'

'Up at Garth.'

'Where? Which room?'

'Can't remember exact... one of the guest bedrooms.'

'You mean in a drawer or a cupboard?'

'No. On the floor. Someone dropped it.'

'Why didn't you just give it to Bea or Francis to pass onto me?'

She was starting to fidget and look uncomfortable.

'It wasn't theirs.'

'Whose was it, then?'

'Your mother's.'

'My mother's? How on earth do you know that?'

'Because I do.'

'But she never came to Garth.'

'Didn't she, now?'

'No. Bea said they never had any contact with her.'

'Well, all I know is what I know.'

'You mean you actually saw her there?'

She began to walk away, along the glistening gravel path towards where David lay beneath the fallen white petals of the roses she had left him. McCall followed close by.

'Did you, Mrs B? Did you see her at Garth?'

'Leave the dead and dying in peace, young Francis.'

'But we're talking about my *mother*.'

'You haven't done much of that in the past, or about your Dad.'

'God, Mrs B. Don't make me feel any worse.'

'Then take my advice. Leave well alone.'

'But you said we could talk about anything that's bothering me.'

'I didn't mean about that.'

'About *what*?'

Mrs Bishop had gone too far already. McCall knew he would not pressure any more out of her. He let her go. She was bitter and old and could get things wrong – but *this*? McCall owed all he was to Bea and Francis. They would have no motive to hold back on something so trivial as his mother visiting Garth Hall. Yet he knew Bea was mistaken to say they had shown him the footage of his father. McCall's story was in those seven seconds. He wouldn't ever have forgotten them. And if Mrs Bishop was right, it would mean he had been misled twice. However frail he was feeling, the journalist in McCall wanted to chase down the lie to source. But these were raw times – for him and for Bea. He could not go in hard.

McCall found her later, struggling down the attic stairs with a bucket of rainwater from the leaking roof. He emptied the others for her though the effort exhausted him. She made him sit with her in the kitchen and he told her he had seen Mrs Bishop.

'We got talking about the past and she started to tell me about the time she'd met my mother, years ago.'

'Old Mrs Bishop said that? I'm sure she's mistaken, Mac.'

'She seemed pretty certain to me. Said my mother had come here to Garth.'

'No, never. Your parents didn't meet until after the war and we'd all gone our separate ways by then.'

'So my mother never came here?'

'No. Why ever would she?'

'Well, Francis knew my father so he might've known my mother as well.'

'You know, it's a bit sad really but dear old Mrs Bishop was always getting things mixed up with the housekeeping and everything. I'm afraid her memory is playing tricks again.'

Chapter Seventeen

Adultery, n.
Violation of the marriage bed, whether one's own or another's. – Chambers's Twentieth Century Dictionary.

It is a grubby, blowzy word, a word with a past, a word that loiters in cheap hotels or back street restaurants where alibis are cooked up.

Bea knows all this. She should feel guilt and shame but doesn't, only a rush of anticipation as she pays off her taxi and walks the last hundred yards to Arie's flat. The afternoon is hot and dusty. She always has to ring the bell twice then cross Gower Street to wait by the bus stop opposite till she sees his curtains drawn. It's all so *Arie* – conspiratorial and a bit shady but exciting, too.

Buses come and go. Then she sees his signal. She walks up four flights of bare wooden stairs. He waits for her in his clerk's serge suit, as distracted as ever by matters he avoids discussing. Bea puts down the shopping bag of curtain material she has bought to explain away her trip to Francis. Arie kisses her lightly on both cheeks, more brother than lover. He smells of French cigarettes and whatever he slicks on his tight gypsy curls.

'There is tea. Would you like some?'

'*Tea*, Arie? I'd hoped for something a little more risqué than that.'

'Please Beatrice. You don't understand how high the stakes are."

But she does. That is what she loves about their affair. Yet how can she tell him Francis would not mind? She knows because she is certain of everything... as certain as only those who believe the world revolves around them can be.

'I will have to go for a bottle of milk.'

'I'll come with you.'

'No. You must stay out of sight.'

'Why? What are you afraid of?'

'Stay here, Beatrice. Do not leave this room.'

His order allows for no dissent. She watches him go then thinks she will take a bath, cleanse herself of the city's dirt and heat. She kicks off her high heels and lets her pleated tartan skirt fall to the floor, then the jacket and white silk blouse and each item of underwear.

Her moves are slow and deliberate as she imagines those of a whore might be... brassiere, stockings, suspender belt, knickers, all cast down on the worn carpet in this shabby little attic. She luxuriates in the freedom of her pale nakedness – her seductive, unsuckled breasts, the smooth unstretched belly arching down to the dark reaches of her sex which yearns for Arie.

She pads softly into the narrow bathroom. The linoleum is cool to her feet. Tepid water, slightly rusty, spits down the knocking pipes and into a bath that needs bleaching. Bea leans against the door as the bath fills. The austerity of Arie's life is clear – one chair, one plate, one suitcase. He lives like an outlaw. There is a trapdoor set in a dormer of the sloping ceiling, leading to a zigzag metal fire escape at the back of the apartments.

Arie could vanish at the ring of a bell.

This is the first time she has ever been alone in his flat. His desk is empty, which is odd. It is usually full of papers or articles he is writing. But they have all been moved away. Everything about this man still intrigues her. She peeps into his empty wardrobe, under the mattress of his metal camp bed, even in the food safe that contains nothing but an onion.

Bea shuts the door harder than she intended. Something wedged between the food safe and the wall falls to the floor. It is a brown envelope. Inside is a page ripped from a London street map and marked with three inked crosses in the area of Westminster. There are several sheets of Hebrew writing she cannot read – and a photograph.

It is of a man in his sixties with heavily framed spectacles and gun metal hair swept back from a wide, belligerent forehead. The face stares directly into the camera, tough and uncompromising. Bea recognises him immediately. This is Ernest Bevin, the British Foreign Secretary. Francis introduced her at a reception after Labour beat the Tories to take power last year.

Arie says Bevin is stopping the Jews that Hitler did not kill from entering their homeland in Palestine. But why does he need a picture of him?

Bea hears faint footsteps on the stairs. She replaces the envelope and makes it into the bath as he opens the door. She splashes herself then wraps a towel around her waist and pulls the plug. Tiny pearls of water course down her neck from strands of wetted black hair and run to the buds of her breasts.

Arie makes their tea at a gas ring and looks up as she leaves the bathroom. She pauses and he smiles. He comes to her. The towel falls between them. In his eyes, she sees a child, an assassin, and all the prepotent forces beyond the weakness of man to suppress. Not a word is spoken. He takes her where she stands against the wall, this gentle, violent, soldier-poet, lusting like only those who have lived with sudden death can do.

When it is over, when they are finished, they sink to the floor, exhausted. They lie on the unbrushed gritty carpet, their chests damp in the warm still air.

Far below in a world beyond the curtains, cars crawl through the sun-blocked streets, a thousand miles away.

'I'd like to meet your husband one day.'

'Meet Francis? Wouldn't that complicate matters for us?'

'It's a risk I would take. Anyone in the British Foreign Office is of interest to me.'

'But Francis is only on secondment. He's not a career diplomat.'

'But I'm told he's taking a special interest in Palestine.'

'How on earth would you know that?

'Keep your friends close and your enemies closer – isn't that what they say?'

'Francis never talks to me about his work.'

'Nor should he. But I might be able to help him.'

'How could you do that? Have you got information?'

'I've told you. We Jews will fight for Palestine. There's going to be a war, and wars are not just fought with guns.'

'It sounds to me as if it'd be more use for you to talk to a military man like Peter Casserley.'

Arie exhales a white flag of smoke.

'Did you not hear about Casserley?'

'No. What happened to him?'

'He got betrayed. Right at the end.'

Bea might have married Casserley once. Now, it is as if she never knew him. War blunts all sensibilities. So many have died, all so horribly. Even the human impulse to give meaning to random, chaotic events is overwhelmed and made redundant.

She gets up and gathers her scattered clothes.

'All I can say is that you're mistaken if you think Francis has any influence with Mr Bevin.'

'He's on the inside, Beatrice. That is what's important.'

'Maybe but he'll not be able to open the gates of Palestine for you.'

'Bevin has made some serious enemies by his actions. Just you ask your husband.'

Bea begins to dress herself. She becomes Mrs Francis Wrenn once more. But she remains an actress after a matinee. There is still another performance before she can rest that night.

'How would I explain to Francis that I knew you?'

'Tell him the truth about how we met, how you got me to England.'

'He might think it very odd that I never mentioned such a thing before.'

'Say it was of no consequence to you but now we've met again in London by chance.'

It would be the truth but dressed up in a falsehood. Bea is not sure.

'Francis is the dearest of men, Arie.'

'Which is why you must have married him.'

'I would hate to cause him any hurt. Do you understand me?'

'Of course. We must all be careful.'

Francis was seconded from the RAF to the Foreign Office shortly after his father died. The old judge, wizened and cotton-haired, held on for the last months of the war, shuffling between the rooms of memory at Garth Hall, not always knowing where he was. He took to his bed as the victory bonfires blazed across London, concerned only that Francis was safe. Lavinia assured him he was and he seemed content at that. His sister held a glass of champagne to his thin, dry lips. He managed a sip or two then fell back on his pillow.

Lavinia telephoned her nephew who drove north early next morning with Bea. The judge lay open-eyed, unable to speak or comprehend. He must have seen that look so many times before, on the faces of those gripping the brass rail in the final assize.

Within a month, Judge Wrenn's coffin – hand-built in oak from the Powis Estate – was carried on the shoulders of his son and Mr Bishop and four Shropshire Yeomanry veterans from the Great War. They trod a slow path under the bird-call canopy of Garth Woods where the old judge had played as a child, across the brook he had dammed and fished, then up the field to St Mary and All Angels. He was placed on a bier with care and

82

respect then wheeled to the altar, above the vaulted remains of his ancestors.

It had been a bright clear day, full of May blossom and promise yet Bea had found it all quite melancholy. Not many relatives answered the summons of the single, tolling bell. The family was thinning out, even then.

All hope turned on her.

A year on and Francis is less of an innocent in Whitehall. He'd had his 'walk in the park' when the funny people from Intelligence gave him the once over and set a few harmless tasks to see if he could spot a tail – or shake one off. He told Bea he was supposed to think it all very exciting.

'I said if they'd ever had a bloody Messerschmitt shooting at their rear ends then they'd know the meaning of the word.'

Bea spends part of the week with him at her mother's old apartment in Great Titchfield Street, refurnished and decorated now for the entertaining they have to lay on for foreign diplomats. On Thursdays, she catches a train back to Ludlow for long weekends at Garth Hall. Francis joins her when he can.

Lavinia keeps the house going with part time help from Mrs Bishop. Most rooms are shut off since the fuel crisis but they have logs enough to heat the ones they use. Bea sometimes feels there is an atmosphere, that Lavinia and Mrs Bishop resent her – this absentee new chatelaine who still has not guaranteed the line. Maybe she is too sensitive, imagining slights that haven't been made. Mrs Bishop's baby girl is nearly two now, a bubbly little thing, toddling about with a rag doll, always smiling. Bea hates it when the child is at Garth.

It brings back the pain.

'Are you sure you've never had a miscarriage or some pelvic infection?'

'Yes, of course.'

'Well, that's hard to believe. There's evidence of scarring here.'

There was. And not just in her tubes. But she had been too afraid to seek help. Her doctor also attended Daddy. How could she dare take that risk? She had scrubbed the flat from top to bottom, fearful his eye would fall on some spot of sin that had been overlooked. She thought she had atoned but God punishes in mysterious ways.

'You do realise what this means, Miss Bowen?'

'No, I don't think I do.'

'What are you... 20, 21? Well, I doubt you'll ever be able to have children of your own.'

83

Bea had stared at him, this bristle-stiff medical officer, not truly understanding his verdict was final and beyond appeal. The weight of his words didn't sink in, not then... not with Arie just gone from her life and the threat of invasion and death on everyone's lips.

'Am I fit enough to join the WAAFs or not? That's all I need to know.'

'Didn't you hear what I just said, young lady?'

'Yes. Perfectly – but there's a war on, isn't there? We must do our duty.'

Now, six years into marriage with Francis, the untellable truth was getting harder to hide as every bloody month went by.

'Anything to report, darling?'

'No, not this time.'

'We'll soon have to get you checked over by that vet in Harley Street, won't we?'

She'd laughed at first. They both had.

It was Francis who suggested Arie should spend a weekend at Garth Hall.

'If he knows as much as you say, maybe I should give him a punt.'

'It's certainly getting nastier in Palestine. The papers are full of it.'

'You don't have to tell me. These damned Jewish terrorists are even blowing up our planes.'

'You know it's all Bevin's fault, don't you, Francis?'

'Maybe it is but we haven't enough rope to hang all the buggers and even if we did, there's plenty more where they came from.'

Bea listens for Francis getting back from Ludlow Station. She had told him Arie looked like a highly strung violinist who'd lost his instrument. Lavinia will join them for supper. It will make conversation easier. Even before Arie arrives, Bea is reliving the high wire giddiness of Prague. But she knows it is a long way to fall.

Mrs Bishop is staying late to help. She needs the money. Alf is finding work in civvie street hard to get. Francis rings from the coin box at The Feathers.

'Just buying our friend a pint of best. Back in half an hour.'

Supper is Welsh lamb and a great success. Francis and Arie could have been friends for years. They talk of war and politics and the seismic shifts in the power of nations. Bea feels almost excluded – and she is afraid Lavinia smells a rat about Prague.

'How could you not have told us about such an adventure, Bea?'

'We simply caught a train together, that's all.'

'But the risks you must have taken. One only reads about such things in novels.'

Arie senses danger.

'Beatrice is guilty only of modesty... a charming trait of the English.'

'And when did you say you met again?'

'Two weeks ago, in Bedford Square. Beatrice was coming out of a shop.'

'What an unbelievable coincidence, Mr Minsky.'

'Indeed, I thought so, too. But it is a very small world.'

'And when you got to England from Prague, what did you say you did next?'

'I enlisted in the British army.'

'In which regiment was that?'

'It was not a regiment, more of an irregular unit.'

'I don't understand. Where did you serve?'

Bea interrupts this time. It is clear Francis's aunt does not like or trust their guest.

'Arie served behind enemy lines in Europe, Lavinia. It was the most dangerous work imaginable.'

'So you were a saboteur, Mr Minsky. How brave of you.'

'You're too kind but I was simply a linguist, a liaison officer really.'

'But Bea just said –'

'No Lavinia, it's Arie's turn to be modest, now. We must respect his wishes.'

'I do, Bea dear. I was simply expressing an interest in Mr Minsky's extraordinary life.'

Francis watches at the margins like a line judge but says nothing.

Mrs Bishop fills their coffee cups and they move to easy chairs by the inglenook. Lavinia soon excuses herself and retires to bed. Bea pleads tiredness, too. She kisses Francis and holds out her hand to Arie who takes it and bows from the waist. Francis pours two decent measures of cognac. Bea closes the drawing room door and hears her men toast each other.

'Cheers, old chap. Here's to friendship.'

'L'chayim, Francis – to life.'

Bea lies on her marriage bed. Through the window, the moon is a thin yellow feather curling between the clouds. Her two worlds are passing perilously close. She feels the magnetism of both – one mundane and secure, the other unpredictable and fast. Each in its own way sustains her. But which would she choose – or is that very thought a prelude to destruction?

Bea rolls across to Francis's side where their favourite wedding photograph stands on his bedside cabinet. She looks again at how they were, held in time under a swirl of confetti, laughing at the fates. On the floor below is the black leather briefcase she had bought him for his new job. It is not locked and should really be in the safe downstairs. The voices of Arie and Francis are barely audible from downstairs. Bea is tempted… just this once.

She slips off the bed and crouches in the shadows and undoes the case. Inside are classified documents about Palestine. One says a Jewish terrorist group called Irgun is behind a campaign of sabotage and murder aimed at destabilising the British mandate to rule the territory. Another is a copy of a briefing note for Mr Attlee, the Prime Minister.

Our agent in Jerusalem says that Irgun have set up a cell in London along the same lines as the IRA.

Clipped to it is an MI5 memorandum.

Irgun is made up of desperate men and women who regard their own lives cheap. They have been training selected members for the purpose of travelling to Europe to assassinate a prominent British politician.'

And there in bold type, Bea sees the name of their target – Ernest Bevin.

Chapter Eighteen

McCall found Francis kneeling by his hospital bed, plucking flowers off the carpet pattern. He did it slowly and with loving care, arranging each invisible bloom into a bouquet only he could see. A male nurse brought him a plastic beaker of tea with a spout so it wouldn't spill.

'Still gardening, squire?'

It was McCall who felt hurt by the mockery.

'His name is *Mr Wrenn.*'

Not all the contempt in McCall's voice was for the nurse. It hid the self-loathing at what he himself was about to do. He gathered Francis close and helped him to his feet. Beneath the blue hospital-issue pyjamas, the bones of his skeleton were hard to the touch.

'Come on, Francis. Let's have a talk.'

'Are you the ambassador?'

'No, I'm Mac.'

'*Mac?*'

'Yes. You and Bea brought me up.'

'Did we?'

He led Francis towards the communal sitting area, past other etiolated patients lying on beds by lockers of photographs of families they could not remember in homes they no longer knew. McCall took a long white envelope from his pocket.

'This is an important document, Francis.'

'Is it?'

'The ambassador needs you to sign it.'

'Never liked him... never told him everything...'

'Really?'

'Some things it was best for him not to know.'

Then Francis slowly turned his gaze on the barred windows that imprisoned him. In that exact moment, McCall felt sure a faint light of understanding passed across Francis's eyes, as if some tiny function in his brain had miraculously repaired itself. Francis had woken up in his own nightmare and was seized by panic.

'Get me out... I must get out.'

'Francis? What is it?'

'Help me, Mac. Help me.'

He rose up and gripped McCall's arm then stumbled towards the door. McCall could not imagine which was worse – Francis being lost in his world or found in this.

'They're killers. They're going to kill me.'

'No one's going to kill you.'

'They are. They've done it before.'

'What do you mean? Done *what* before?'

McCall held him by his shoulders and stared into his face, desperate to keep him talking.

'Francis – answer me. Who are you talking about, Francis? Who?'

Yet as quickly as his eyes had filled with understanding, so they died back to indifference.

'Say something... please, Francis.'

But the resurrection was over, the real Francis gone. McCall had no choice now but to betray this innocent, mannish child. He put a pen in Francis's hand and guided it to make his signature. McCall felt only disgust with himself.

'I want my flowers...'

'All right, Francis. You can show them to Bea this afternoon.'

'Yes... such beauty.'

Francis returned to his secret garden, barefoot and feeble. McCall bent down on the patch of carpet with him. He put his head close to his.

'I always loved you, Francis...'

McCall could hardly hear his own voice.

'You know that, don't you?'

But Francis just picked the prettiest flowers he could see.

McCall parked near Mr Fewtrell's office across the street from the ruins of Ludlow Castle. Edgar Fewtrell had always acted as Francis's solicitor. They had been grammar school boys together – Francis, physically strong, intellectually lazy, Edgar the opposite, shy and bookish, limping in heavy metal callipers after infantile polio. Francis was his protector. Whoever would torment Edgar had Francis to deal with first.

Fewtrell would not know how to retire. He sat behind his father's old desk, head sunk between his shoulders like a turtle in glasses, peering at the document Francis had just endorsed.

'Good, good. All seems in order.'

Both knew that was not true. Francis lacked the mental competence to sign over his financial affairs to anyone. Nevertheless, Fewtrell added his witness signature. Bea was owed a duty of compassion in all her troubles.

'Beautiful she might be but Beatrice never had Francis's head for business.'

'It's the roof that's worrying her.'

'Well, it needn't now. You'll soon be able to bring the builders in.'

McCall was about to drive away when Fewtrell emerged on the pavement carrying three black box files tied with string. He said they weren't important – just unwanted papers Francis had long since forgotten about.

'Put them on a bonfire if you want because I will if you don't.'

McCall was due to meet Evie at Ludlow Station next day. She had a week's leave and suggested they both needed to get away for a break.

'It'll get rid of our cobwebs, Mac.'

She had become anxious about him... adrift on his own in no-man's land where Francis lay dying and the father he had replaced was beyond reach.

McCall found space for Mr Fewtrell's files in the dacha with all the other boxes and books and paper trails of a man's life. Here was ambiguity, the living, the half dead and the dead who lived in the heart. Not for the first time, it struck McCall how little he knew, how little he understood.

'Was my other Daddy brave?'

'The bravest of brave men, yes.'

'Tell me all about his job in the war again.'

'Well, he had to shoot down the horrid Germans before they could shoot us.'

'But why didn't he sit at the front of the plane with you, Francis?'

'Because we all had different jobs and he was the gunner at the back.'

'Where was my other Mummy then?'

88

'I've told you. She was like Bea, working with the other ladies to get the aeroplanes ready.'

'What was my other Mummy like?'

'As beautiful as the loveliest princess you've ever seen.'

'Like Bea?'

'Yes, that's right. As beautiful as Bea.'

'And are they coming to get me one day?'

'Who?'

'My other Mummy and Daddy, of course.'

'No, little friend. I don't think they'll be doing that.'

It went dark. The stars came out and the canopy of Garth Woods trembled in the gentlest of breezes. A farm dog barked and beyond the soughing trees the waters of Pigs' Brook ran black over its cobbled bed. All of nature seemed subdued.

'Come on, Francis. Let's play a game.'

'All right, little friend. What game shall we play?'

'Cowboys and Indians.'

'Right, then. Got your bow and arrow?'

'Yes. Have you got your gun?'

'It's right here. Now, I'm counting to fifty then I'll be after you.'

'No you won't. I'll get you first.'

'We'll see – one, two, three, four…'

Now he's running and slapping his thigh like he's on a horse and dodging the bullets of the white man's six-shooter.

All his senses are heightened and he can smell the mushroom rot of decaying beech and the musk of ferns as he slides into a hollow by the muddy brown banks of the stream. He's panting for breath from the hard ride but no one will find him here. The stream's a roaring torrent cascading down from the high mountains where his Indian braves are trapped unless he can escape. He crawls on his front and sees the white man getting nearer. But he's not alone. Another man is with him. A stranger. He can't make out his face 'cos the sun's in his eyes. But they're closing in and they've both got guns. He must get to safety. Yet the cloudless sky is so hot. He stops and looks again. There's nobody there… only insects, floating with the grains of pollen that drift between the meadow sweet and the moon daisies, all swaying in the soft warm wind to lull him to sleep and dream.

Then there is a shot – a gun shot, so loud, so near that it echoes inside his skull and explodes out of his eyes. There is another and he doesn't know where he is, except he's lying in a field of corn… a field of corn swaying with poppies.

Deep, red poppies with petals that drip and soak into the bloody earth.

Everywhere in the dacha, there was Francis. A fingerprint in the dust on a shelf, the hint of fading aftershave, strands of silvery hair caught forensically in the teeth of his ebony comb. McCall could hardly bear to look. He untied the files Fewtrell had given him – more boxes of film, more documents.

McCall felt himself starting to sink between fatigue and inertia, wanting no more reminders of what he was soon to lose. He would stay in the dacha overnight, another vigil of sorts, stretched out between Francis's two old armchairs.

Tomorrow, there would be Evie.

He switched off the desk lamp. The blackness was sudden and total and he knocked into the table. Fewtrell's box files banged to the floor. McCall found the light switch and started collecting up the fallen papers – accounts from tradesmen, carbon copies of Foreign Office reports, old passports belonging to Bea and Francis. There was also a block of five cheque book stubs, held together by an elastic band so perished it snapped when he touched it.

These were from Francis's Number Two Account at the District Bank in Castle Street, Shrewsbury. McCall flicked through them. They covered the period from just after he was born in September 1946 till June 1950. Francis had made payments every week – sometimes more often – starting at £4, rising to £7. Each stub was dated and detailed in his scrivener's hand.

The payee was always the same – McCall's mother, Elizabeth.

Chapter Nineteen

Evie saw McCall from the approaching train, alone against the platform railings in a waxed jacket and jeans, thin body closed against the world and lacking its usual insouciance.

She was coming to understand the depth of McCall's depressive side. It lay hidden in grief unappeased since childhood. A shrink would call it *attachment loss.* The fear of losing Francis was unearthing what had been long buried and forgotten.

McCall clung to her as they kissed. He needed a shave – and a haircut. They went hand-in-hand through the narrow shuts between Ludlow Station and *The Feathers* for a Saturday lunch of lamb casserole. At least he was eating… even if he wasn't saying much.

Bea had gone to visit Francis by the time McCall and Evie arrived back at Garth. It was a cold clear day and a tide of bluebells washed through the woods to the door of Francis's dacha. Evie wanted to look inside. It smelled of creosote, fire ash gone damp and *old man*. On the shelves were internal Foreign Office reports she suspected should never have left Whitehall.

McCall seemed preoccupied as he lit the little stove and made coffee. Evie sensed he had something to tell her, something he needed her to know. She waited for him to break the silence.

'I don't know why but I think Bea and Francis have been lying to me.'

'Lying to you? In what way?'

'About my mother and father.'

He told her of Edward McCall being in the wedding footage they had kept from him, how Francis sent his mother cheques but Bea denied Elizabeth had ever been to Garth – despite what Mrs Bishop now said.

'But McCall, these are all elderly people. They're not well, they get things mixed up in their minds after all these years.'

'Yeah, I know, but I think there's something more to it – '

'Only because you're down in the dumps at the moment. You're only seeing the black side of everything.'

Evie got him to rig up the Eumig. She wanted to see Arcadia herself, to witness Bea's wartime marriage, its beauty and simplicity, the dead being resurrected. Neither spoke in the four minutes it lasted. Then McCall laced in the seaside reel – him as a boy playing cricket, Francis and Bea dancing a can-can. Evie felt herself being pulled ever closer into these stories she did not fully understand.

'How fascinating – starring in your own life. Do you feel any connection to that kid on the screen?'

'I know it must be me but I don't know who I am, if you can understand.'

'That's your trouble, isn't it… not knowing?'

'Yes… I look at these people and they're all strangers.'

'Don't you remember that day?'

'No. It's fallen between the cracks. If Francis hadn't taken his cine camera everywhere, I'd have nothing of it in my mind.'

91

'So you don't remember who else must have been with you at the seaside?'

'What do you mean?'

'Well, there's a sequence where all three of you are shown together. There must have been a fourth person to operate the camera.'

'Probably just someone passing by.'

They walked back to Garth and Evie told him again he needed to find his real family and put them to rest – as he would have to with Francis before long.

'You've got to do what you're afraid of, McCall... start digging up the past.'

What remained unsaid was her fear that if he didn't, he would be stalked by depression for the rest of his life – exactly like Phillip, the husband she had just made herself leave.

If photographs cannot lie, neither can they reveal the entire truth.

A shutter closes on an instant of existence and those captured within become their own little mystery. Beyond the frame and out of shot, what tensions, what secrets, lie between them? McCall examined the blow-up he had had made of the tiny Box Brownie print Mrs Bishop sent him all those years before. This was the only image of his mother, the only evidence of his *otherness*. He had no recollection of voice or scent or touch connecting him to her. Francis said she was artistic like Edward. But of her origins or relatives, McCall knew nothing, still less of the lottery of attraction that led to his creation.

Elizabeth stood between the sunshine and the shade, a pace apart from her Edward. She was attractive, not beautiful. Just doing her best. Her eyes were dark like her son's but subdued, allowing no hint of emotion.

McCall looked at the belly wherein he would have grown, the breasts that had fed him, the hands that once held him close. All her clothes were mis-matched and shabby like Mrs Bishop's church fete cast-offs. Her coat was missing some buttons and the open blouse beneath looked creased and un-ironed. The poverty of it all saddened him. No wonder Francis sent her money.

As McCall stared into the enlargement of his mother's lost face, so he began to realise that hers were the features he had crawled across like an insect in the desert in that recurring nightmare of childhood. He recognised at last that this was the unmapped landscape of his infant subconscious, a place of fear without end that he had never understood then – and still didn't now.

Evie took the picture from him. She allowed herself the gentlest of smiles. McCall's mother had been as impoverished as her own. There was comfort of sorts in that.

The sea beyond the register office at Weston-super-Mare churned brown and a salty wind tore at the plastic macs of trippers making pilgrimages from one gimcrack entertainment to another. It was a vulgar, dismal, place. McCall and Evie waited their turn to see the duty clerk.

When she came, McCall said he wanted copies of his parents' death certificates and gave their details. The woman went through the 1950 register.

'You're sure that's the year they died?'

'Yes, in June or July.'

'I'm sorry but we've no entries for anyone called *McCall* dying in 1950.'

'That can't be right. That's when they died.'

'I'll look again but –'

'It was a road accident... near Churchill. That's in your patch, isn't it?'

'Yes, but there's nothing about people of that name dying then.'

It did not make sense. Bea and Francis became his guardians soon after his parents were killed. That is what they had always told him. The crash happened about three months before his fourth birthday. He had still got Bea and Francis's card – a golliwog riding a toy train with a big red number 4 on the front. It was in his memory box.

'I'll try the registers for1949 and '51 just in case.'

But they were blank, too. Evie suggested they check McCall's local newspaper story about the accident. The cutting Francis had given him was undated but torn from the *Weston Mercury & Somersetshire Herald.* They went through the town library's bound copies for 1950. The paper was an old fashioned weekly broadsheet with a gothic masthead and a front page of classified adverts for whist drives, faith healers and ex-soldiers offering to dig gardens.

Not a single road fatality occurred anywhere in the *Herald's* circulation area that year. In the twelve months either side, a boy was knocked off his bike and died and a farm worker got crushed under a tractor. These were tragedies but not the ones McCall wanted to read. His unease grew.

Both the cutting and McCall's birth certificate gave his family address as Mendip Cottage, Churchill. The village was ten miles inland, straddling a crossroads beneath a wooded escarpment. The post office was closed but a woman mailing a letter said the postman always had lunch at *The Crown.*

They found the pub at the bottom of a stone track rising over a hill pitted with old lime workings and colonised by scrubby trees, all bent by the winds from the Bristol Channel. The postman sat smoking a pipe in a corner seat. He remembered *Mendip Cottage* but said it had been pulled down long since and a new house built on the site.

'Wasn't fit for pigs to live in, that hole.'

'Did you know the people who lived there around 1950?'

'Can't say I did, no.'

'They were called Edward and Elizabeth McCall. He'd been in the RAF during the war... in bombers.'

'No. Lots of people lived in that place at one time or another.'

'But this couple were killed... in a car crash, here in Churchill.'

McCall put his *Herald* cutting on the table in front of them. The postman read it and shook his head.

'I'm born and bred here and I never knowed anything of this.'

He told McCall how to get to where the cottage had stood, along a back lane to a farm, a mile away. The new place was called Mendip *House* and had a conservatory full of cane furniture and pot plants. Whatever humble signs of habitation McCall's parents might have left had disappeared. He and Evie stood at the white wicket gate, trying to work out where Mrs Bishop's photograph would've been taken. A woman in her late sixties and dressed for gardening came from a greenhouse and asked what they wanted. He showed her the picture of himself as a baby with the parents he never knew. She softened and invited him to look round.

'Bits of the old cottage are still visible.'

They followed her to an orchard of leggy apple trees strangled by ivy. Close by, McCall could see the archaeological remains of his family home... a bumpy outline of grassed-over foundations like those of a hovel in a village emptied by plague.

He stepped into where the two main ground floor rooms had been. They were lawns now, with circular rose beds and a wooden bench on a square of red clay tiles where the chimney once stood. McCall thought how small it was... so cramped and mean. Yet this was his first world, the place where he would have learnt to walk and run to the people in the photograph who'd have picked him up and felt joy that he was theirs. He tried to imagine his mother preparing meals here or his father framing the pictures Francis said he painted so well. But McCall's own canvas had neither shapes nor colours.

Only the cottage's lean-to scullery remained intact under a roof of orange pantiles. McCall put his hand to the thumb latch of the door, worn smooth by those long gone.

The woman went inside and brought back a photograph of the original cottage, derelict and abandoned. The windows were covered over by sheets of corrugated iron and the front door nailed up with planks.

The caption underneath read: *Mendip Cottage June 1949.*

94

McCall looked closely and said the date wasn't accurate. The woman bridled slightly.

'I can assure you it is because we moved into the new house in the June of 1950.'

'No, that's the month when my parents were killed.'

'I'll show you our deeds if you want.'

'But that's when *we* were living in Mendip Cottage... the three of us.'

'You can't have done. It was already demolished and the stone used for this house.'

McCall looked at Evie, unable to understand how twelve months of his life story had gone missing. She had no explanation, either.

McCall still hadn't figured out sex. Not properly. You search and find, couple up and pleasure away, panting and promising. It is all a lie but your fingers are crossed so it doesn't matter. Then it is over. You wash and dress and do something else till the next time. What did it truly mean? McCall knew what it was supposed to mean but that was with *her*. To have died in those moments after... those moments after with Helen, that would not have been so bad. But she'd been crossing *her* fingers so where did that leave him? He hardly knew anymore. Now, on his back in a cheap seaside guest-house and holding onto the iron bars of a strange bed, he didn't much care, either. It wasn't Evie's fault. But as she tried to take him with her lips and her tongue and her little white teeth, he lay wounded and damaged like a warrior on the field being finished off by the enemy. She told him not to worry. It didn't matter. It wasn't important. They drifted away into the night.

Think back, McCall... interrogate memory.

He is a child again, in a wheat field sprinkled with poppies. The flowers wave in the wind, redder than a sunset, back and forth, back and forth. And as they do, so the moist petals are shaken off and fall into the yellowing corn. It seems as if the flowers themselves are bleeding – onto his bare legs, his hands and face and clean white shirt, into the very soil itself. He gets up and runs away to cower in fear in some dark place. The air he breathes smells of decay, of more dying petals and the sweet rot of dead birds and rabbits, tied by their feet to a nail on the wall. Then he sees a long low box made of pale wood and grown-ups he has never met before who incline their faces to his, mouthing words beyond his understanding.

He wants only to get out, to escape, but there are no doors and his eyes are drawn again to the box that is lifted up and carried away by the strangers. Women kiss him. His cheeks are wet with their tears. Then he is alone in the back of a big car, driving through a place of statues and stones

95

where jackdaws swoop about his head. And all the time, a voice in his head keeps asking questions.

Who is in the box, little boy?

He doesn't know.

Tell us... tell us now or we'll nail you in there instead.

He cannot answer. It is all a flickering newsreel from long ago. Nothing is in the right order so he is adrift in all his memories and the shadows they cast.

Chapter Twenty

'You're getting quite friendly with Arie, aren't you, Francis?'

'He's a very intriguing chap and that's a fact.'

'How do you mean?'

They are in Garth Woods, clearing brambles and saplings so Francis can build a shack like those the Russians call *dachas* and live in during weekends in the country. He straightens up and holds the sickle loosely by his side.

'Well, for a start... for a man as cultured and urbane as Arie Minsky to be working hand in glove with a gang of murdering terrorists is intriguing, don't you think?'

Bea stops what she is doing, exactly as she is meant to. She has already guessed Arie is up to something dubious, dangerous even. But it does not lessen the shock of being told what it is. Francis says he has proof Arie is connected to the Zionist underground that has just blown up British military headquarters in the King David Hotel in Jerusalem. Ninety people were killed, hundreds more injured. Bea does not want to hear this. She wants to believe Arie is a journalist in London. He cannot be involved in such wicked things. But Francis says for Arie, London is simply a second front in the same war.

'Arie knows the importance of being able to shoot, Bea.'

'Meaning what, exactly?'

'That intellectuals like him have to be willing and able to fight for the Jewish cause, which is getting their own homeland.'

She demands to know how he can be sure of any of this. Francis says Arie confessed it himself. The bonfire of slashed undergrowth they are making crackles and smokes high into the yellowing crowns of the autumn beeches around them. Far in the distance, a bluish mist clings to a fringe of trees like the bloom on grapes. It unsettles Bea to think Arie is sharing confidences with Francis. Even worse, Francis says Arie was smuggling European Jews to Palestine from Prague before she met him – exactly as Peter Casserley suspected back in '39.

She covers her ignorance by blaming all the bloodletting on Britain's refusal to admit more Jewish settlers from the very death camps the Allies fought to liberate.

'That may be so, Bea, but if we let thousands of Jews from Russia settle in Palestine then the Soviets would infiltrate their spies amongst them and Palestine could quickly become a puppet state run from Moscow.'

'If our government believes that then they're more fool than I thought.'

'Possibly, but there's always a bigger picture to think about in diplomacy.'

'Not nearly as big as six million people being murdered.'

Bea walks away so he cannot see the anger in her face. She tips a wheelbarrow full of brambles onto the fire that sends smoke swirling into her face. She retreats to Pigs' Brook and sits on the bank with a handkerchief to her eyes. Francis puts his arm around her and says he is sorry. He remembers how quiet and crushed she had been after seeing the newsreels from the concentration camps.

'It's always interesting, isn't it?'

'What is?'

'Someone's motivation… what makes a person take the line they do.'

'What are you getting at, Francis?'

'Finding the motive… find that and you've found the man.'

'You've got to get inside his head, first.'

Francis considers her as he always does, dog-like in his gentle devotion to all that she is and all that she means to him. They walk back to where Francis's dacha will be built. Bea thinks of all he has just said – and all he has not. Arie's position is easily understood. But hers? She is not a Jew. Won't Francis think it strange she is this upset about their plight? He will never ask, though. But what if he suspects? There is nothing in the flat anymore. There are no clues. All the evidence has been removed so who is to know what was ever there?

Only Bea herself.

Francis leaves to meet Arie at Ludlow Station. Bea listens to the Alvis bubbling down the lane till only silence and uncertainty remain. She tosses more brash on the fire and sees it blaze and die like obsession itself. How odd that such a friendship should develop between lover and cuckold. She thought she knew their hearts so well... these boys, lying in her arms all *petit mort*, hers for ever more. Yet she bears no sin, has no need of priests. Her way from Prague winds on and she alone is destined to find it.

But in her bones, she cannot be sure who is spying on whom.

Bea carries a tray of tea to where the trenches are being dug for the brick pillars to support the dacha. Alf Bishop is the only one who really knows what he is doing. Francis's sleeves are rolled up and Arie has taken off his shirt. He is really brown, not a spare ounce of fat on him. Francis looks pink and sweaty, very English.

Bea had seen them arrive home, talking intently. Arie did not even stop to say hello. They went straight to Francis's study and she heard him make a trunk call. That must have been to London.

It was not until later that Arie actually spoke to her. She had sensed how on edge he was. He said he had been to Palestine but not when or why.

'Francis has told me the situation's pretty grim out there.'

'Yes, full of soldiers and secret agents to keep your Mr Bevin's police state going.'

'It sounds awful, Arie. I'm so concerned but what can I do here?'

'Nothing. It is as it is – and there's worse to come.'

Then he and Francis shouldered their spades down to Garth Woods where Alf Bishop, just back from the pub, had already pegged out the site to get the levels and footings right.

Bea hands out the cups of tea and scones Mrs Bishop has made. Then Mrs Bishop herself comes running towards them. Someone from Francis's office has just rung up. Francis glances at Arie and goes quickly to the house. Alf Bishop lights another Park Drive and disappears to relieve himself behind the trees. Bea takes Arie aside and demands to know what is going on.

'Stop treating me like an idiot. The pair of you are up to something.'

'Beatrice, please. Prague's over.'

'But *I* want to help. It's me – remember?'

Francis returns before she can press Arie further. The slightest of nods are exchanged between the two men. Bea asks Francis what his office wanted. He says it was something and nothing. Pen pushing never stops – even on a Saturday. Bea turns her back.

They are hiding something from her and they have no right to.

Everyone drinks too much at supper. They eat fish – trout tickled near Ludford Weir by Alf Bishop. Arie's mood darkens. Bea sometimes wondered if he might be jealous, seeing her and Francis as husband and wife. She had only ever viewed their little triangle from the apex of having two men love her to make up for the father who didn't. But on this night, it is closeness of her lovers that threatens her.

They all move to the chairs around the fire which Francis stacks with logs. There is only small talk, no conversation that matters, nothing to include her in their unspoken business. Yet she's damned if she is going to bed early to leave them alone with their secrets. She refills her glass with yet more Pinot Noir from the old judge's cellar.

'Come on, Arie – sing for your supper. Tell us what you're really getting up to these days. Your life's always been so full of excitement. Share it with us.'

Arie doesn't reply immediately. He holds her gaze in a way that suddenly frightens her. She sees again the man she had helped down from his crucifix in Prague, that woodcut etch of a face and its seer's eyes which saw the suffering to come.

'Since you ask, Beatrice... I have been searching for something.'

'And what might that be?'

'It is the courage within myself to ask questions and then to listen to the answers.'

Orange flames spread between the logs that pop and spit above the hearth's broken bricks. Arie looks into the fire as he speaks... into the fire where he sees the faces of those who have been turned into flecks of ash.

'I have been forcing myself to consciously find out what happened to my family.'

It is too late for Bea to call back her words, to regret their selfish conceit. She must wait for Arie to break the silence.

'They called it the "small terror" in the early days... just a few Jews beaten to death or a synagogue burnt down, nothing the old people hadn't heard about in the pogroms of the past... nothing new. How could they know the future... how could anyone? But slowly, by degrees, the Nazis made us outcasts, pushing us ever closer to the abyss.'

Arie pauses, takes a breath, sips his wine. Neither Bea nor Francis can take their eyes off him. A great hurt is being confronted.

'No one truly understood the catastrophe we faced but the movement I joined never accepted that our enemies should think that if we Jews were beaten or killed, we wouldn't be offended, just because we were used to it. I was in Prague to help people escape. But the net was always being pulled tighter and I was ordered to get to London by any means I could.'

No one moves, no one speaks. The embers in the hearth glow red.

'In Vilna was my wife, our children. What chance did they have with sixty thousand people crammed in a ghetto of a few streets? No food, disease everywhere... despair, also. The Nazis...so cunning...promised work in a town called Kovno. These Jews, thousands of them, piled into the train. But it didn't go to Kovno. It turned off to a place called Ponar where the people went for picnics in happier times. The Jews knew something was wrong and began to break out but the Nazis opened fire, shot them to pieces. Those who weren't dead already were marched to some huge pits and shot. Word spread through the ghetto that Kovno was an illusion, a trick to get the Jews to go quietly to their slaughter so now they knew...that afternoon the clouds settled low over the ghetto and those inside felt so trapped and close to death... so ashamed of their helplessness.'

Arie closes his eyes. His shoulders heave, his chin goes onto his chest. He seems on the point of breaking down and Bea wants to comfort him but Francis shakes his head.

'The pits filled with more bodies and even the earth began to spring with blood. The riflemen weren't Germans but Estonians, Ukrainians and our fellow Lithuanians, neighbours of ours once and now they complained that their shoulders ached from all the shooting they had to do. And so the Vilna ghetto was emptied but the Nazis needed to hide the evidence of their crimes so a group of Jews was chained together to excavate the pits and burn the corpses on pyres of logs...'

Arie's head is in his hands. His tapering fingers twist the coils of his greying hair.

'...These prisoners were no longer human beings... how could they be? They in turn were killed... all but one who escaped, and he is one I have now met. One image remains above all others for him... a woman who'd been with child. When the prisoners lay her on the logs, her womb splits open and the baby inside is seen to be on fire.'

Arie's last words come from the emptiness of his heart.

'This man knew this woman, knew who she had been in life... she was Ruzhka, my little sister.'

Francis drives Arie back to London next morning. His visit should have lasted longer but it was clear over breakfast that no one drew any comfort from the presence of the others. It was a time for reflection, for measuring one's life and purpose against what had been revealed the night before.

Bea walks to the village shop and buys a *Sunday Express*. The bells of St Mary and All Angels peal through Garth Woods, over a gentle landscape that has not seen invaders for a thousand years.

A Stop Press paragraph catches her eye.

> *Five men of Middle Eastern appearance arrested in London yesterday for entering Britain illegally will be deported on Monday morning.*

Chapter Twenty One

Nothing Evie could say persuaded McCall to come out of his angry self and not cut short their week away.

'Bea's an old lady, Mac. You can't confront her like some baddie you're exposing on television.'

'They've kept the truth from me. I haven't the faintest idea why but they've lied to me.'

'Maybe they'd very good reasons. You owe her the benefit of the doubt. Her husband's *dying*, McCall – the guy who helped to raise you... dying.'

'I still need Bea to give me some answers.'

'Look, you're too close to all this. Why don't you let me talk to her?'

'Because this is *my* life, Evie – *my* story.'

They drove back to Garth that morning. McCall didn't say another word on the entire journey.

Bea was not feeling well – not from any definable ache or pain, more the shiver of an ageing tree as the gales of winter set in. She had had more than her three score years and ten so the future was unknowable and short. She released the catch to the bureau's hidden compartment and removed a specific envelope from those inside – but with great care, so her fingers did not actually touch the armband next to them. It was as if the spores of some contagious disease were sewn into its emblem of evil and the silvered cloth threads of the word *Schutzmann*. Bea would have burnt it years ago but for the terrible fascination it held for her.

She made for the wooden seat by Pigs' Brook which always caught the late afternoon sun. The envelope she carried contained four black and white photographs. Bea held them like a hand of cards, remembering what she had been dealt and how she'd gambled. In the first, Arie stood alone on Westminster Bridge with Big Ben in the distance. His hair was neatly cut for once, his businessman's suit double-breasted bird's eye with wide lapels. The second showed Bea in a short-sleeved striped dress with her hair piled high in the pin-up girl style of the late 1940s. How glamorous she looked then, how remote from the old body she now inhabited.

She put the pictures side by side on the seat. Even apart like this, she and Arie could only be lovers. They'd had lunch with Francis that day. He got a bit tight because he had told the Foreign Office he would not accept a Moscow posting if it meant leaving Bea behind...

Francis doesn't just love Bea. He worships her. He displays her on the London diplomatic circuit like some rare creature he has captured but cannot entirely tame. That is her attraction. The lustful eyes of others watch her every move, see her bestow little encouragements to whichever foreign official Francis has chosen for grooming and wait their turn. Bea causes men to be indiscreet.

Her husband basks in the envy of those who would bed the woman who sleeps at his side each night. She is his and always will be. Francis indulges her, delights in her, denies her nothing... and would forgive her anything. Francis cannot conceive of life without Bea. She is aware of this. So is Arie.

'Do you think he suspects us?'

'I couldn't swear he doesn't.'

Francis has gone back to his office after their long lunch. She and Arie are in his apartment, naked on the rough blankets of his iron-framed bed. The room is airless and hot.

'I don't understand your Francis. Why does he not move against us?'

'Because he loves me. By doing nothing, he is showing just how much he loves me.'

'You mean he forgives you all this... our liaison?'

'Yes.'

'Most men would come after me with a gun.'

'But Francis knows he would then lose us both, wouldn't he?'

Some nights, she would not arrive back till after midnight. Her excuses wore thinner each time. But affairs induce blind recklessness. She would never deliberately humiliate Francis but could not function without Arie – not when he was in London.

Bea attends Francis's tedious diplomatic parties, smiling and coquettishly gossiping then slips away into the night. Sometimes, before she edges ever closer to the door, she would catch him looking across a room at her... maybe pretending he was not sharing her just as he had pretended not to be terrified in his bomber.

To articulate fear is to make it real, to make it happen so Francis keeps quiet. Besides, nothing is forever. Everyone knows that.

She draws Arie back inside her again and cries out as the moment comes and they fall from the heights together... down, down onto the bed below where they cling one to the other until the light is gone.

It is just before ten, two days later. Bea is at Victoria Station exactly as Arie had instructed – but without saying why. The concourse heaves with people pushing and waving farewell in shafts of dusty sunshine. It is Prague again but without danger. She sees a man coming towards her who looks like Arie but cannot be. This man is carrying two suitcases so it seems like he is going away. But it *is* Arie.

He takes her to a cafeteria and buys her a coffee she doesn't want.

'What's happening, Arie? Where are you going?'

Arie doesn't reply. She remembers a different morning... the one when Peter Casserley took him from her and she never saw him for years. He lights another of his French cigarettes then answers – straight and blunt.

'I'm going to Jerusalem.'

'Jerusalem? No, Arie... please... not that. Don't leave me again. I can't bear it.'

'I'm sorry but I have to. I'm more use there, now.'

'But you've got all your writing here – your journalism.'

'Yes but I have other work I must do, too.'

'What other work?'

'I've been told if I set up as a freelance out there, the BBC will use me.'

'But if you've known this, why didn't you tell me before? Why must you always be so damned secretive with me?'

'And spoil everything?'

'So it's not spoilt now – me waving you off once more till God knows when? Christ, Arie, don't you understand how you're twisting me inside out like this?'

Bea is angry and tearful, the child denied once more. She deliberately knocks her coffee into his lap then hurries onto the platform so her crying is lost in the noise of engines and station announcers and the feet of those who are running late.

Arie holds her and she knows there is not enough time to change his plan. She thinks of telling him about Liad, their son. But what is one more death to someone like him?

'Beatrice, come on. Be strong like you've always been.'

'You've done this on purpose – tricked me here.'

'It's best this way. It has to be done – and quickly.'

'For you, maybe.'

'And for Francis. Think of him, Beatrice.'

'Francis? That's a bit bloody steep – '

'No, there's a bond between us all. And I am coming back, Beatrice. I really am.'

'When? When are you coming back?'

'I don't know yet but there will be something I'll need your help to do.'

'What sort of thing?'

'It's safer you don't know for now, just yet.'

'You're lying, Arie. I know you are.'

'No. Listen, I've got to go. There isn't time to explain but just think of Prague. It'll be like that again.'

'I love you Arie.'

'I know – and I love you both.'

Before she can say another word, he takes a packet from his overcoat pocket and gives it to her. Inside are the photographs they had taken on their last day together. He'd had them specially developed.

'In photographs, it is possible to be happy forever.'

'Please don't go, Arie.'

'I have no choice.'

Then Arie smiles with those infinitely sad eyes and is gone into the crowd and the rolling waves of steam from the train that pulls him out of Bea's world once more.

Alone in the empty flat one evening a week later, Bea answers the telephone. A woman asks for *Mr Wrenn* in a voice that is hesitant and unsure. For an irrationally jealous moment, Bea suspects Francis is having an affair of his own.

'I need to speak to him, you see. It's very important.'

'Have you tried his office?'

'I don't know the number.'

'But you seem to know our home number.'

'Mr Wrenn gave it to me.'

'Well he's not here. Is there anything I can help you with?'

'No, only Mr Wrenn can help me.'

'Who shall I say called, then?'

'Elizabeth.'

'Elizabeth who?

But the caller's money runs out and the line goes dead. After supper, Bea remembers to give Francis the message. There is a slight distance between them since Arie left. But Bea's period has come again and these perpetually barren days create their own friction. Francis puts down his official papers when he hears Elizabeth's name. Bea wants to know who she is.

'Edward McCall's wife, that's who.'

'Didn't he serve with you?

'Yes, rear gunner. He was at our wedding. Morose sort of chap.'

Bea remembers him – troubled and darkly introverted but umbilically joined to Francis and the rest by all they had seen and done and survived over Germany.

'But why's his wife ringing you?'

'Edward's still in a bad way, apparently.'

'So she's rung you before?'

'Yes, but you know I keep in contact with all the old crew.'

'What's wrong with him?'

'He's been drinking all the housekeeping, apparently.'

'Selfish pig. But that's no concern of yours, is it?'

'It is, rather. I'll have to drive down and see if he can't be made to mend his ways.'

The clouds shifted across Garth Woods, shutting out the sun. Bea felt chilled and thought about getting home. In her hands were the remaining two photographs Arie had given her all those years before. If the first pair brought back memories of joy, these revived only hatred and the desolation of incalculable grief.

Six million dead.

Say it quickly. It could be the entire population of London... all murdered. Children, women, men, old, young, sick, fit, clever, stupid, deaf, blind, gassed, shot, hung, beaten, tortured, burned. All Jews.

How could the human mind conceive such a crime? Who could be an instrument in this meticulous slaughter and ever sleep again?

Bea held a picture of some who had found it no trouble.

Nine men pose in grey army tunics, fastened up to the neck with seven silver buttons. Most are about forty, some younger. They carry side arms in polished leather holsters and have just arrived in a town square wearing black riding boots polished till they gleam. Each has a stout suitcase with heavy brass locks. Their rifles are reared up on the pavement like the poles of a wigwam. The unit's tenth man takes the photograph to send home to his wife and children for the album about Papa's war.

There is little of note about any of them. One has prominent ears; another, rather thick lips. Two more have aped their Fuhrer and grown absurd toothbrush moustaches. They are tradesmen or innkeepers or men passing by on a tram, never to be remembered.

They are also killers, these fathers and husbands and brothers.

This is an *Einsatzgruppe* – a travelling squad of executioners from the SS whose function was to murder Jews wherever they could be cornered by collaborators in every desolate square mile the Nazis overran.

They are the monsters within us all.

Never forget.

105

That is what Arie told Bea. Nor would she. The other picture made sure of that. A line of women and children stared out from beyond death itself. They pleaded with the viewer to pause a while, to think what they and their issue might one day have become. Here were some of the six million as they wait to be murdered – real faces in the abstract arithmetic.

Bea would always try to imagine their names and stories, how their voices sounded and their smiles would have been. The women might just have come from market in headscarves and pretty floral dresses. The children are in bonnets and boots and white socks. Those too tired or too young are carried. One mother's fingers are spread in support behind her baby's tiny head. And just beyond where they all wait are the cattle trucks that had brought them to this spot.

There are no Nazis visible, no guns or whips or savage dogs. Yet they are there, out of frame, waiting... not wanting to appear in a family photo album. Not this time.

Bea's gaze went – as it always did – to the face of a girl of about twelve. She reminded her of the prescient child she'd cared for and had to abandon in Prague... thin straight legs, clumpy black shoes, gripping a small woven straw basket in her right hand.

And in that eye-blink of time as the shutter opened and closed, so her other hand went to her gaping mouth to cover that human reaction of shock and fear. She had suddenly realised what was about to happen on the ramp of the Auschwitz railhead that day.

This picture always had the power to tear at Bea's heart. She felt such an affinity with these women and their children. Wasn't the father of *her* child a Jew? Hadn't she been as forlorn as these pitiable mothers when her baby's blood ran through her hands? Her son should've been a grown man by now – a scholar, a poet, a musician... and so much more. She couldn't bear to think about it. The Nazis didn't just kill the living. They stole the future.

Bea looked at the girl again. History was always in black and white. It made such dread events seem so long ago, less to do with us now. And that was a blessing. God would never allow such cruelty to happen under a clear blue sky... would He? But Bea knew from Arie's picture that the sun did shine on Auschwitz that day.

The little girl threw a shadow across the earth where she waited. That was all she would ever be.

That was what she had understood.

A sudden faintness welled over Bea. She rose unsteadily knowing she must get back to the house and safety. Her heart was thumping out of her chest, her legs ready to buckle. She opened the wicket gate onto the orchard lawn and heard Mac's car.

She cried out and McCall came running with Evie close behind. Bea fell then, couldn't stop herself folding beneath the apple trees as surely as if she had taken a sniper's bullet.

McCall was with her in a moment, full of guilt and remorse at his anger but at being cheated of the truth, too.

'No, Bea – please. Not now.'

'For Christ's sake, leave it, Mac. Phone an ambulance, quick.'

'Bea? Bea? Listen to me.'

But she was slipping from them, seized by the same fear of those forever condemned to die with her on the grass where she lay.

Chapter Twenty Two

Garth Hall was hidden behind scaffolding and long drapes of protective blue plastic, waiting for the builder to start repairing the roof. A slight wind ruffled the sheeting and waves of aquamarine-tinted sunlight lapped through every window. It seemed to Evie as if the house was sinking to the bottom of the sea. McCall was still not back so she was alone in this lost world of other lives. Going from room to room, she experienced again that feeling of being gathered in by the spirits of this place, even before those of Bea and Francis had departed. Evie did not believe in a god's will theory of pre-ordination. That denied all human choice in the infinite randomness of existence. Yet everything happening to her now simply felt as if it was meant to be.

She sat at Bea's dressing table – a trespassing child trying on a brooch of Baltic amber and spraying her neck with perfume from a cut glass globe. The room filled with the warm summer scent of azaleas. And as she breathed it in, so Evie caught the memory of another's face, imprisoned within her own in the mirror.

She had thought her mother beautiful then, back-combing her Titian hair, reddening her cheeks with lipstick. Then it would be a kiss and a smile and she'd disappear, a painted moth drawn by the arc of light over Liverpool, glowing like the setting sun in the night sky. Evie would imagine her mother in ballrooms swagged with velvet curtains, an orchestra playing and handsome men turning as she glided by. She could be gone for days, to sing and dance who knew where and without a thought to all the love she had left behind.

Evie raised the lid on Bea's little ivory musical box and listened to its tinny, sad song.

Goodnight, go to sleep.

Bea must not die. It wasn't only McCall who didn't know her well enough yet.

Bea survived her blue-lit ride to hospital but the stroke she suffered weakened her entire right side. Her speech might never fully return. They had given her a pad and pencil and she'd already summoned her solicitor, Edgar Fewtrell. McCall was to have power of attorney over her affairs. He got his anger under control though Evie knew it still blew about in his head. But the sight of Bea being fed and washed like the infant Francis across the corridor was the cruellest of images. The socialite and the spy, locked inside themselves with all they knew.

McCall went to Mr Fewtrell's house in Mill Street. It had a fine eighteenth century brick façade hiding a much earlier building set with oak gone silver with age. They sat in Mr Fewtrell's ordered study drinking dark aromatic tea from Africa without milk or sugar. The solicitor had a venerable presence but the impatient directness of a don.

'Upsetting, for you, Mac... seeing them the way they are now.'

'Very painful, yes.'

'And are you coping with it?'

'I'm trying to.'

'It's like being inside a tent that collapses when one's mother and father die.'

'Oddly enough, it's making me think more about my natural parents.'

'Why is that odd?'

'Because I haven't done much of it before, I suppose.'

'We all need to know who were are, where we've come from.'

'I was never sure that applied to me.'

The hour chimed from a long-case clock with a painted face of fruit and roses.

'Francis always told me about the scrapes you got up to, out in war zones and such.'

'Nothing I've ever done compares to his scrapes, I suspect.'

'He was always so proud of you, Mac... never forget that. I doubt if your natural father could've loved you more.'

108

Mr Fewtrell poured himself another cup and held the saucer below his chins so nothing spilled on a waistcoat that would no longer button up properly. McCall steered him back to what he really wanted to know.

'Why can I find no paperwork about how the Wrenns become my guardians?'

'Fewer forms and regulations back then, I suppose.'

'You mean orphans could just be handed out, no questions?'

'Not exactly, but why do you ask?'

McCall sensed Mr Fewtrell's guard going up.

'Because I think there's more to what happened to me than I've been told.'

'What makes you say that, Mac?'

'I believe Bea and Francis could have misled me about my parents.'

The old solicitor's wire wool eyebrows drew together. He put his cup and saucer on the desk with some delicacy.

'Misled you? In what way?'

'Oh, little things... like when they died, where they died, maybe even *how* they died.'

'I must say that doesn't sound like them at all in my experience. Are you sure?'

'I've been looking through the public record.'

'And what have you found?'

'That there's a year missing from their account of my early life.'

'But what possible motive could they have to mislead you about such a matter?'

'I was hoping you might know.'

'Well, I don't and that's a fact.'

Another hint of unease passed across the solicitor's unblinking eyes. McCall pressed on instinctively. It is rarely the lie that sinks the guilty. It's the cover-up.

'I now know Francis was sending cheques to my mother every week from when I was born until the time she and my father were supposedly killed. I think that's curious, don't you?'

Mr Fewtrell stood up, suddenly every inch the advocate. He became at once the Wrenn family's legal adviser, not just their friend.

'You should take great care in this matter, Mac. The situation demands nothing less.'

'What situation?'

'My advice is to do *nothing* to jeopardise your position as sole heir and beneficiary.'

'I don't follow. I'm only trying to find out what really happened to my parents.'

'I'm sure you are but let nature take its course.'

'You mean let Bea and Francis die first?'

'That's precisely what I mean.'

'But why?'

'I can't know the accuracy or otherwise of what you may or may not have discovered but I do know that were Beatrice or Francis to get wind of it, however unlikely that might seem, it could cause them untold upset when they are no longer in a position to speak for themselves or explain what may or may not have happened years ago.'

The phone rang in the hall and cut short his submission for the defence. He excused himself and limped away to answer it.

McCall scanned the study with a hack's eye for anything interesting. A photograph on the mantelpiece showed a group of unsmiling men on the steps of a sombre official building. The caption read : *United Kingdom Legal Team, War Crimes Tribunal, Nuremberg 31 August 1946.*

He immediately recognised the patrician gaze of Hartley Shawcross, Britain's chief Nazi prosecutor. And three places to his right stood Mr Fewtrell, younger, thinner but with those same uncompromising eyes.

McCall had never figured out why Francis's unorthodox affairs were handled by a country town solicitor and not some whiz of a firm in London. Here was a clue. This inconspicuous, crippled man had helped to put a rope round the necks of Hitler's willing executioners.

There was more to Edgar Fewtrell than anyone might guess.

McCall was aware of Evie watching him from a landing window. She had wanted them to walk down to Garth Woods together, for him not to be on his own. But solitude was exactly what he wished. He was grieving – but whether for the dead or those about to die, he wasn't sure. His loves and loyalties were never more confused. He thought ahead to autumn, to when this ordeal might all be over and the leaves would drift to earth once more as they had when he had first arrived at Garth Hall.

'Do you think he'll ever grow to like us?'

'Give the poor little blighter a chance.'

'He looks like the wind could blow him over.'

'Then we'd best hold onto him, hadn't we?'

He might have been witnessing his own delayed birth, emerging fully formed from a long gestation into a world of colour where everything was new and exhilarating and he could run and climb and do anything he might want… anything except speak, that is.

110

So in those early times McCall existed in his head and acted out the stories he told himself.

Agent M is hiding under the bridge across Pigs' Brook and the Germans are combing the countryside for him. They've got guns and dogs with sharp yellow teeth and orders to kill on sight because Agent M's uncovered top secret information. It's so important it'll save lots of lives. He's got to get a message to London. He crawls on his belly through the thick undergrowth to the hideout where he's left his transmitter. *Agent M reporting in. Stop. Nazis have put special device in Daddy's plane. Stop. Will explode over water. Stop. Warn Francis repeat, warn Francis. Stop.*

He's tortured ten Nazis for this, now they're after revenge. The stream will put the dogs off the scent but Agent M slips on the pebbles and his sandals are soaked. But it doesn't matter. Daddy *must* be saved. He's never been in so much danger.

Agent M pushes on through nettles and thorns then scrambles into his camp under the big holly bush. He hears voices. Two voices. *Real* voices. One of them is Bea's. The other belongs to a man.

'It won't be easy, Beatrice. He's got protection at every level.'

'Our friend thinks it's almost certainly Cologne.'

'Yes but we've got to make sure of it.'

They pass by, not six feet away and Agent M hears no more. He doesn't see the stranger's face but he must be one of Bea's best ever friends. He's holding hands with her.

McCall watched a nuthatch pecking for insects in the rot of a shallow-rooted beech, felled by winds two winters before. The composting trunk gave off an earthy smell of decay. Unseen and deeper into the trees, owls waited to hunt, foxes sniffed the late afternoon air for prey. Here was the inescapable natural order of things – an unforgiving cycle of life, death and renewal, without sentiment or regret.

He unlocked the dacha and sat in Francis's ripped leather chair, unconsciously assuming primacy. At the hospital last night McCall had broken a bar of chocolate into tiny pieces and gently put them between Francis's lips. He had taken them into his mouth in some latent instinct to survive. His misted eyes never left McCall's face, though the clouds did not part this time. There was no sunshine of recognition, no words uttered... just the taste of sweetness remembered.

Now, McCall crumbled the last of his Lebanese Black into a joint and wished he could sue for peace – with his parents for getting killed, with Bea and Francis for lying. But these were new wounds on top of those Helen had inflicted and that were yet to heal.

Yet Mr Fewtrell's advice about McCall's chimerical parents was sound. They would not harm to wait a while longer for their son to find them. So he put a record on Francis's gramophone to remember how the music of Elgar, Beethoven and Bach and the voices of Callas and Caruso would come through the woods as he had skimmed stones across the brook or laid on his back, watching the clouds being ripped to shreds by the branches of the mile-high trees.

The four photographs Bea dropped when she collapsed were spread out on the dacha table. She and the unknown dark-skinned man on Westminster Bridge were dressed in the styles of the late forties, early fifties. Why Bea had pictures of Nazi soldiers and concentration camp victims, McCall couldn't think – unless they were mementoes from Mr Fewtrell's war crimes trials. He wondered if that was where the Nazi armband had come from, too.

McCall set up the Eumig to go through the remaining footage from Fewtrell's box files. He watched sequences of Bea cleaning the Alvis, another of arty shots of sunlight streaming in through the stained glass windows of St Mary and All Angels and even a reel of McCall in a cowboy outfit in Garth Woods, firing a toy six-shooter at the camera.

Bang! Bang! You're dead.

He was lacing up the last cassette when Evie knocked and came in.

'I've made supper.'

'Shan't be a minute; just watching this.'

The picture wobbled up from Francis's shoes, across an ill kept muddy garden to reveal a place McCall could now never forget.

It was Mendip Cottage – his first home.

'God Almighty – '

The roof bellied in and the walls bellied out. Some of the windows were broken and the kitchen door was half off its hinges.

'Look, Evie. It's my house.'

A woman emerged into shot, carrying a child not yet three years old.

'Christ… that's my mother.'

The camera moved in closer and Elizabeth's pride filled the screen with a smile so much more pretty than in the still picture he had seen. The child overcame his shyness and turned to face the visitor. Elizabeth hugged her precious boy.

'That's me, Evie. Me and my mother.'

These silent images mesmerised McCall. This was who he had been, where he had come from… and in his mother's arms. And it had all been kept from him.

But why?

The shot panned from Elizabeth, across a few scratching chickens to establish another female figure smiling, almost coyly. It was Bea... Bea who said she didn't know Elizabeth and hadn't had contact with her. Here was proof of yet another lie. McCall waited for his father to appear. But he didn't. A different man walked into frame instead. Elizabeth handed her son to him. He lifted McCall up onto his shoulders and beamed at the camera, full face. Then the screen went blank.

The man who had held McCall was the man in the photograph... Bea's foreign looking friend on Westminster Bridge.

Chapter Twenty Three

Francis Congreve Wrenn died soon after six the following morning. A nurse rang McCall thirty minutes before the end. The phone bell tolled down the long landing and through all the empty rooms before he and Evie woke and knew at once a death was being announced. They arrived at Francis's bedside a few minutes too late. The curtains were already drawn and porters were on the way up from the morgue. McCall touched Francis's face and felt life cooling from it. He had rehearsed this moment for months yet could never be word-perfect. In the clay of this shrunken effigy was McCall's past. Somehow, it must be understood... understood then laid to rest.

'Where's Bea gone, Francis?'

'She's had to go away for a few days, little friend.'

'Is she coming back?'

'Oh, yes. She always comes back, doesn't she?'

'But who will look after us if she doesn't?'

'You mustn't fret about that, little friend. She'll be back in her own good time.'

'What shall we play till then?'

'Let's make a camp fire in Garth Woods and see if we've any sausages in the pantry.'

'We'll tell Bea all about it when she comes home.'

'That's right. We'll do just that and she'll be so upset she's missed such a treat.'

'Why's she gone away again, Francis?'

'Best not keep asking me, little friend. I haven't the answer.'

'So we'll just have to pretend to be brave till she gets back, won't we?'

And so it was. Always pretending.

A nurse eased the plain gold ring from Francis's wedding finger and McCall signed for it. He was told that a doctor could break the news to Bea if he wished. He said he would do it himself. This was a filial duty. Evie waited in reception. McCall felt weightless, as if observing himself from above, slowly floating down a corridor towards an intense blaze of white light. Death and fasting keen the senses.

Breakfast was being delivered to the ward. All the female patients looked alike – pale bed jackets, paler faces. Bea saw McCall before he saw her. No words were needed between them. McCall took her left hand and placed Francis's ring in the soft warm palm and gently closed her fingers over it.

For Bea, Francis had died long since. She had already mourned his passing, wept in silence for the man she'd loved and hurt for so many years. What else was there to say in a world where she could no longer speak? How fitting for Mac to bring the final silent message. Why had she never had the courage to tell him the truth? There was still anger in the sadness of his eyes. A falsehood repeated often enough attains a sort of reality but is still a lie at its black heart.

But Francis always said only the present and the future mattered, that the past was a foreign country beyond our power to conquer and change. He believed we were the sum of our experiences, good or bad, and the drama of life flowed from how we dealt with the calamities our foolishness created.

Bea wanted to think she had always done her best, done what was right. So had Francis. But now, as she too could see the end of it all, Bea was required to offer up a more persuasive plea of mitigation.

'Mac? Where are you?'

'Come on out, little friend – don't hide from us.'

'Francis has got something for you. Come and see.'

They are in Garth Woods with Arie. Francis has just collected him off the London train. Arie is soon to leave for Budapest to cover the political crisis there. They have bought a present for Mac on the way home from the station. It's a cricket set.

114

'You'll never guess what's here for you, Mac.'

Bea is worried about Mac. Mrs Bishop's boy died last week and Mac saw her almost fall into the grave with grief, screaming David's name. David was Mac's friend and Bea didn't think the teachers should have allowed the children to see the burial. Mac could go mute again, as he had been when they first took him in – and when Lavinia passed away, too. They had seen a specialist who said Mac's only way of dealing with loss was to disappear inside himself. But it is frightening when he does. He shuts himself down mentally and it is as if there's no one inside him for days on end.

There is movement in the big chestnut tree overhanging Pigs' Brook. Mac drops from a branch and runs towards them, shorts torn, shirt filthy. He has always been a ragamuffin of a child.

'There you are, Mac. Come and meet a friend of ours.'

'Hello Mac, I'm Arie.'

'Hello.'

'You can call me uncle if you want.'

'Hello, Uncle Harry.'

They laugh but Mac doesn't know why. Then Arie gives him the new cricket bat so he doesn't care. They knock the wickets into the orchard lawn and try to teach Arie the rules. But he doesn't understand them and Mac bowls him out. The child immediately trusts this stranger – and that is rare in itself. He takes Arie back into the woods and shows him the rope swing over the brook and says he bets Arie can't guess where his dens are hidden. Arie's skin is very brown and Mac has never seen anyone this dark before.

'Are you from a long way away, Uncle Harry?'

'Yes, a long way away.'

'My other Daddy's name was Edward. You're not a German, are you?'

'No, I'm not a German, Mac.'

'My other Daddy and Francis killed lots of Germans in the war.'

'Why did they do that, do you think?'

'Because the Germans are bad people, that's why.'

Over supper, Bea watches Mac's commensal eyes study their visitor with a child's fascination for the exotic. Arie's hair has grown long again and hangs in girlish ringlets over the open collar of his blue shirt. He stresses words and ideas with an invisible baton between finger and thumb and his coal-black eyes can still go afire with all the passion Bea remembers. They talk of Hungary and what is to happen now its communist rulers have become a hated elite. Francis dryly asks Arie if this is the socialist paradise he espouses.

'Of course it isn't. Socialism has no place for torture chambers and show trials.'

'But that's what it's come to, hasn't it?'

'Yes... the secret police are no better than licensed murderers.'

'And what do you think the ordinary people will do, Arie?'

'My guess is they'll rise up and demand their political freedom.'

'And mine is that Moscow will answer in the only bloody way it knows how.'

They drive to Anglesey early next morning. Arie sits in the front of the Alvis with Francis. The weather is hot and the white sands of Aberffraw are deserted. Mac chases off to find the gang of smugglers he feels sure is hiding beyond the waving grasses on the dunes.

Arie uses Francis's cine camera to film him and Bea dancing across the beach. Their feet leave a trail of happiness across the watery sands. Then Mac and Francis play cricket and Bea goes to the car to fetch their lunch of fish paste sandwiches, apples and bottles of beer and lemonade. She pauses, holds back her breeze-blown hair with a free hand and gives Arie a movie premiere smile.

They finish eating and Arie takes Francis to the water's edge where they walk and cannot be overheard. Their friendship is very masculine. They trade secrets. Information is power in their lives. Bea feels more left out than ever. But then, so must Francis when she travels away for *her* reasons. And he never questions her.

Maybe he doesn't need to. Someone in Francis's deniable world probably tells him what is going on. She hopes he realises she loves them both... equally and forever.

How could he possibly not know that?

Mac is digging a moat around a sand castle and talking to the commanders of his invisible army who will lead the attack he is planning. He trots to the sparkling sea to fill his bucket. The air is filled with the sounds of waves and gulls. Bea lies on a large white towel... lies very still with her left arm under her head and her right folded across her stomach.

Mac runs back to his castle. He sees Bea and stops. He stands absolutely motionless. The tin bucket drops from his fingers and the water soaks into the sand.

In a moment more, he's at Francis's side, grunting not speaking but terrified of something he cannot describe. He keeps pointing toward Bea's prone body. Francis is alarmed and takes Mac in his arms. The child is breathing so hard that his little chest pumps against Francis's like bellows. They run back to Bea who is obviously only asleep. She stirs and comes back to life. Mac turns away and hides his face against Francis's shoulder.

116

Three weeks pass before he says another word. He never told them what was wrong. But they knew, anyway.

The funeral director was not happy when McCall said Francis's coffin had to be carried from the house, through Garth Woods and across the brook to the church field and St Marys and All Angels beyond.

'Might it not be more dignified for the deceased to be driven to the service?'

'Mr Wrenn wished to be carried. It is a family tradition.'

'What if someone trips and we drop the casket?'

'I'm sure Mr Wrenn wouldn't mind in the least.'

All repair work on the roof was suspended for that day. The mourners assembled in the stable yard. Mrs Bishop was there with her daughter, Mrs Craven, and a dozen or so villagers. Mr Fewtrell attended with a few other elderly men, black-coated and rheumy-eyed at yet another funeral for a friend. Only Bea would be driven to the church, accompanied by a nurse. Bea's attendance was against all medical advice. But she had scratched a jumbled message on her pad – *funeral, must go. I not be stopped.*

The procession filed behind the coffin, carried by six suited bearers. They followed McCall across the orchard lawn into the woods where he paused them outside the dacha and closed his eyes. All that could be heard was the slow tic... tic... tic of a cock pheasant and the swilling waters of the stream. McCall moved on. Each slow step was a retreat from the past... by the clump of ash trees where his play dacha rotted in peace and by all the hides and secret places in the world he had lost forever.

The rector stood at the bridge over Pigs' Brook and led from there. Bea waited in a wheelchair in the porch below the bell tower's clacking black crows. She could see where the sexton had been digging, close by the yews where she and Francis first lay together on that windless summer morning in 1940 and he had died his little death, knowing it might happen for real before many weeks were out. The symmetry of life is only revealed to those about to depart it.

McCall wheeled her to the Wrenn family pew where they sat together. Even through her fur coat he could tell how reduced she was becoming, how impermanent. He looked round for Evie who had promised to take time off work to come.

The church was barely half full but he could not see her. The choir sang *The Lord Is My Shepherd* then the rector spoke.

'Today, we must pray for ourselves, not just for Francis. There may be those here who need to search their souls, to ask what they are running from. Maybe it is God himself so they must answer honestly the question *Who am I in his purpose?*'

McCall mounted the pulpit steps. The untruths Bea and Francis had told him seemed less important, now. His mouth was dry, his eyes wet. He started to talk, but almost inaudibly. Two people entered the church from the porch. One was Evie, the other an old man he did not recognise.

'We each have our memories of Francis and that's what they should stay... our own. All of us here have somehow fitted into his extraordinary life, a life that was complex and exciting but about which few people know much. It's probably better that way. But we who are left salute a hero, a patriot, a man of honour and integrity we all loved and were proud to call husband, friend, comrade... or father.'

He looked down at Bea. She was close enough to touch the coffin. But there were no tears behind the veil of her black velvet hat, just the faintest of sad smiles.

The choir ended with Housman.

> Take my hand quick and tell me
> What have you in your heart.
> Speak now, and I will answer;
> How shall I help you, say;
> Ere to the wind's twelve quarters
> I take my endless way.

Then they put Francis in his grave.

Bea and the other mourners left for Garth in three polished funeral cars. But McCall set off alone, walking down towards the woods. Evie hurried to catch up and began dragging him back towards the church.

'Quick – there's someone you've got to see.'

The man who had arrived late with her was saying goodbye to Mr Fewtrell by the lych gate. He'd been tall once, straight-backed and sinewy, but looked a little arthritic and bent now, like an old soldier on Remembrance Day, anxious to be out of the cold.

'It's *him*, McCall. I swear it.'

'Who?'

'The man in the cine film – the one holding you as a baby.'

'*Never*. Really?'

'I've just been sitting next to him, haven't I?'

They were about a hundred yards away. McCall immediately began running towards the graveyard. But the man's chauffeur was already closing the rear door of a silver Daimler. McCall shouted and waved but the car accelerated away. All he could see was its diplomatic plates as it disappeared down Church Lane.

Chapter Twenty Four

The hospital nurse fussed over Bea in the back of the lead funeral car.

'Your husband wouldn't have wanted this... you risking your health today of all days –'

Bea prayed for her power of speech to return, if only to tell this drone to shut up.

'– You're very wilful and if I'd had my way, you'd still be on the ward.'

Bea closed her eyes. Francis was gone. It was all over – done and finished forever. The future was Mac's alone, now. Yet how ruined he had seemed at the graveside, more so than even those others who'd played the great game with Francis.

Mac might never truly forgive her, nor stop worrying the bone he had dug up. She could not even beg him to anymore. What an odd little boy he had been... robust enough on the outside but God alone knew how fragile within. Francis said they must see him as a blank sheet of paper on which they could write any story they wished. Nothing was that simple – not when the child was the sum of its terrors.

At least Evie showed up. Such a striking woman should not be in church for a funeral. She and Mac could make much of a life together. Everything in Garth would be his. They had only ever wanted the best for him... only the best.

'Mac – I've got the biggest surprise ever for you.'

'Tell me. What is it?'

'We're going on a long journey in an aeroplane.'

'Are we, honest? An aeroplane like Francis used to fly?'

'No, not quite like that. One that carries passengers. We're going on a holiday.'

'Where to?'

'To see Francis... to where he's working.'

Francis had wangled a Foreign Office jaunt to lecture on Cold War politics at a NATO training base in the Bavarian mountains. Mac was missing him and his face lights up at Bea's news. A week later, they're in a London taxi heading from their hotel to the airport. He's excited at all the capital's famous sights but grips Bea's hand during take-off, afraid yet trying to hide it. A stewardess asks if he would like to meet the crew. Mac

119

is led to the flight deck, wide-eyed. His only question is to ask if the pilot is going to drop any bombs.

'No, 'course not, young man. All that's finished.'

'Francis was a pilot.'

'And who's Francis?'

'He's my new Daddy and he and the old one used to bomb the Germans.'

'Well, the war's over now. We're all on the same side.'

The aircraft banks low for its final approach into Munich. Through the cabin window Bea sees specks of humanity moving ant-like in the streets below. Here are shopkeepers, mothers, teachers, railwaymen, plumbers, clerks, librarians, architects, decorators, scientists, doctors... unremarkable citizens. Ordinary people. Just like us. But for Bea, each was the tiniest of cogs in the factories where Hitler industrialised murder. They obeyed his order to hate their neighbours, the Jews; hounded them into ghettoes, stole their belongings and ensured every cattle truck was full of human cargo for the journeys so few would survive.

Bea feels nauseous with revulsion. She will soon have to move among them... to smile and talk and eat with them while never believing they stopped being Nazis the moment their Fuhrer fired a bullet into his own brain. It had become politically expedient for all the untold crimes of these new allies to be forgotten. Yet why should the agony of the unavenged dead go unheard? But Bea knows she must rein in her loathing. If Arie can operate here, so must she.

Francis has organised a NATO driver to meet them in an official car. Mac sleeps in Bea's arms on the long journey through streets once brutally controlled by the fascist Brown Shirts. Then it was out into the countryside towards their hotel, high in a mountain village.

Mac remains underweight for his age. There is still a vulnerability about him that's immune to all the security they offer. She pushes the flop of brown hair from his innocent face and wonders about the man he will become. Francis says he will need to go away to school soon if he is to toughen up and make anything of himself. He is sure Mac will be able to cope. Bea is not convinced.

She looks at the passing scenery. It is an overcast day and there has been a shower. There are birch trees everywhere... hunched and heavy with rain and paler than bones, like markers in the land of the dead.

What in the name of Jesus must it have been like?

She puts her free hand close to her face and peers through the bars of her fingers. That is all there would have been – thin cracks between the metal-strapped planks of the wagons to gulp a breath of air or lick a flake of snow. No food, no water, no space to sit or rest. Each was a coffin, deep in human waste into which the sick would die and those without hope go mad.

Iron wheels on iron rails, the beating machinery of destruction, all day, all night... screaming, screeching, pouring out smoke to blow like wraiths through the branches of trees.

Birch trees. Everywhere.

Birkenau.

Bea and Mac leave the *Hotel Alte Post* and go to meet Francis in the square. The village sits in a deep bowl of mountains, high-peaked and oppressively close. Mac stares at all the life-size bible scenes painted in bright colours on the outsides of shops and houses. He has seen nothing similar before and doesn't like the frightening depiction of Christ nailed to the cross, oozing blood.

'Why do they paint these pictures, Bea?'

'It's the way the people round here have of thanking God.'

'What are they thanking God for?'

'For keeping them free of the plague a long time ago.'

'What's the plague, Bea?'

'It was a most terrible disease.'

'Why was it terrible?'

'Because big red marks suddenly came on people's bodies then they died soon after.'

'Was it to do with the war, then?'

'No, Mac. This happened hundreds of years ago when there wasn't any medicine.'

'So weren't the people here marked by the plague?'

'Some of them were but most of them escaped so that's why they still paint their houses and put on special plays to give thanks.'

They see Francis and Mac runs to him to be lifted high in the air with delight. Bea and Francis embrace and Mac babbles his news about what he's seen and done in Garth Woods.

They go to a small restaurant and sit below a wall of antlers from deer shot in the forests nearby. Francis orders spätzle for them – small egg noodles, gently cooked and served with a basket of black bread. All around are German men... chewing slowly and efficiently. Mac feels their gaze upon him because Bea and Francis are speaking English. He has only ever seen Germans snarling orders in comics and heard stories of how they tried to kill Francis and his first Daddy. Mac thinks they are even nastier in real life. He moves his food round the plate and fixes them with all his impotent hostility.

'So, little friend... what would you say to another surprise?'

121

'What sort of surprise, Francis?'

'Well, the Germans are very good at making toys and in this village there's a shop that sells the finest wooden toys in all of Bavaria.'

'And I can have one?'

'Yes, but only because you're the best little boy in the world.'

Francis leads the way through cobbled streets full of more weirdly painted houses. The shop they are looking for is in an alley of three-storey buildings between a bakery and a jeweller's. The window is cluttered with every sort of toy – puppets, dolls, Noah's arks full of beasts and birds. Inside, Mac doesn't know what to look at first. A young woman emerges from a back room. She has golden hair coiled in a bun and a long white pinafore stuck with wood shavings. Francis could only be English in his tailored Norfolk jacket and brogues. But he remembers enough German from the days when he might have had to bail out of his bomber.

'The lady says to choose anything you like, Mac – whatever takes your fancy.'

Mac picks up a wooden car and a helicopter then sees just what he wants – a fort with a working drawbridge. Francis insists Bea has a present, too. She selects an exquisite Madonna and Child which the assistant herself carved from a log of lime wood. Francis pays cash and praises her great ability. Then he gets out his cine camera and asks if he might film her at work. She's embarrassed but Francis is all charm and she agrees.

They are taken into the little grotto of a workshop behind a beaded curtain. It smells of linseed oil and sawdust. One shelf is lined with the decapitated heads of clowns waiting to be painted with sad or smiley faces.

Francis goes down on one knee to shoot his sequence then pans across to another wood carver whittling a thin plaque of alder on his bench. The man's hands are a fascinating contradiction – thick, heavy, almost brutish, yet able to guide a narrow-bladed chisel with the skill of a surgeon. Every trim and slice of the pale-grained wood slowly coaxes out the tormented despair of Christ crucified hidden beneath.

For Bea, what is being revealed is the face of another anguished Jew.

Francis moves in closer. The wood carver doesn't let his concentration lapse. He is in his mid fifties, fit and strong with the leathery bald pate of an Alpine climber. Francis switches off his camera and bows in gratitude.

'Wie heissen, Sie?'

The wood carver hesitates, but only for a moment.

'Frank... Wilhelm Frank.'

Breakfast next day is hard boiled eggs, ham and radishes. Bea and Francis tell Mac to eat up as they are going mountain walking. They set off down a street named after King Ludwig, cross the clear, icy waters of the Ammer river and pass chalets with big gardens and trees full of linnets and blackbirds. The metalled road gets steeper and gives out to a dirt path. It hairpins up and up, through woods of spruce, linden and birch. Mac loves it. He has brought his toy pistol and runs ahead to make sure it is all safe. They turn a corner and see a huge sculpted Christ hanging on a cross, thirty feet high and made from blocks of cloudy Kelheim marble. Mac jumps out from behind a tree.

'Bang! Bang! You're dead!'

Bea and Francis pretend to fall down then find a bench where they sit and admire the scenery. Mac heads back into the trees to look for spies. Far below, the bell of the village church marks the hour and echoes round the circling mountains from its golden-domed tower. Francis checks his watch. Bea calls Mac to her and gives him a bar of chocolate.

'Can I go and play again now?'

'In a minute, Mac. Just be good and wait here till I say.'

Beyond the figure of Christ, a man appears from within the semi circle of trees that are its backdrop. Mac spins round and points his gun at him.

'Bang! Bang!'

'No, Mac. Stop it. Don't do that now.'

Francis quickly walks across to the man. They shake hands and talk for a moment. Then the man disappears back into the trees and Francis returns to the bench.

'What's Uncle Harry going here?'

'That wasn't Uncle Harry.'

'It was. I could see him –'

'No, Mac. It wasn't anything like him. It's just someone I had to meet here.'

'But you gave him something.'

'No I didn't. What a story-teller you're becoming, little friend.'

Bea and Francis both laugh. But Mac knows what he saw.

123

Chapter Twenty Five

Evie wondered if she should rescue McCall from the female mourners who had backed him into a corner with their wan smiles and sympathy. Yet it did not need a wake for his vulnerability to bring out their mothering instincts. It was always in his face. Evie made no move. She was too sensitive to her own position. Shun any prominence, attend only to Bea's wishes. Critical eyes were watching, alert for gold diggers.

The windows remained covered by the builder's blue plastic sheeting which cast a theatrical ghostliness across the drawing room. Bea looked ill, even without stage effects. The more people nodded over her as though she were a stupid child, the angrier she became at being unable to answer back.

McCall reminisced about Francis with some stiff old Foreign Office types. They were the last knockings of Empire and the darker arts beyond politics. The flag would soon be lowered on them, too. After an hour, Bea could take no more. Evie and McCall helped her into the nurse's car. Bea tried hard to form words to express what she was feeling but nothing came so she just held tight to McCall.

When everyone had gone, he sat with Evie at the kitchen table and talked about the VIP in the diplomatic car.

'If he was a friend of Bea's, why didn't he come back to the house?'

'Mac, how would I know?'

'Are you sure it was actually *him*?'

'Absolutely.'

'But that footage was shot years ago.'

'I know but those high cheek bones, the penetrating eyes – he's still got them.'

'But you were only side on to him in the church.'

'Listen – I'm trained to remember faces. It's part of the job, OK?'

A door to McCall's past had opened as another closed. He had to locate this man, ask about Elizabeth and why Bea and Francis had airbrushed a year from his life. The film of his mother, like that of his father, summoned her back from the grave. McCall had seen himself in her arms and all he had meant to her. It did not matter that they had lived in a condemned house or were church-mice poor. His mother cried out to be acknowledged for who and what she had been. Evie knew what was in McCall's mind – and why.

'I can find out which embassy the Daimler came from, if you'd like.'

'That'd help.'

124

'There's someone in the diplomatic protection squad who owes me... and listen, McCall – you've no need to upset Bea with any this.'

'Why should it upset her?'

'Come on, you can see how she is. Another stroke and that could be the end of her.'

Once a week, Edgar Fewtrell put on his best court pinstripe and ate supper at The Bale of Cloth restaurant in Lower Broad Street, close to where the weavers of the middle ages once toiled in their damp riverside cottages. He always reserved the same table and high-backed settle by the cast iron grate, ordered the same meal of spinach, new potatoes and three lamb cutlets, well grilled, with a glass of house red. He would usually be gone by nine.

Soon after the funeral – and when Evie was back in London – McCall rang him to make an appointment but was invited to The Bale instead. They talked about the progress of roof repairs at Garth, Bea's sad deterioration, McCall's gathering depression.

'I can't seem to sleep or concentrate and the thought of work... I just dread it.'

'It's called grieving, Mac. Let it happen.'

The other tables gradually emptied. Coffee was brought. Mr Fewtrell poured and asked what else was on McCall's mind.

'There was a man you were talking to after the funeral... a bit stooped, had a walking stick and a chauffeur.'

'I think he was just one of Francis's old pals. Why do you ask?'

'So he wasn't someone you knew, then?'

'No, just another mourner.'

'He looked a bit foreign to me.'

'Really? I couldn't detect an accent.'

'Who invited him?'

'I suppose he must have seen the death notice in *The Times*.'

'But he didn't come back to the house as I would've expected.'

'No, well he probably had to get back down to London.'

Mr Fewtrell clasped his hands across a tight waistcoat. He had a rather aldermanic face, soft cheeks flushed pink in the firelight. Yet McCall sensed a steeliness behind his pernickety bachelor ways and said he had seen the Nuremberg photograph in his study.

'Oh, that. All our yesterdays, Mac.'

'I never realised you'd been such an important witness to history.'

'Well, in truth I was only a clerk but it was a fascinating experience.'

'How did you get onto the prosecution team?'

125

'My father knew Hartley Shawcross. He thought it'd be interesting for me.'

'And was it?'

Edgar Fewtrell moved position slightly and stretched out his withered leg.

'You know, Mac, there are some artists who sit in a landscape for days and don't paint a stroke because first, they have to absorb the *essence* of all they see, to get to the very fundamentals of what touches them as human beings. In a way, Nuremberg was like that for me... however dreadful the details of what I saw and heard were, they became secondary to the central truth of the whole experience.'

'Which was?'

'Something quite obvious really...that we must never underestimate man's capacity to bureaucratise evil and wickedness for his own purposes.'

'Yes, but surely Nuremberg proved that man lives by law and is civilised by law.'

'To some extent, it did. But the truth was we hanged a few of the ringleaders... that's all.'

'But that is justice, man's ultimate decency, the formalised triumph of right over wrong.'

'Mac, Nuremberg was a symbolic, political, act as much as anything else. The dock has yet to be built that could've accommodated all those who should've stood in it.'

'I don't see the alternative. There was a trial with evidence, prosecution, defence –'

'True enough but remember this... the law doesn't always deliver justice.'

Mr Fewtrell paid the bill in cash and they walked into the fresh night air. A slight mist rose from the river. Above them, the sky was a clear sweep of stars. The old lawyer and his callipered leg couldn't get into McCall's low-slung Morgan so they stood talking for a moment longer.

'We need to meet again soon, Mac. There are papers to sign, things like that.'

'About Francis?'

'Yes, but you, too.'

'Me?'

'Yes, you're going to be very well off and we shall have to make plans.'

Was she awake or dreaming or dead? Who kissed her in the half shadows?Bea was laid out under the tightly drawn sheets of her hospital bed, arms by her side, head sunk into the snowy white col of her pillow. It was neither day nor night. Figures seemed to hover above her then dissolve. Cleaners, nurses, doctors and the families of those like her, clinging on to whatever remained, came and went like the spirits who kept her company.

'Elizabeth McCall's rung me again, Bea. Edward's still giving her a bad time.'

'You can't carry on being his skipper, Francis. The war's over. He's not your responsibility any more.'

'But he's only like this because of the war.'

'Come on. He's a damned excuse of a man.'

'He wasn't always.'

'Well, his wife can't keep running to you every five minutes.'

'But there's no one else… and there's their boy to worry about. I've told her I'll drive down tomorrow.'

'But Arie's coming –'

'Then we'll all go. Get a hotel, make a weekend of it.'

They find Edward McCall at The Crown in Churchill. Bea hasn't seen him for years. He sits on his own in a brown overall made messy by oil paint from the pictures he tries to sell. The pub has just opened but he has almost finished his first pint of bitter. His eyes are red from crying or insomnia. The smell of self-pity and failure is all about him. Edward looks up and meets Francis's eye.

'Edward, good to see you again. We were just passing.'

'Pull the other bloody one, skip.'

He is introduced to Arie who buys a round of drinks. Bea asks about McCall's son, young Francis.

'He's well enough, I suppose.'

'We'd love to see him – and Elizabeth, of course.'

'Well I'm busy. There's a man coming who might buy some of my pictures.'

Bea hopes he is telling the truth. They leave for McCall's cottage without him. Elizabeth looks worn down from trying to cope. Little Francis scrambles behind her legs and hides his face from the strangers' smiles.

Elizabeth's kitchen is small, dark and squalid, the table covered by newspaper, not cloth. The red floor tiles are furred white with salts coming up from the bare earth on which they are laid. She boils a kettle for tea.

Arie feigns a liking for the framed paintings stacked against the stairs. They're chocolate box views of thatched cottages and country scenes. No originality, no flair – not like his pre-war efforts.

Arie tempts young Francis outside with a promise of candy. They all follow and Francis senior records the gathering on his cine camera. Then he takes Elizabeth across to the orchard to talk out of earshot. Arie asks Bea what has made Edward the way he is.

'Something happened on a mission. Francis hasn't ever told me the full story.'

Edward McCall returns from the pub a few minutes later. His mood is even darker. The would-be buyer failed to turn up. Arie makes an offer for 'Farmhouse at Dawn' and refuses change from the five pound note he puts in McCall's hand. Then Francis starts recounting war stories about how he and Edward survived their hairy raids over Germany. Edward turns away, almost angry.

'Leave it, skip. I'm sure you have to be somewhere else.'

He gathers up his boy and carries him inside. Bea sees the child's eyes looking at her, not understanding. Elizabeth looks at her, too, on the point of tears. She goes inside and they hear the door being bolted.

They drive from Mendip Cottage knowing they have brought distress, not comfort, to those within. Arie asks why Francis takes Edward's problems so personally.

'Because I know he was a brave man, once.'

'What happened to him?'

'Cracked up spectacularly on a raid... fell victim to the *eighth passenger*.'

'The what?'

'Fear. That's what we called it.'

They check in at the Cliff Hotel in Cheddar then set off walking a path along the limestone ridges of the Mendip Hills. Bea can think only of how much she pities Elizabeth and despises her husband. He seems incapable of understanding what a blessing a child is.

They rest a while on a seat above a steep-sided ravine. The quilt of England's soft green hills lies beyond. No one speaks. Arie and Bea are waiting for Francis to finish the story of Edward's downfall. When it comes, his account is somewhere between a debriefing and a confession... and one that was long overdue.

It is October the 14, 1944. Two hundred and fifty Lancasters from 5 Group take off from bases in Lincolnshire. Their target is Brunswick in Lower Saxony, thirty miles from Hanover. It's a medieval city of timber-framed buildings but has factories making aircraft as well. Each Lancaster carries two one-thousand-pound bombs of high explosives and sixteen canisters of multiple incendiaries. They fan over the North Sea in three great wedges of destructive power. The target will be reached by midnight. Each crewman is about his business. The navigator is curtained off with charts and instruments and signals are coming in to the radio operator. Crouched in their turrets are the gunners – forward, mid-upper, rear – each watching for enemy fighters in the fearful vastness of the night sky. Tedium and routine are but preludes. Ahead will be confusion, panic and the ferocity of combat... and the prospect of instant death. Within each man, there is all this – this and the conflict between the instinct for self-preservation and the demands of duty. Those who accept they are likely to die will suffer less stress. More imaginative men see only the horrifying end that might await them.

They are seventeen thousand five hundred feet above Brunswick. The city's streets are running with white fire from the first storm of Lancaster bombs. Francis and his aerial warriors begin their run. They are about to be tested to destruction once more.

Then they hear screaming on the inter-com.

'I've had it, I've had it. I've fucking had it!'

It's the rear gunner, Edward McCall.

'Do you fucking hear me, you bastards – I've had it!'

There is terror in every word. At that moment, the bomb aimer should be signalling weapons away so Francis can peel left and descend below German radar. But he doesn't. Something's terribly wrong. Francis hears scuffling from behind then McCall lunges at him.

'Out of the bloody way, skip. Get out of my way.'

He tries to wrestle Francis from the pilot's seat to get at the escape hatch. McCall wants to bale out... wants to leap into the hell that is below. Francis is fighting to keep control of the aircraft. McCall punches him in the face again and again and they go into a dive, hurtling towards the flaming city at two hundred miles an hour. The forward gunner manages to scramble up from his turret and grabs McCall. The flight engineer pitches in, too. They sit on him and bind his hands with webbing. But still McCall kicks and thrashes about till they hit him so hard he goes unconscious. Francis struggles back into position and levels them out just above the inferno.

Bea shakes her head in disbelief. Arie asks what happened when they got Edward back to base.

'In war, Arie, a man's courage is his capital... but he's always spending. Edward was broke in every sense yet they still accused him of cowardice.'

'But he'd been a good man till then. How could they do that to him?'

'I had to make a report, you see. I felt bad about it but he'd endangered all of us so he was put on a charge...lack of moral fibre, they said.'

'How very English.'

'They'd have called it shell shock back in the Great War but our top brass thought if the men started getting out of combat duties by having breakdowns, it'd spread like a contagion and there'd be no one left to fight the air war.'

'So he had to be punished, made an example of?'

'And very publicly, too… stripped of his rank and put to shovelling coal in the boiler house.'

'Not just treated like a coward but like a criminal, too?'

'Exactly.'

'How cruel.'

'Edward wasn't seen as top drawer, you see, not from a class where courage was a matter of breeding and character. Those of us who actually flew aeroplanes and not desks knew this to be utter rot, of course.'

Bea tried to open her eyes beneath the bright hospital lights. She felt her hand being lifted and put to the lips of a visitor. Then she was kissed on both cheeks and her untidy hair pushed back tenderly from her forehead by a lover's long, tapering fingers.

He had come back to her as she always knew he would.

Chapter Twenty Six

In the hours before dawn, Garth Hall had the feel of a studio after the actors and technicians had gone but before the scene-shifters had created a new reality. Sleep was not coming easily to McCall. Evie called it brain whiz – the uncontrollable pinballing of fears and doubts in the mind. He lay on the chesterfield in the drawing room, counting the minutes till seven thirty when he knew Winnie Bishop would have had breakfast, maybe put fresh flowers on David's grave and be busy with housework. Then he drove to her bungalow.

'I need your help on something important, Mrs B.'

'Today's washing day young Francis, so I'm busy this morning.'

'I understand but I need you to look at something. It shouldn't take long.'

McCall saw she was intrigued. He drove her back to Garth and they went through the woods to the dacha where he had already set up the Eumig and screen.

'This is all a bit mysterious. What's it all about?'

'You'll see, Mrs B. Just watch this little bit of film.'

Then he played the footage of himself as a toddler with his mother. Bea stood smiling in the garden of the McCall family home as young McCall was handed to a dark-skinned man who laughed at the camera and put him on his shoulders.

'Who is that man holding me, Mrs B?'

'Why are you asking me this?'

'Because I think you know him.'

Mrs Bishop sat in Francis's old chair, plucking the hem of her dress as she always did to cover uncertainty. But she had not looked surprised at what she'd seen.

'What's his name, Mrs B?'

'He was a friend of the Wrenns, that's all I know.'

'Yes, but what was his name?'

'I don't rightly remember. There were so many people coming and going here.'

'OK, then what about his job... do you know what he did or where he came from?'

'This isn't fair, Francis. Like I says, it's all a long time ago.'

'But you've usually got such a good memory, Mrs B.'

'For some things, yes.'

'Then why not this?'

'Like I've said before, leave people in peace. What's done is over.'

'But this man obviously knew my mother... and he was at the funeral so he's still alive and I can talk to him about her if only I can find out who he is.'

'That's as may be but I want to go home.'

If nothing else, it was interesting she did not tell him to ask Bea. They drove back to her bungalow in silence. McCall regretted ambushing her, making such a big deal out of it. Mrs Bishop turned to him as she unlocked her front door.

'You've had no breakfast, have you?'

She scrambled some eggs and watched him eat as she always had. They sat drinking tea, still saying nothing but smiling when their eyes met. McCall thought he should go but she motioned him to stay where he was.

'You see things when you work in other people's places, young Francis... you see things and hear things but it's best to keep your mouth shut in service.'

She looked out of her window, over the graveyard towards the trees of Garth Woods that hid the big house beyond.

'Your mum was up here on her own more than once... came here when you was just little, before you was brought here for good.'

'I never knew this, Mrs B.'

'Well, it's true... on David's memory, it's as true as I sit here.'

'So you actually met my mother... talked to her?'

'Many's the time, yes.'

'Tell me what she was like as a person.'

'She had trouble at home, that was clear as day but a nice enough little woman, only ordinary like the rest of us but a decent soul.'

'What did she tell you about her family, where she came from?'

'No, nothing... she didn't seem to have no people of her own.'

'And the man in the cine film... who was he, Mrs B?'

'All I know is he was on the wireless a lot, reporting wars and such, like you.'

'You mean for the BBC?

'Like from places where you've been, yes.'

McCall could not understand her reluctance to tell him any of this. Nothing she had said could offend anyone. Yet she started ruching her skirt again.

'Is there something else about this man, Mrs B?'

'Gossip, yes.'

'What kind of gossip?'

'About him and Mrs Wrenn.'

'You mean they were having some sort of affair?'

'I never said that. It wasn't my business to know and I never stuck my nose in.'

'No but that's what you meant, isn't it?'

'Always going away, she was. She'd get a phone call and she'd be away.'

'With this man?'

'I don't know who she went with or where she went but all as I do know is that's why you had to live at my house so much.'

Evie was due to meet Phillip on Westminster Bridge at eleven thirty. He would be late. He always was. Brilliant academic he might be but he couldn't find soap in a sink. That was Phillip. Manic depressive, too – and with insecurities even worse than hers. No wonder their marriage was on the rocks. But he kept phoning her, still desperate for reconciliation after all these months. Everyone needed hope and she had loved him, after a fashion, since Oxford. So she agreed to counselling, if only to ease the final separation when it would come. Not till then did she ever think she could tell McCall she had been married.

Big Ben struck twelve. Tourists pointed, cameras clicked and the city bustled by. Evie wondered about all the countless trysts and discreet moments that would have begun on this bridge. Bea had stood here once... Bea and the man with no name who had looked so happy holding McCall, the child. What was the story there?

Then Phillip approached, odd socks, no tie, waving with one hand and just about holding onto a plastic bag of history text books in the other. Evie smiled and they hugged. What a shambles. He should never be let on the streets without his mother.

McCall saw Bea naked once... in the room where he now stood, about to play the burglar. At six years old, it had been the most confusing sight he'd ever seen. He had cut his finger so ran to the house for a plaster. All the old lead pipes were gurgling so he knew she was emptying her bath. Some primitive compulsion seized him and he found himself crouching on the step of the maid's stairs, peeping down the long landing. Part of him was playing out a made-up story about secrets and spies. Part of him wasn't.

Bea came out of the bathroom and walked towards her bedroom. She was completely undressed... just as something inside of him wanted her to be. It felt naughty but he went to Bea's door and stood watching her towelling her glossy hair. As she did so her breasts swayed above the inexplicable black bib at the root of her soft white belly. Here was infinite strangeness, compelling but beyond his understanding.

Bea looked up and smiled. She didn't shout or make him feel dirty but just pulled on her nylon stockings then selected her clothes from the wardrobe and dressed for the day. No words passed between them.

McCall had pretended concern for his cut finger which he held so tight that it dripped little poppies of blood onto Bea's carpet.

Now it was all different. Bea had had an affair and betrayed Francis... *their* Francis. She'd been no better than Helen. Bea's bureau was open but its hidden compartment wasn't and he had no idea how to spring the lock. So he stole through her other belongings like a thief. He turned out every drawer, cupboard and closet and even the pockets of her dresses and coats. But there was nothing – not a scented envelope or a coded note. He even checked the floorboards but none was loose enough to make a hiding place.

How any of this would help him to find the truth about his real family, he neither knew nor cared. It just got rid of some of his anger.

133

He was interrupted by someone knocking at the porch door. It was the rector's wife who doubled as village correspondent for the *Ludlow Advertiser*. She wanted to check Francis's war record for an obituary. McCall made her coffee and saw she'd a list of mourners from the funeral.

'Where'd you get those?'

'We leave cards on the pews and people fill in their details.'

McCall went down the names. All the old Whitehall spooks were there – Evie, too. But no one whose name sounded foreign. The missing mourner had not signed in.

Bea was a stubborn and awkward patient, much given to stick banging and glaring at speech therapists and nurses. But they did not object to her annoyance and frustration. It showed a will to fight the depression that can overwhelm those who have suffered a stroke.

She was still grieving, not just for Francis but for the person she had once been and whose freedoms she'd taken for granted. Yet after a visit from an elderly man as smart and elegant as Bea herself, the re-hab nurses saw improvements. He had sat holding her hand, his head close to hers. They heard him whispering in a silk-soft voice and saw the tears. Yet after he had gone she was happier than they'd ever seen her. The specialist thought she might yet recover some speech. It seemed she had something to live for.

Bea was propped up against her pillows when McCall visited. A hairdresser had been in to wash and set her hair. She had make-up on, too. Bea gave McCall a guarded, lop-sided smile and wrote him a message on her pad. *Go home, I.* It'd be a while before her mental grammar improved. *Soon go.* McCall nodded encouragement. *Garth go, me.*

McCall had felt rather ashamed after rummaging through Bea's possessions. It had been a sordid intrusion into her privacy, however upset and mistrustful he'd become with her. Yet what he was about to do was more of the same.

He took out the four photographs she had dropped on the orchard lawn and laid them out to see her reaction… the Nazi soldiers, the concentration camp victims, herself and her alleged lover. He watched closely, for though the stroke had twisted that once beautiful face, it could not take the truth from her eyes.

'What is his name?'

Bea shook her head. If she was not aware before, she now knew what McCall was after.

'I missed him at the funeral, Bea. I want to write and thank him for coming. I thought he could be one of Francis's old diplomat friends.'

She scowled and waved him out of the ward. McCall's audience was over. Bea turned her back and didn't even watch him go.

Next morning, McCall received a registered parcel and a note from Edgar Fewtrell.

> *I enjoyed our supper. Can we meet at my office next Wednesday morning at 10? We can conclude the business I mentioned to you. The enclosed packet is from your guardian who left me instructions to post it to you exactly a fortnight after his death. I have no idea what is in it so I hope he has left some explanation of his own.*

He hadn't. Inside, McCall found four more reels of cine film that Francis had labelled *A, B, C,* and *D* in red felt-tip pen. With them was a large black and white photograph of a well-dressed, intelligent-looking man with a small swastika badge in his left lapel. Beyond that, the package was empty. Francis never lacked a sense of theatre.

McCall did what he knew he was meant to and hurried down to the dacha. The first cassette was Super-8 with integral sound. McCall laced it in and the screen showed a locked-off shot of Francis's leather armchair by the pot-bellied stove. Someone could be heard moving behind the tripod. Then Francis walked into view and sat down. He looked at the camera, fiddling with his glasses like a politician about to do an election broadcast – but in gardening clothes and from a shed.

> *Bit awkward this, Mac... know you'll understand, though. Couple of things I want to get straight with you. First off, if we'd been able to have a son, you're just the sort of chap I'd have wanted... we had some good times, didn't we? A few larks and stories and I only wish I'd been around more in the early days and we could've spent longer together. Anyway, wasn't to be. Drawn a veil over most of those times, now. Best thing, too... not that anyone's going to let a scribbler like you get wind of them. I've not always been proud of some of the things I've been involved in... bit late to make amends now, I know. But see what you can make of these bits of home movies I've asked old Fewtrell to send on to you. I had some others once upon a time but can't seem to keep track of everything. Still, you always liked a challenge and these'll give you that, all right. Steer clear of the Official Secrets Act if you can and all those silly buggers in bowler hats who go round snooping. Never liked them... anyway, that's about it. Good luck in life, Mac... goodbye, little friend.*

Francis half smiled and began to rise out of his chair. He was stopped by a final thought, one last little message.

Don't forget me, Mac... will you? I've always tried to do my best. Remember me...

He moved out of frame to switch off the camera. McCall stayed where he was, unable to see anything else, anyway.

Chapter Twenty Seven

He has died too often,
And something has been said
that makes him aware of the bodies
floating face downwards
in his mind.

McCall ran a deep bath in the roll top tub. The wall mirror misted over but he could glimpse the nakedness of someone he once knew...skin drawn tight across the crib of his chest, heart yet to heal. He sank into the warm, amniotic darkness.

Why? It was always the most important of questions.

Francis's poignant message from beyond the grave he understood... but why had he willed him the riddle of this other footage? Francis had always been a camera nut but why had *this* material been shot?

McCall dressed then packed a Moroccan leather overnight bag. Francis's photograph of the Nazi lay on a chair. It had been credit stamped to a Berlin picture agency, 'Presse Bild Zentrale, Friedrichstr 214' but bore no caption, name or date. The face was handsome but aloof, lit from the side so it was in half shadow, accentuating the pitting caused by adolescent acne. His fair hair was parted on the right and he wore a suit of finely woven stripes with a pale shirt and silk tie patterned in tiny triangles. McCall guessed he would be under forty – maybe a lawyer on the up, a mid-career civil servant or a party apparatchik. Not an obvious thug but not an innocent, either.

And there he was in, this same Nazi, some years older and being secretly filmed by Francis in Reel B.

What was Francis up to – and *why?*

He had caught him walking down the steps of a municipal building in a dark overcoat. To get this tight, Francis could only have hidden in a vehicle parked close by. The shot panned with the man till he disappeared behind a Mercedes convertible with a sloping grill. Two blackened church spires were visible at the end of a long thoroughfare of shops.

The camera must then have been switched off, but whether for days or weeks was unclear. The next location was in open country. The pictures showed skid marks veering off a main road wet with rain, and patches of charred undergrowth by a tree.

The final sequence on Reel B was a bag job – a covert walking shot taken in a scrapyard behind a garage to reveal the burnt-out wreckage of an early Volkswagen Beetle with a split rear window. McCall didn't get it.

So he had pressed on with reels C and D.

And that is when he had really sat up and taken notice.

McCall made three phone calls before driving to Hereford for a fast train to London. He checked Bea was still improving but left no message. Then he rang a TV facilities house in Soho to book time to make several freeze frame enlargements from this new 8mm footage. His last call was to fix a meet with Gerry Gavronski, a contact he had known and trusted for years.

An almost guilty feeling of relief came over him. His own illness, Francis's death, Bea's lies – these stresses lifted. He was a driven hack again, back on the road with a sniff of an intriguing story. Nothing and no one would get in his way.

Evie rang as he was about to leave.

'I've got something on the missing mourner.'

'Terrific. What?'

'No name yet but his car is shown as belonging to the Israeli Embassy.'

'Christ, really?'

'Yeah, our man's well over retirement age so he's unlikely to be a diplomat himself but he must have connections to borrow an official limo.'

Evie never let him down. McCall told himself to remember that.

Gerry Gavronski was an unmarried, overweight, poor-sighted lump of a man with an electric shock of gingery grey hair. He worked – and seemed to live – in a landfill of an office three floors above Tottenham Court Road tube station, editing a small circulation anti-fascist magazine. His knowledge of fascists, past and present, was encyclopaedic.

McCall showed him Francis's photograph of the man with the Nazi lapel badge.

'I'm looking for a name, Gerry – a name and anything you can come up with about this guy.'

Gavronski pushed his glasses high onto his head and stared at the picture. He began banging through the drawers of his metal filing cabinets. On the wall above Gavronski's typewriter McCall noticed another scrawled death threat had been pinned up since his last visit. Gavronski held to a single belief – that fascism was a latent and ineradicable pestilence.

His little magazine charted any new sign of infection. For that, he had been stabbed, beaten up and had acid thrown at him.

'So, McCall... here he is in the files. *Jakob Rösler.*'

He handed McCall a picture showing Francis's Nazi addressing a meeting. A paragraph from a German paper glued on the back confirmed Rösler's name.

'So what did Rösler do, Gerry?'

'He was an SS officer, not that senior but dedicated enough.'

'Dedicated to what?'

'To killing people, stupid. That's what they did. That was their purpose.'

Gavronski sat back, eyes closed affectedly as if about to give a tutorial. McCall took the cue and began scribbling in his notebook.

Summer, '41... systematic SS sweep... Minsk, Bialystok, Lvov, Vilna, Kovno. Jews killed wherever found. Most shot. Other atrocities – some pumped with water till exploded, others forced into buildings, burned alive. SS men in units of ten called Einsatzgruppen. Very mobile. Aided by local collaborators, militiamen. In Lithuania, raids by Einsatzkommando 3. By December, 200,000 Lith. Jews eliminated.

'And was Rösler somehow involved in all this?'

'From memory, I think he played some organisational role, yes.'

'So he wasn't actually on the front line... not pulling the trigger?'

'I can't be sure but you must remember, it didn't take an education to shoot a queue of naked women and children. but it needed lots of logistical brains to get all the killers in place to do it.'

'Have you any idea what happened to Rösler later?'

'On this I'm hazy but I think he was captured quite a while after the war.'

'Any idea what happened to him after that?'

'He'd have got hard labour but he wouldn't have been locked up for long.'

'Yet he was a murderer, in effect?'

'As were thousand of others and for them, not even a parking ticket.'

Gavronski went back to his filing cabinets and retrieved a sheet of paper.

'One of these gentlemen kept a diary that came to light years later. I've long given up trying to fathom the minds of such people but you try if you want.'

He handed McCall a translation of an Einsatzgruppen man's entry for July 14 1941.

We go into the woods and look for a suitable place for mass execution. We order the prisoners to dig their graves. What can they be thinking? I believe each has the hope of not being shot. I don't feel the slightest stir of pity. That is how it is and has got to be. Slowly, the grave gets bigger and deeper.

The grind of traffic along Oxford Street faded to nothing. McCall heard only the scuff of polished boots in the soft sandy floor of a pine forest, a shouted order, the whimpering of those about to die.

Money, watches and valuables are collected. The women go first.

McCall imagined the iron echoes of gunfire and the flap of wings as birds lifted in panic from the tops of trees and circled the pit below.

The shooting goes on. Two heads have been shot off. Nearly all fall into the grave unconscious only to suffer a long while. The last group have to throw the corpses into the grave. They have to stand ready for their own execution. They all tumble into the grave.

How obedient everyone was... compliant, even. No revolt, no attempt to rush the firing squad and tear at those bored faces and die content. Just a queue. An orderly queue. No one causing any trouble.

'So, Mac – what is your interest in Rösler?'

Gavronski was a long time on the earth and McCall wouldn't insult him with a lie... not a big one, anyway.

'I've been given some information but I don't know where it's leading.'

'But why's it come to you?'

'Good question, Gerry. If I find out, you'll be the first I'll tell.'

'You know Rösler didn't die in bed, don't you?'

McCall glanced up, trying not to appear overly intrigued.

'No, I didn't. What happened to him?'

'A car crash, I think.'

'When was that?'

'Early fifties, mid fifties, something like that. I'd have to check.'

'Was there anything unusual about it?'

'What an odd question. It was a car crash. Why should you think otherwise?'

McCall blanked him with a grin then wrote a cheque for £75 and put it between the rollers of Gavronski's typewriter.

'A donation, Gerry.'

Then he told him about trying to trace the mourner who had attended Francis's funeral in an Israeli Embassy car. Gavronski had friends in such places.

'Is this connected to Rösler in some way?'

'No, Gerry. This is strictly a family matter.'

Sometimes, only a fib will do.

The pissy reek of cannabis hung about the cutting room where Evie met up with McCall in Soho. She did not approve of him smoking dope nor did she buy into his irrational excitement about the footage Francis had bequeathed him. McCall had been under great emotional strain – and it was showing. He was an obsessive by nature. But he was searching for patterns or answers in something he had been left by a man who'd lost his mind. Evie also sensed it somehow threatened Bea and that bothered her.

'You must keep a sense of proportion, McCall. Francis had dementia when he put all this together.'

'Listen to me, will you? Look at the footage.'

She watched Reel B and agreed the blow-up freeze-frame of the man leaving the civic building and the one in the photograph could be the same – Jakob Rösler. McCall insisted the spires in the background were of the cathedral in Cologne because that was where Rösler lived after the war. The crash site and the wrecked Volkswagen followed next.

'And guess how Rösler died.'

'Don't tell me... careless driving. But you don't know this was his car.'

'No, not yet but just watch the screen.'

Another freeze frame came on – the face of a man Rösler passed as he came out of the civic building. McCall told her to remember this image.

Reel C played in and there was Bea with all the style of an actress on set, walking into frame with McCall as a little boy with sparrow legs and hair like a bird's nest. They crossed a market square hand in hand. Behind them was a vast sugar loaf of a mountain covered in fir trees.

The picture changed to the inside of a toyshop hung with puppets and dolls and wobbled through to a workshop and a young woman carving a figure in wood. The camera then panned to a bald man chiselling the face of Jesus from a large, coin-shaped piece of timber. The man looked up, but only for a moment. As he did, so the camera caught something like fear in his eyes. McCall paused the footage.

'This reel was shot in a place called Oberammergau in Bavaria where we went for a holiday because Francis was working out there. Now look at this.'

The sequence resumed in the street outside. A man stood on the corner but only for a second or two before he moved away. McCall stopped the footage again.

'Recognise him?'

'No.'

'Well look again.'

He'd had another freeze-frame blow up made of this Reel C man and ran it alongside the image of the person Rösler passed walking out of shot in Reel B.

'They're the same man… in both places.'

'Come on, McCall. They're far too indistinct to tell.'

'Believe me. They're the same guy. That's our shy mourner.'

'Mac… it never is. What you're saying doesn't stand up.'

'You said yourself he had a memorable face.'

'Sure, but this image is all blurred. You're seeing things because you want to see them.'

'Francis left me this stuff for a reason. He wanted me to follow it up.'

'McCall – his mind was skewed. He was sick. None of this truly means anything.'

A receptionist came in and said there was someone on the phone for McCall. He was back a minute later, serious and calmer.

'OK, maybe this helps. That was my contact. He says our mourner is an Israeli guy called Arie Minsky.'

'Minsky? Was he a diplomat?'

'No, not a diplomat – a war correspondent. Very well connected.'

'But what does any of this *mean*, Mac?'

'Too early to say but I can tell you something else – Minsky and Bea were lovers.'

'How the hell do you know that?'

'Because Mrs Bishop suggested as much… and in a way, Bea's told me herself.'

'Bea? How could she do that?'

'By her reaction when I showed her his photograph.'

'You heartless bugger, McCall. She's ill –'

'She's always been tougher than she looks. But she wouldn't tell me his name.'

'I don't damn well blame her.'

'Maybe not but she knew I'd recognise it if she did.'

'How would you do that?'

'Because I knew him as *Uncle Harry* when I was little. I'd just forgotten his face.'

McCall played her the last of the three mute cassettes, Reel D. His notes read : *high angle cityscape, pans l to r / low rise office blocks / big advert "Garry Finance Corporation" on wall of medium skyscraper / Odeon Cinema / cars driving on r h side / 50s-60s America? / location change / camera in bag / suburban street, trees, white clapboard houses, tended gardens / railroad track / grain silo / man getting into car / same man hailed by cameraman, points (maybe giving directions) drives away.*

'I didn't spot your Mr Minsky.'

'Maybe not. But he'll be there... wherever it is.'

Evie had not seen McCall's journo blood lust before. It was not attractive. The story was everything and he would get it.

She didn't doubt that. His callousness frightened her. It took no account of casualties along the way – especially those on his own side.

'What are you going to do, now?'

'Go to Germany.'

'Mac, no. You can't do that. Please don't.'

'I have to. That's where the evidence leads.'

'Think about what this could do to Bea. She doesn't deserve any of this.'

'Maybe not. Then again, neither did I.'

Chapter Twenty Eight

Rösler's death was reported in the *Schwäbische Zeitung* in March 1955. A young librarian saw McCall struggling with a pocket dictionary so she volunteered to help. He bought coffee in a pavement café later and re-read his note of the translation.

A businessman, Jakob Rösler, had a fatal car accident with his wife yesterday on the autobahn south of Düsseldorf where they lived. The police say that for as yet unexplained reasons, their Volkswagen crossed the median line, narrowly missing other traffic, and crashed into a tree on the other side. Through the force of the collision, Herr Rösler's car caught fire. His wife was thrown thirty metres and both were pronounced dead at the scene.

Those five words – for as yet unexplained reasons – gave McCall reason to be cheerful.

He watched the strolling passers-by, the elegant, the fashionable and the elderly in whose name the Nazis had put the feeble minded to death and rid the Reich of all its social undesirables – Jews, gypsies, homosexuals, communists.

Most of the Germans he had met in Cologne and now in Düsseldorf, made special efforts to help him, as if by such little acts of penance their inherited guilt for history's greatest crime might be mitigated. But

142

McCall's hostility to their nation had been osmotically absorbed from Bea and Francis and childhood comics so was incapable of being unlearnt overnight. It had taken Francis a lifetime.

The burning rubble he and his crew left behind was buried beneath shimmering glass offices now. The stench of the entombed dead had long since blown away. For those taking their ease in the Königsallee that sunny day, only the future mattered. The old shall die and the world will move on. The God of Profit forgives all in the end.

McCall paid his bill and plotted a route on his street map. He crossed a paved square towards a district of solid, four-storey tenements built of red engineering brick during the Kaiser's time. It took only a few minutes to locate Bruckner Strasse. Inside the large communal hall of Number 7, a row of mail boxes showed *Herr Theo Rösler* living in Flat 5 on the first landing.

McCall walked up the wide stone steps and heard a piano being played, the closer he got to Rösler's door. He knocked and the music stopped. Someone approached a Judas hole to peer at him. Here was the joy of journalism… either being told to sod off or offered the key to a box of secrets that hadn't been opened for years. Whichever it would be, he got ready to pitch.

Evie could tell Bea was improving. Her eyes sparkled again. The depression of those first days in hospital was much less evident. She was trying her hardest to speak, struggling to make herself understood and not depend on scratching illegible messages. But the speech therapist still had much work to do.

'Gone, Mac. Not here, Evie, why?'

'He's working on something, Mrs Wrenn… a story he's picked up.'

'See me, when?'

'As soon as he comes back, yes. I'm sure he'll be in to visit you straight away.'

'Where gone?'

'I'm not sure. Abroad somewhere, I think.'

'Why?'

Evie could lie for her country but confronted by Bea's unblinking stare, her hesitation was an answer in itself. Bea's mood changed. She became quite distracted. Evie now knew McCall had shown her the photograph of Minsky and asked his name. Bea must suspect a link between that and why McCall had gone overseas.

'He'll be home soon, Mrs Wrenn. Please don't worry.'

Bea's face suggested it was too late for that. She found her pad to write a note.

Stay, you stay.
'Of course I'll stay.'
Talk, us. Talk.
Evie was about to reply when she heard the sound of a metal tipped walking stick striking the tiled floor behind her. She turned quickly. And there stood Arie Minsky, the missing mourner, smiling at them both.

Theo Rösler was his father's son. He had the same silvery hair, the strong, intelligent features but much warmer, kinder eyes. McCall said he was researching a possible television programme for the BBC and would like to discuss it with him. Rösler pondered, but only for a moment, then stood aside and gestured him in. McCall never expected it would be that easy.

He was offered English tea and left alone in the main living area. It was a room of rare serenity. The pale walls were empty save for a single oil painting of a child by a tree in a garden. Six vermilion tulips in a glass vase formed a centrepiece on a table of plain alpine sycamore and one entire corner of the apartment was dominated by the Bechstein piano he'd heard being played. Rösler returned from his kitchen and served tea in white Wiesenthal cups with chocolate biscuits on matching plates.

'So, this is about my father, yes?'

'If it's painful for you, I apologise.'

'All pain passes one day but it is strange to me that you should come all this way to talk about him all these years later.'

Hacks always play with a marked deck. They also hide cards up their sleeves then deal from the bottom. It's what cops do, too. But with Rösler, McCall could hear Mrs Bishop's voice. *Honesty's always the best policy.* McCall needed Rösler more than Rösler needed McCall.

'It's about the car accident in which your parents died.'

'Why is that now important to create such an interest for you?'

McCall told him of the covert footage – but not his true relationship to the man who shot it.

'It was filmed by someone who was then working for the British government.'

'I do not understand why such a person should make such a film.'

'Nor me – but he did.'

'For what purpose would he do such a thing?'

'I would love to have asked him myself but unfortunately he is dead so I can't.'

'How do you know what you have seen is the same accident of my parents?'

'I've checked your father's picture in the public record and he is the man in the film.'

144

'And tell me, please, how this material came into your hands.'

'A lawyer gave it to me but I cannot give you more than that just yet.'

'So, will you tell me what sort of motor car my parents had?'

'We call them Beetles, a Volkswagen from the early 1950s... split rear window.'

Rösler nodded then put down his cup. He told McCall to wait and went into another room. A short haired cat with only half a tail moved with stealth across the dove-grey carpet and lay in a patch of sunlight by the glass doors to a narrow balcony. Rösler returned with a box of photographs. He spread them on the table – women in long frocks and big hats, men with whiskers, stiff and pompous. McCall immediately recognised the pictures of Rösler the Nazi – but in civvies, strolling across a lawn, seated at a desk then standing with his wife by the very car in which they were to die.

'Is this the same man in your film?'

'Yes. That's him.'

Theo Rösler went to his piano as if distracted and needing refuge. He began the opening bars of a prelude. McCall knew Rösler was stalling, playing for time.

'Do you know the works of Schumann?'

'No, I'm sorry. I don't.'

'Some of it is said to represent the opposite states of mind... even the duality of characters he saw within his delusional self... you might think that quite fitting for us Germans.'

Even to McCall's tin ear, Rösler's playing was sublime.

'You must understand we were not always barbarians in this country... always having to atone for the sins others committed. I was a child when Hitler rose to power and I can remember all the excitement and those parades and my father being swept up in the fervour of this great national renewal. Only later did we begin to understand... about the camps and the Jews. You will know, of course, the Jews wore yellow stars to mark them out as the damned but there were other coloured badges in the camps.'

Rösler suddenly stopped playing and advanced on McCall.

'The criminals wore green triangles and the political prisoners red and homosexuals pink. What colour badge do you think I would have been made to wear?'

'I'm sorry, I couldn't say.'

'A pink triangle. That is what I would have been made to wear before I was shot or gassed and thrown into the ovens.'

'But your father was in the SS, wasn't he?'

'And do you think that would have saved me?'

'Your politics were obviously not his.'

145

'No, not then, not later. I became a music teacher and I would never talk to him about those days.'

'Do you think he was guilty of war crimes?'

'My mother swore to me he never killed anyone. He was in business before the war and then in the army and was no more than a clerk. That is what she said.'

'Did you believe her?'

'I cannot know what the truth was from those times and if you ask me if my mother did then I would say she probably did not, either. It was convenient for people to forget.'

McCall asked if he thought his parents were killed accidentally.

'What is behind your question?'

'I've looked at the newspapers of that time and they reported that your parents' car veered off the road for no reason.'

'That is so. The car was not old, nothing was found wrong with it.'

'So how was the accident explained officially?'

'It wasn't, but if you are saying someone made it crash deliberately, why should anyone do such a thing?'

'Your father had been an SS man. Maybe he had enemies?'

'No, he was not important in the war or after it. He was in jail for what he did and it makes no sense for anyone to kill him, whatever you are seeing in your bits of film.'

Rösler stood up almost angrily. He insisted McCall should see the place where his parents died. It was if he needed to convince not just McCall of what he believed but himself, too.

They drove into gentle farming country in Rösler's Audi, parked off the main road then walked towards a large tree half way down an embankment. It was a Norway maple, the sort that folklore says protects against witches. This was where Jakob Rösler burnt to death like a heretic. His cultured son went very quiet.

'Beyond the tree, my mother was thrown there…. they told me she didn't suffer.'

McCall began to detect a profound need in Rösler to believe his parents died through an act of God, not man. The alternative was unbearable. They would have been murdered. Their sensitive, artistic son would then have to ask why anyone should do such a thing… and the answer would scar him for life.

And so it was with McCall.

When Evie left Bea and Arie, her affection and regard for the old lady was even greater. People like Evie, ones with little known personal history, are readily dazzled by those with ancestry to spare.

146

Bea and Arie were sure it had been right to tell her the truth, as much for their sakes as for Evie's. When they waved her from the ward, Bea felt her soul being released from its cell. Arie had explained everything when Bea's words wouldn't come and she could not write quickly enough to keep pace with her jumbled thoughts. Evie listened and questioned until at last she, too, understood. They did not bind her to secrecy but urged discretion about how and when she let McCall into his own life.

With Evie gone, Bea had a final confession to make. She got Arie to push her wheelchair into the patients' lounge. It had a view across the Shropshire hills, to all that was and all that might have been. She drew him to her and kissed his face again and again then held his hand to her belly.

He was not sure why Bea was doing this then she pointed at him, at herself, at her womb. She sketched the outline of a baby on her pad... a boy baby. Arie began to speak. Bea shook her head.

Below the image of the child, her uncertain hand formed the crudest representation of a gravestone. On it, she wrote *'Liad, RIP September 3 1939'*.

At last she had told him. They had had a son. Arie knelt and held her close. He shut his eyes and all those he had once loved came before him again and in their arms, each cradled this unbodied child, this new holy innocent whose smile he had never seen, whose hand he had never held.

Arie Minsky could only weep then.

Chapter Twenty Nine

The Röslers were killed some thirty years earlier. Any police, fire or ambulance officer who might have attended the crash had retired or died. Their records no longer existed, either. McCall checked. Even the back street garage where Francis filmed the Volkswagen being scrapped had closed down. No independent evidence existed to cast doubt on Jakob Rösler and his wife dying in anything other than a freak accident. On its own, Francis's footage proved nothing. But there had to be links, common factors in a bigger story. Somewhere. McCall just needed to find it.

He caught a train to Munich, then on to the town of Murnau where he waited for a local connection to Oberammergau. He sat on a wooden bench vandalised by a newly cut swastika in the blue paintwork. His train climbed a single line through rich green pastures spotted with yellow and white alpine flowers.

The landscape got steeper and more wooded as they clattered through tidy little villages – Bad Kohlgrub, Saulgrub, Unterammergau. Each had ordered rows of well maintained houses with tended gardens and neat stacks of split logs, drying for winter fires to come.

Most of McCall's fellow passengers were elderly. None would meet his gaze with their watery pink eyes. He wondered whether these people were as guiltless as Theo Rösler wished his father to be or if their hands, bent and liver-spotted now, had saluted the Fuhrer and torn down his enemies.

McCall checked into the *Hotel Alte Post* in Oberammergau where he had stayed with Bea all those years before. He walked into its remembered streets, a religious toy town of a place, hardly more than a painted backdrop to the Passion play its people had staged every ten years since escaping the plague three centuries back.

He stood once more by buildings decorated with high priests and garishly coloured angels then gazed again at Christ's execution – an image of mob hatred, intrigue and revenge that had so terrified him as a child.

'They've banged nails into him, Bea… he's bleeding all over himself.'

'It's only a picture.'

'But why are they hurting him?'

'They were cruel times, Mac. Horrible things were done.'

He doesn't like Germany or Germans. This is where mass murderers come from. He's frightened but mustn't show it. The Germans tried to kill Francis and his other Daddy but they were more clever and killed the Germans first. The people passing by look ordinary enough but they could try and murder him at any time 'cos that's what they do in the comics. But he's got his cowboy gun and they'll not take him without a fight.

'Bang! Bang! You're dead.'

McCall headed to the outskirts of Oberammergau and the NATO school where Francis once taught. It was a fortress, bulwarked on two sides by walls of the blackest stone he had ever seen. The Nazi secret police had used it and all Bavaria's mountain air would never cleanse its stench of evil. He hurried on up the dirt path to the marble statue of Christ on the cross, high in the woods above the village. It was as he recalled, a brooding, silent place with rags of misty clouds caught in the fir trees. He went to the same bench where he had sat with Bea and looked across to Francis passing something to Arie Minsky – *Uncle Harry*.

They said it wasn't him. But even as a child, he'd known the truth.

After dinner in the hotel, he rang Evie. She wanted to know what he had discovered about Rösler.

'Not much more than I knew already – except Frau Rösler died in the crash, too.'

'You can't still feel this is worth all the effort, McCall.'

'I've only just started.'

'Bea's coming out of hospital tomorrow. She's still quite feeble.'

'She's bound to be.'

'I'm going back up there this weekend. Shall I give her your love?'

'Sure. Why not?'

McCall's search of the *Garmisch Partenkirchner Tagblatt's* files for the six months after the holiday he and Bea had had in Oberammergau failed to produce a single story remotely similar to the suspicious deaths of the Röslers'. The village librarian, a woman of infinite goodwill, tracked through every copy but finally opened her hands to heaven.

'Nothing. We find nothing, I am so sorry.'

McCall tried to stay positive. He walked the streets till he found where the toyshop was – or used to be. It had been converted into a private house. An elderly man answered his knock but understood nothing of McCall's phrase book German. He called inside for his young granddaughter who was learning English. McCall said he was searching for the two wood carvers who ran the toyshop in the mid 1950s. She translated for the old man who gabbled a defensive reply and turned back indoors.

'My grandfather says he doesn't know anything.'

'About the wood carvers?'

'No, about all that happened.'

'I don't follow. *What* happened?'

'We only live in this place for nine years.'

'You mean something happened here before you came?'

'Yes. There is a policeman, very old now. You can talk to him.'

She gave directions to a house beyond the church on Ettaler Strasse, under the shadow of Mount Kofel. When McCall reached it, he saw a sandy-haired man digging manure into his front garden. His hands were chapped red and soiled by the shit of cows. He had been big once, well over six feet, but was shrinking with age and wore his skin like an overcoat several sizes too big.

McCall smiled and got out his deck of marked cards.

They sat in an untidy, widower's, kitchen eating cold veal and cheese. Konrad Wetzel had been a sergeant of police – steady and astute, the sort of dependable country cop the authorities left alone. Not that crime was

149

rife in a village devoted to the glory of God. Wetzel chewed with ruminant efficiency and waited for McCall to open.

'I came here with my parents when I was very young and my father has just died. My mother is very ill now so I'm on a kind of pilgrimage, I suppose.'

'But why are you looking for the wood carvers?'

'Because when we were here many years ago, we bought some religious carvings from these people and I would like to take some home for my mother.'

'Many shops sell carvings in Oberammergau. Go there.'

'Yes, but I want my carvings from these same people.'

'Well, it is not possible now.'

'Why not?'

'Tell me first, what is your profession?'

'I am a legal representative. I work with many lawyers and the police.'

Wetzel left the table. His head almost bumped into the beams of his ceiling. He lit a briar pipe and moved to an armchair by his kitchen range. Old cops, old cases...

'The wood carver was Wilhelm Frank... him and his daughter. One day, he goes.'

'He goes? You mean he left Oberammergau?'

'Goes, disappears. His daughter is upset, wanting us to search for him.'

'And did you?'

'Of course. We look in the mountains and the rivers... in all places but nothing.'

'You didn't find him?'

'No. His daughter gets a husband and closes the shop and she goes away also.'

'I see.'

'Yes, well many years pass and some children, some bad children, got into our tunnels.'

'Tunnels?'

'In the war, we have much secret work in Oberammergau to make a jet plane in a factory under the mountains here, in tunnels so your English bombers cannot see it.'

'Ah, so did the children find something in the tunnels?'

'You are a lawyer, you say?'

'I do para-legal work in London, yes.'

Wetzel went to a cupboard and brought out a file of papers with two black and white photographs attached. These he unclipped and pushed across the table to McCall.

'Wilhelm Frank... the wood carver.'

150

Or what remained of him.

All McCall could see were the bleached bones of a crucified skeleton assembled unnaturally on the stone floor, arms outstretched, right foot over left and the mouth of the skull open in a scream that would never end. And in the claw of his right hand was a photograph – a copy of one of those that Bea dropped on the orchard lawn at Garth when she had collapsed.

It showed the nine uniformed soldiers newly arrived in a town square, boots polished, handguns in holsters, standing by their rifles and stout leather suitcases. All keen to get on with their work. But it was not exactly the same as Bea's picture. A cross had been pencilled on the face of one of the soldiers... Wilhelm Frank.

The man who had once carved the face of Christ with such delicate perfection would have died in the dark under the eyes of the patient rats.

McCall cleared his throat.

'So you had a gruesome murder to investigate, Herr Wetzel?'

'Not a murder, no – an accident.'

'An *accident*? How could this man's death have been an accident?'

'A fall of rocks, probably. That is what we felt.'

'But the way the skeleton was left... crucified like that. How could that be from a fall of rocks?'

'Those children could have done it...or others before. A joke in poor taste.'

'But the photograph in his hand – how do you explain that?'

'Anyone could have put that there.'

Wetzel stared through the foul smoke of his pipe with peasant defiance.

'Herr Wetzel, you couldn't possibly believe this was an accident, could you?'

'Officially, that is what was decided.'

'But unofficially, it must have been murder... surely?'

'That is your opinion –'

'But based upon these pictures.'

'The police in any country need evidence, proof. We find no proof of murder.'

'But did Wilhelm Frank have enemies, someone who hated him enough to do this?'

'Who is to say? We found no obvious cause of death so we found no murderer.'

The camera flash in the confined tunnel had caused the skeleton to appear luminously pale against the black rock. The image seemed almost painted, like a crude medieval depiction of man's descent into hell.

'Was this man an old Nazi, Herr Wetzel? Is that why you didn't start a proper murder investigation?'

Wetzel removed the pipe from between his yellow teeth and knocked its bowl of burnt ash into the hearth.

'There were meetings here afterwards, many meetings. Important people came.'

'You said this was only an accident. Why would important people come for that?'

'Oberammergau is a holy place, religious people visit us from all places in the world and we want it to stay like this.'

'You mean you didn't want any fuss?'

'Only *good* Germans are here, only good things.'

'So you covered up this man's murder?'

Wetzel rose out of his chair and opened the door to signal his hospitality had run out.

'I do not know who you are or why you are really here but you should know the past is best buried... like Wilhelm Frank himself.'

Chapter Thirty

Evie's bloodless response to the mysterious death of Wilhelm Frank annoyed McCall.

'In my trade, we call this red meat.'

'It's gone off, McCall. It'll poison you – and worry the life out of Bea, too.'

He had arrived back from Germany that morning. Bea had been doing the *Telegraph* crossword in her chair by the drawing room fire. They had exchanged smiles and touched cheeks, almost formally. Evie was around so he had no chance of asking the questions Bea would not want to answer, even if she still had the full power of speech. What he observed, though, was a mutually protective closeness developing between the two women. Everyone fell in love with Bea, eventually.

'Don't you see, Francis *did* know the significance of what he was leaving me.'

'How's a bit of film of a man who died in a car crash significant?'

'So you don't think there's anything strange about Wilhelm Frank's death, either?'

'You've no proof he was murdered.'

'He just broke his own arms and legs did he? Lay down to die like he'd been crucified and lo and behold, he'd once been secretly filmed by Francis, too.'

'That's just how the skeleton was found.'

'And I suppose it's just another coincidence that there was a copy of Bea's photograph wedged in its mitt –'

'Pictures like that were ten a penny after the war.'

'And that Minsky happens to appear in the footage of both these dead men?'

'That's your *belief,* McCall. Those blurry images aren't evidence he was there.'

He shook his head in disbelief. Evie tried softening her tone.

'Look, even if this conspiracy happened the way you say, it was years and years ago and all those who might've been involved are either dead or not the type to talk anyway. What's the point?'

'You might as well ask what's the point of journalism.'

'I'm not convinced it is just journalism, Mac. I think you're off on some very personal displacement activity.'

'Spare me the analyst's couch, for Christ's sake.'

'Look, Francis has just died. You've been ill, you're upset and confused about Francis, Bea, your birth parents. Everything. Your life's turned upside down, Mac. You're desperately trying to make sense of it all but the last thing you need right now is a mission impossible like this.'

McCall was out of patience. Evie was full of psycho-crap because she couldn't get her civil servant's head around what he was uncovering. He left her in the kitchen and took refuge in the dacha on his own.

Gerry Gavronski's background research on Arie Minsky arrived in the post. The Nazis murdered every member of Minsky's family. He had fought behind enemy lines with British commandos in the Special Operations Executive and was at the liberation of Belsen. Details of his rumoured role in the Jewish political underground were harder to find. But he was regarded as a fiercely independent freelance for Press and radio.

Gavronski attached a cutting from the *Baltimore Sun* which ran one of Minsky's pieces when the Soviets invaded Hungary in '56.

> So this is "Socialism", is it? I have seen for myself what Moscow's forces have done in the name of this great cause, not against fascists or counter-revolutionaries but against the weak, the poor and the defenceless who dared to question the puppet politicians in Budapest. And now they lie, dusted with lime in the streets where they fell to the invaders.

The gallows and torture chambers of the Hungarian secret police, once the stock in trade of the hated Nazis, are busy again under the protection of "friendly" Socialist tanks. No doubt revenge will be taken for those of their communist comrades whose bodies I saw hanging from street lamps. Lynchings are ugly in any language but understand why some occur before rushing to condemn.

Then Gavronski relayed an interesting rumour.

'Someone suggested Minsky was a bit part player in the Mossad team that ambushed Eichmann in Argentina and brought him to Jerusalem for the big Holocaust trial in '61. Maybe. What I know for sure is that he's divorced, no children, not involved in journalism anymore. Sits on the board of a publishing house in Akko where he lives. Hope this helps.'

It did, rather. Arie Minsky grew more fascinating by the day.

Two Nazi nobodies had come to violent ends, however officially explained away. But what role had a BBC stringer played in all this...and why had Francis and Bea agreed to help him?

It remained a tantalising Russian doll of a story, each clue having another hidden inside itself. McCall might go mad at not knowing. But if Francis's last reel could be linked to a third death – and if Minsky made another guest appearance in the footage – he was airborne.

McCall knew he should be grateful to Evie for spending time with Bea, especially till the builders finished. But his mind was elsewhere, not least on all the administrative papers Edgar Fewtrell needed signing for the property and wealth Francis had willed him. Mr Fewtrell asked whether his trip to Germany had been fruitful.

'How do you know I've been to Germany?'

'I'm not sure. Beatrice probably told me.'

'But she wasn't supposed to know.'

'Well, maybe it was your delightful Evie.'

McCall let this pass. He drove back to Garth to re-examine the third reel in the seclusion of the dacha. Francis must have been about nine or ten floors up to get the aerial pan across a grid of streets in what looked like a Mid West prairie city.

It showed a commercial district of early brick-built skyscrapers with heavy traffic driving on the right hand side. He'd had enlargements made of every frame that might possibly identify the location. An entire wall of one building was an advert for the Garry Finance Corporation. But it revealed neither telephone number nor address. US directory enquiries had no listing and three hotel signs and street names were all too blurred to read.

The only positive result came from a blow-up of the Odeon Cinema's frontage. It was showing *The Bridal Path,* which his film guide said was a British-made comedy released in 1959. At least McCall had a base-line date.

He retrieved Bea and Francis's old passports from the box file that Mr Fewtrell had given him. They had criss-crossed Europe throughout the 1950s yet neither had ever set foot in the United States during that whole decade. But on May 27 1960, Francis entered Canada. Eight weeks later, so had Bea.

McCall had been looking in the wrong country.

From his shoebox where memories were kept, McCall retrieved all the birthday cards and letters they had ever sent him. In September that year, Francis wrote him a short letter with a postcard of a Cree Indian, daubed in ceremonial paint.

> *Dear Mac*
>
> *Won't be long now. We'll be home for Christmas, loaded with presents and shan't we have a lovely time? Canada's such a big place, mostly wilderness. I'm still desk-bound, so haven't seen any cowboys or Indians worth speaking of. How are you getting on with your lessons at "Mr Whackmore's Academy"? Can't wait for term to be over, I'm sure. Still, keep at it, little friend. Bea sends all love.*
>
> *As always,*
> *Francis.*

It was written on notepaper from Canada's Air Command Headquarters in Winnipeg, Manitoba. McCall rang the city's main library that evening. He asked if a company called the Garry Finance Corporation ever operated there. It had – in the downtown Lindsay Building at the junction of Ellice and Notre Dame avenues. Then he called the *Winnipeg Free Press* cuttings library to check which reporter worked the crime desk in 1960.

'That'll be our Mr Ted Cleeve. He *was* the crime desk.'

'And does he still work on the paper?'

'No, he retired a while back but he's still knocking about the city.'

Within an hour, he had spoken to Ted Cleeve at home. He promised to dig out his old shorthand notebooks and ring back collect. Cleeve was as good as his word. Not only that, he remembered something that hadn't made sense all those years before. McCall knew then he would be going to Canada – whatever Evie's objections might be.

McCall walked into the drawing room and for a painful instant thought he was seeing Helen again… that tossed-back laugh of hers, the marmalade hair and Bea all smiles, eyes full of the grandchildren she craved. Evie

155

made it real, made it seem possible once more – to Bea, at least. McCall felt a splinter of resentment that they appeared such friends. They looked up at him and went quiet, as if he had interrupted something private from which he was excluded.

'Hello, Bea. You're seeming much better.'

Bea couldn't help her smile being twisted but McCall saw the suspicion in her eyes. She began writing on her pad.

Where been?

'I've been away on a story for a few days.'

Where?

'London… Germany.'

Why there?

'I have to see people, go to where they live. It's what I do, remember?'

Bea's frustration at being unable to write words as fast as they came into her head was obvious. She retired early to bed. Over supper later, McCall told Evie he had now established that Francis's third reel was filmed in Canada. She was not impressed.

'So was there a mysterious death there, too?'

'You'll find out if you come with me.'

'You're not seriously going, are you?'

'Why not? I've found this old reporter who knows part of the story.'

'And what about all the stress and grief this could cause Bea?'

'If she's not told, she won't know.'

'Come off it, Mac. She knows you're digging away on Minsky.'

'What's she said about him?'

'Nothing – but she's not stupid. She knows you're up to something –'

'– because there's a great TV show in all this stuff from Francis.'

'And that's more important, is it – another Golden Turd of Cracow for McCall's mantelpiece and to hell with the consequences for anyone else?'

Evie began to clear the table noisily.

'Well, I'm going nowhere with you. In fact, Bea's asked me to go on a cruise around the Med and I've said I will.'

'A cruise… you and Bea? What the hell's that all about?'

'You just don't get it, do you? You just don't see you're about to destroy something neither of us ever had.'

McCall didn't need any shrink to tell him he was always haunted by a fear of rejection or that all his relationships ultimately foundered on questions of trust and betrayal. Evie was supposed to be his ally in the search for his real parents and why he'd been lied to about how they were killed. Yet she, too, had now switched allegiances and gone over to the other side. It

156

was not by chance his stepmother always got her own way. Bea could get the devil himself pissed on holy water if she tried.

The evening was still light so McCall went back to the dacha where the newly leafing trees were shifting in the spring wind. He had pinned up the photographs of Bea and Minsky, the concentration camp victims and the nine Nazi soldiers with guns. He checked again with a magnifying glass and Rösler definitely wasn't one of them... unless it was him who had taken the picture.

But Wilhelm Frank, the wood carver, stood second from the right – solidly built, broad at the shoulder. It would not have been easy to persuade such an individual to do anything against his will, let alone walk to his death in a maze of tunnels under a black mountain.

How the hell was it done? And why kill him and apparently let his comrades live? McCall decided to stay in the dacha. He wouldn't sleep but maybe Francis's spirit might take pity and guide him through the night.

Chapter Thirty One

No one escapes their history. All are pinned like butterflies to a board by what has gone before.

The cruise liner *Aletha Delyse* slipped its berth and cut into the Adriatic. Venice sank behind it. Ahead lay Mikonos, Athens, Palma. Evie sat on the upper passenger deck with Bea – movie star glamorous, even in a wheelchair. She wore dark glasses, floral headscarf and a pale yellow orchid cotton trouser suit with leather Persian slippers stitched in golden thread. Evie, in jeans, smocked peasant top and wide-brimmed straw hat to keep the sun off her freckled face, remained happily in Bea's shadow. A warm wind blew from the Dalmatian coast. Bea seemed to have blood in her veins once more, aware she might now cheat death and be born again at the end of this ocean.

Beneath the stars and by the water, Evie and her Mother Confessor had already seen what Canaletto had painted. As with Bea and Arie, so Evie carried emotional burdens she wanted to set down. But only to someone who could not speak might she have admitted how torn apart she remained at her own mother's disappearance. Bea responded with her eyes alone, wrote nothing on her pad and only smiled when at last Evie had nothing more to say. Of Bea's stepson, there was no mention.

McCall's plane made landfall over the polar desolation of Labrador. He could see countless little lakes sequined on the vast shield of iron bedrock below. It looked a place of perpetual wind, inhabited by creatures howling from the wastes of tundra and ice which they say was God's gift to Cain. For McCall, three miles high and jammed into a metal tube with two hundred strangers, the future had never felt so uncharted. He still was not well enough to return to work and yet had assigned himself a story... a story of which he and his were somehow a part. The usual safety barrier between the professional and the personal had been taken down. Nor was Evie around to keep him grounded in reality. Yet Francis had willed it all.

Toronto was still three hours away. McCall would change planes there for the final sixteen hundred miles west over the Great Lakes of Huron and Superior and the prairies of Manitoba then to its capital, Winnipeg.

Hang on, little friend. Keep pretending.

That is what Francis would say.

Arie Minsky's morning exercise for his arthritic leg was to walk from his house to an Arab café across from the green-domed Great Mosque of Akko. They served cold lemonade with mint and he would sit listening to the doves in the palms of its stone-flagged courtyard.

A muezzin summoned the faithful to prayer from the mosque's tapering minaret that dominated this city of a thousand years and more. It was still only April yet the air was already sultry and scented by bougainvillaea. In the bazaar, Arab women clad head-to-toe in their black hijabs, moved like liquid between racks of rainbow-coloured silks that shimmered in a breeze from the pewter sea. Akko's ancient city walls had never been high enough to repel the ships of the invader... Greeks and Romans, Crusaders, Turks and the British all came, conquering and killing. In these times, Jews learnt that whoever does not want to be defeated has no option but to attack.

Minsky was untroubled by this philosophy, not to begin with. It was his own, and that of the Irgun – and therefore his fellow saboteurs, hanged by the British from a girder in an Ottoman citadel just along Al-Jazzar Street from where he now rested. But if their blood had irrigated the nascent state of Israel, all the ensuing wars of survival gradually unhinged the psyches of those living under the constant threat of death

Yet to admit such a psychological cost would be to appear weak, uncertain that the cause was right. So any emotional damage to Arie

158

Minsky and those like him was held within their heads till, in time, what remained became so brittle it could collapse at the slightest touch.

He finished his drink. An important phone call was expected and he needed to set off home through the narrow, hewn-out passageways and lanes of the old city. Here was shade but heat, too, places where the scent of flowers gave way to wood smoke, piss and sewage and the snarling of emaciated cats, fighting in the dirt for their lives.

McCall met Ted Cleeve in The Second Cup coffee shop in central Winnipeg. Cleeve came over as an irreverently cynical soul. They talked first about stories they'd covered, bastards they'd dealt with. It was a ballet of the bullshitters, each weighing up how much to trust the other. Cleeve only got to the point as they walked to the city's main library under a granite-grey sky threatening snow from the Rockies.

'OK, McCall. Here's what I know. The cops tell us a guy's strung himself up in his garage out in this little town, Carmen – miles from any damn place. A bunch of us reporters head out there to interview the wife who found him. Ella Virbalis, she was called. Pretended not to speak English though we knew she was a clerk in a furniture store downtown in Winnipeg.'

'Maybe she was in shock, Ted. Must've been pretty grim to find him like that.'

'Yeah, sure. Anyway, her daughter's there and we're getting nowhere and it's all a bit tense. The kid wants us to leave so I ask to use the bathroom. When I come out, I'm on my own with the wife and I snatch a last question – why did she think her husband would kill himself?'

'And what did she say?'

'It takes her off guard. She stops dabbing her eyes and stares at me and says in English, "He didn't. My Yanis didn't tie the knot himself. He'd have left me a note".'

'Maybe she needed to believe he wouldn't do such a thing. Made it easier to bear.'

'No, McCall. I was there. She *meant* it, believe me. She *knew*... like she knew immediately she should've kept her mouth shut to me.'

'But you asked her what she meant, yes?'

'Sure I did but she looks real scared and pushes me out the door.'

'What about the police investigation? Was this a lead they followed up?'

'You're joking – those guys couldn't find a cat up a tree back then.'

'But there must have been an inquest.'

'Of course but the cops haven't found any evidence of any foul play so everyone agrees old Yanis Virbalis finished himself off for reasons no one could figure out.'

The library's file copies of the *Winnipeg Free Press* from the autumn of 1960 told of espionage and paranoia – US spy planes over the Soviet Union, Polaris nuclear subs operating out of British bases, a political crisis developing in Cuba. The world was on the brink of destroying itself. At last, McCall found Cleeve's story, buried below the fold on an inside news page.

> *The widow of a Lithuanian-born man found hanged in his garage told the Free Press that she did not think her husband would have killed himself.*
>
> *'Yanis wouldn't have tied the knot,' said Mrs Ella Virbalis at her home on 9th Street, Carman.*
>
> *The couple, who have a 14 year old daughter, Rosa, came to Canada as penniless immigrants after the war to build a new life. Mr Virbalis, aged 55, worked at the railroad depot in Carman where his colleagues said he was well liked and had no reason to take his life that they knew of.*
>
> *Mrs Virbalis, employed three days a week as a clerk at Wilson's furniture store in Main Street, Winnipeg, insisted if her husband had intended to kill himself, he would have left a note. She had telephoned him less than two hours before she found his body when he seemed in good spirits, according to Mrs Virbalis. Police are carrying out an investigation and would not comment further.*

The story carried a single column photograph of Virbalis. It was the eyes that caught the attention – deep-set and dark, too close together under such a wide forehead. He had cropped, receding hair, jug ears and full, womanish, lips. Beyond that, he was an unmemorable face in the crowd.

But McCall recognised him immediately. He was in Bea's photograph – the one showing the nine Nazi soldiers. Virbalis had stood next to Wilhelm Frank, the wood carver... in whose skeletal hand precisely the same picture had been found.

More than that, Yanis Virbalis was the man Francis had filmed in his final reel.

Chapter Thirty Two

Next morning, McCall and Cleeve met for breakfast of barbequed smokies in the echoing, marble departure hall of Union Station. The old reporter had to catch a train to Calgary where his brother was in hospital. McCall felt tetchy and washed out after a sleepless, jet-lagged night in an over-heated truckers' motel.

'Your story didn't make much of a splash, Ted, whatever your suspicions.'

'Too damn right, it didn't. I was pretty sore about that and told the City Desk, too.'

'But Mrs Virbalis couldn't ever prove it wasn't suicide, could she?'

'You mean she couldn't or wouldn't?'

'Well, she'd bugger-all evidence.'

'Maybe not but the cops asked her why she'd said it wasn't suicide to me but she refused to say anymore.'

'So where the hell does it go from here?'

Cleeve smiled and pulled out another notebook he'd unearthed overnight. He had interviewed a customs source who said Virbalis and his wife landed in Halifax, Nova Scotia, by boat from Genoa in 1947.

'He claimed to our authorities he was escaping the communists who'd taken over Lithuania from the Nazis and who were just as bad. He'd been a factory worker and was forced into some kind of local militia by the Germans then posted as a guard or an orderly at various camps. But when the commie tanks rolled in, they were killing his fellow countrymen on any pretext so with his wartime record, he'd have been up against a wall as a collaborator.'

'The Canadians let him stay, then?'

'Sure, him and thousands of others with their cockamamie stories from Europe. The difference was most of them didn't end up dead.'

They walked to the platform and stood by Cleeve's carriage.

'Is there anything else that makes you think that what happened to Virbalis was suspicious, Ted?'

'You mean apart from his wife being terrified when I spoke to her?'

'Or mistaken.'

'Well, they'd no money worries, the marriage wasn't in bad shape, the daughter was bright enough at school and they'd a vacation planned.'

'People under stress do crazy things on the spur of the moment.'

'This guy wasn't under any stress, McCall.'

'Not that we know of.'

'No, but then there was the undertaker.'

161

'What undertaker?'

'Maybe a year later, I met the undertaker who'd collected Virbalis's body and we got to talking and he told me that our friend had shat himself.'

'What's unusual about that if someone's hanged?'

'The undertaker said in his experience, only those poor mutts who were about to be executed shat themselves because they lose all control through fear. Suicides don't do that.'

'Did you write a follow-up piece about all this?'

'No, my paper didn't think it would be in the public interest.'

'Christ, Ted – why ever not?'

'Some decision upstairs, I guess. *If* he'd been bumped off, that'd just draw attention to all the other Nazis we'd let in and the Russians would've exploited this for their anti-west propaganda. It was the Cold War back then – remember?'

Cleeve heaved himself on board and stood wheezing a little by the open window. The train began to move. McCall trotted by the side, still asking questions.

'Look, even if you're right, why was Virbalis singled out from all those others?'

'Like I said, I've no idea.'

'He was a no-mark guard, a nothing.'

'Not to somebody, he wasn't.'

'But why kill *him*?'

'You tell me, Mac. That's why you're here, isn't it?'

McCall hired a big, lazily sprung Chrysler and set off through an ugly urban sprawl of lumber yards and muffler companies then out into open country for the fifty mile drive south to Carman. Time and history had closed over the death of Yanis Virbalis like grass on a grave. Kennedy became president, man walked on the moon. And Ella herself died from throat cancer, according to Cleeve. But what of her daughter? If Cleeve was right, only Rosa might know what her mother had not dared to say.

The road was monotonously straight. McCall began to lose concentration. He was tired and nauseous from the lack of proper food. And somewhere deep in his subconscious, a little knot of fear was beginning to form around the implications of all he was bent on uncovering. His sort of hackery relied on base, primitive instincts – stalk, trap, kill. It didn't suit to know your prey.

He stopped the car and got out. Flurries of snow crystals twisted between the corn shoots in the surrounding pan-flat fields as he hunkered down, retching till his empty stomach could take no more.

Carman, when he reached it, was a compact little town of three thousand people, descendants of Celtic settlers who'd staked a claim on the winding banks of the Boyne River. He parked beneath the clock tower of its prissy Victorian library and bought chocolate and milk from a grocery store nearby. The town's voter records showed Yanis and Ella Virbalis occupied number 12 Ninth Street from 1955. He had disappeared from the list by 1961 and Mrs Virbalis two years later. No one living in Ninth Street at the time of Yanis Virbalis's death was still registered there.

McCall booked into a guest house and fell asleep fully clothed. It was three in the afternoon, local time. The radio weather forecast – which he missed – warned of heavy snow setting in.

Evie suggested they both go ashore at Piraeus but Bea shook her head and wrote out a message and telephone number on her pad instead. Bea indicated that Evie must find a post office and have an international operator connect her to the number at noon precisely. A man would answer. She should read out only what Bea had written and say nothing else.

After Evie left, Bea went to her bunk, wearier than she thought. First, Germany, now Canada. Mac was ruining the future – for himself, for Garth, maybe even his life with Evie. This could only be Francis's jealous doing. Only he could have put Mac on this demented, destructive path. But she had taken measures, now. Nothing more could be done. Bea closed her eyes. Through the open porthole, she heard the sea and allowed herself to be lulled back to the womb, innocent of all sin.

McCall woke early. There was no sunrise. The dawn sky simply became a less dirty shade of grey. The blameless uneventful town beyond the curtains stirred as he ate his eggs and ham.

He drove to Ninth Street and located the small brick-built house where Yanis and Ella Virbalis had lived with Rosa. It was the only one in a street of forty homes to be screened off by cottonwoods and spruce like some witch's cottage with something to hide. These were modest homes, mainly timber-clad and painted in pinks, greens and yellows that had flaked and faded in the extremes of Manitoba's weather. Decent, dependable people lived here, blue-collar workers who tended their unfenced lawns and raised their kids just right. In the distance, beyond a row of Dutch elms, McCall saw a sentinel grain elevator by the railroad track. Everywhere was tranquil and neighbourly.

It remained exactly as Francis had filmed it.

McCall started doing the shoe leather – knocking on every door in the street. All he got was colder by the minute. No one knew anything. No one remembered anything from back then. Someone said his English accent was 'real neat'. Someone else asked if he had ever met the Queen. By mid morning, anyone who was at home had been spoken to – all for no gain.

But the young couple at the Virbalis house had let him see inside the garage. He'd stood for a moment, trying to imagine what might have happened amid the ladders and planks and tins of old paint. It must have been a miserable place to die.

McCall walked back to his car, despondent. Evie's warnings kept coming back to him. Then a woman he had seen earlier called across to him from her front door.

'Hey, mister – there's someone I've thought of.'

'Someone who knows something?'

'She could do, yeah. An old lady who lived in the street for years.'

'And she's still alive?'

'In a care home across town. She's blind, though.'

'Doesn't matter. She's my kind of witness. What's her name?'

'Miss Deware.'

Eunice Deware was closer to eighty than seventy, snow-haired and as thin as her white stick.

She wore a long plain dress the colour of a mouse's back and a knitted cardigan to match. Miss Deware was rarely visited. Someone calling on her from the BBC in London raised her profile real swell. Such a day merited tea being brought on a silver tray as Miss Deware held court.

'We'd no scandals in our street before, you know... no need of the Mounties, not us.'

'Did you know the Virbalis family well, Miss Deware?'

'Well enough. Quiet sort of folks they were, good neighbours if you'd needed them.'

'So what happened to Mr Virbalis must have been a shock. What sort of man was he?'

'Not afraid of hard work, he wasn't. Railroad man.'

'Why do you think he killed himself?'

'Mental problems, they said. Couldn't cope with what life threw at him.'

'What a tragedy. Do you know what became of his daughter?'

'Rosa? Went away after her mother died. Nothing to stay for, had she?'

'And where did she go... do you know?'

'Brandon, I think. That's where they said. Became a teacher, I know that.'

'At a school in Brandon itself?'

'Maybe. But then the last I heard, she'd moved to Elm Creek.'

McCall thanked her and stood up to leave. But Miss Deware hadn't done with him yet.

'Why's all this of interest to you over in England?'

'It's something to do with the war, Miss Deware.'

'The war? He wasn't on our side, you know, not that Mr Virbalis. My roomer told me that.'

'Your roomer... you mean your lodger?'

'Yes, my roomer. They came from the same place, they did. Some communist country now.'

'Really? What was your roomer's name?'

'Can't rightly remember. He wasn't with me long but they worked on the railroad together. He'd sit over there with Mr Virbalis most evenings, playing chess, talking about the old country, I expect.'

'Did the police come and take a statement from your roomer?'

'He never said. Anyway, he was gone soon after. Just upped and left.'

'And you can't remember who he was?'

'No.... but I remember one thing. His accent sounded more like an Englishman's than someone from wherever he came from.'

McCall shivered in his parked car, engine running, trying to keep warm. He felt sick again but doubted it was from hunger this time. He was alone, five thousand miles from base, not a step nearer his real mother and father but about to fit his adoptive parents into a conspiracy to murder. He was sure now they and Arie Minsky were too close to be innocent in the suspicious deaths of the three ex-Nazis.

Bea was with Francis in Germany when he'd secretly filmed Wilhelm Frank, the wood carver, then in Canada immediately before Yanis Virbalis's apparent suicide. McCall was certain Minsky was in the street footage of Jakob Rösler and outside Frank's workshop, too. The identity of blind old Miss Deware's lodger was hardly a mystery.

He could understand why Jews might wish every Nazi dead – even now, forty years after the death camps were liberated.

Who among us – Jew or not – could have walked amid such sights of wickedness and not felt a great rage, a human urge to punish those responsible? He'd heard tell of Allied soldiers doing just that – shooting Nazi guards out of hand. But after the blood of Jew and gentile alike had cooled, after Nuremberg and all its juridical accounting, what was the tracking down of an enemy for years to bring about his death but murder by any other name?

And why, from beyond death itself, had Francis implicated himself and Bea in what might be these murderous acts of revenge?

McCall had no choice but to press on.

As the scorpion who stung the frog while being saved from the flood said, it was what he did.

McCall drove back to Ninth Street and retraced the steps Francis must have taken to film the service lane behind Virbalis's house. His death – like Wilhelm Frank's – could not have been brought about by Minsky alone. These were Einsatzgruppen men who knew no other trade but killing. They would have fought like the dogs they were.

Yet somehow, they had been subdued, made quiescent. If Minsky had left Virbalis strung up and returned to Miss Deware's as usual that day, his accomplice could have exited by the rear door and hidden in the carigana bushes in the service lane till dark. From there, it was a only short run across a field to the road where a car could be waiting.

McCall started mapping out a route to Elm Creek. He could be there before nightfall. If Miss Deware was right, Rosa Virbalis would not be hard to find.

As he drove away, he had no reason to notice a man getting into another car and following him at a distance.

Chapter Thirty Three

McCall was half asleep and laid out across the Chrysler's bench seat when someone started banging the driver's door window with a bunch of keys. Right then, he had no idea where he was or what he was doing. It was nearly dark but he could see a woman staring from the other side of the glass. McCall stumbled out of the car almost freeze-dried and fell at her feet.

'Sorry, sorry. Didn't mean to frighten you.'

The woman was Rosa Virbalis, gripping a tyre lever in her fist. He pulled out his Scotland Yard press pass for her to check the ID photograph.

'I've nothing to say to any reporters.'

'You don't know why I've come.'

'Don't bet the farm on it, mister.'

The arctic cold bit through McCall's thinly padded anorak. He started shaking so much he could not speak properly.

166

'Not here as reporter... your life, mine... they've crossed.'

'What are you talking about?'

'About your father.'

'What about him?'

'His story... fits into the missing... bits of mine.'

She looked at him hard, assuring herself he'd not escaped from an institution.

'You're dressed all wrong for Canada, mister. Best come inside.'

He sat in one of the armchairs by a log burner. Rosa Virbalis left him to thaw out and went to the kitchen.

It had been easy finding her in the tiny township of Elm Creek. The man who ran the liquor store knew her well. He described what she looked like, where she worked and lived – three miles from nowhere off Highway 2.

McCall did a discreet recce of the junior school where she taught. She was about his age, a bit overweight and no pin-up but with pretty hair the colour of dried straw and cheeks slapped pink by the prairie wind.

Then he had parked by her house, a shack of a farmstead under low cloud pressing down on an earth gone like stone.

Rosa returned with a plate of *piroshki,* little pastry pockets of meat and vegetables she served with large measures of vodka. The warmth of the liquor and the stove made him want to curl up and sleep again. But Rosa was waiting. She had the palest sea green eyes. McCall felt only pity for her, for what she must have witnessed. The sins of Yanis Virbalis were not hers any more than those of Jakob Rösler were his son's.

'Look, this all starts with your father... how he came to die.'

'He committed suicide. So what?'

'Yes, he did but why did he do it?'

'Listen, who knows... he just did. It's years ago.'

'But your mother never thought it was suicide, did she?'

'How's this relevant to anything, mister? It's all in the past.'

'It is but I'd guess you're still bothered by that one question, Rosa... why he did it.'

'Not me, no. It's of no interest anymore. Life moves on and we have to move with it.'

McCall didn't believe her. He doubted she did herself.

'I've spoken to the newspaperman your mother talked to after she found the body.'

'My Mom said things back then she didn't mean.'

'But she said them, Rosa. She said your Dad hadn't tied the rope himself.'

'Yeah, but for Christ's sake, she was just upset. She'd just cut him down.'

'No, not *upset*. Your mother was terrified, according to this man I've talked to. He said she was seriously scared of something and I want to find out why.'

Rosa returned his gaze for several seconds.

'You know why... don't you, Rosa? You know what she had to be terrified about –'

Some sort of audit was going on in her head. She filled her glass with more vodka then, still without saying a word, rolled a joint.

'It stands to reason that you do... mother and daughter together. The pair of you against the world. Who else could she tell but you?'

Rosa leaned back and watched her exhaled smoke spread across the rough plank ceiling. The wall clock struck six. She passed the joint to McCall. That was promising.

'I've never talked about any of this before.'

'No? Well, we all have need of a priest one day.'

A car drove by and she sat up nervously. McCall asked what was wrong.

'Nothing. It's just we don't get cars going by this time of night.'

She opened the stove doors to put in more logs. Her cheeks burned even redder.

'You got a wife back in England, mister... kids of your own?'

'No. That never happened for me. What about you – married?'

'No, still single after all these years.'

'You must have boyfriends?'

'One or two. No one that stays the distance.'

Rosa filled her glass again. McCall knew he only had to wait. She began at last to talk, to purge herself of what had troubled her for so long.

'We'd had a guest speaker at school that day, the day Dad.... you know, some woman from I don't know where, and I was one of those she got talking to afterwards. I arrived home later than usual. Mom was in the street shouting like a mad thing. I'd no idea what was happening but I got her inside before the neighbours came out but she kept pointing to the garage so I went and looked inside and saw my Dad lying on the floor. He wasn't moving and Mom just kept screaming so I rang for an ambulance but I knew there was no point. The police turned up and started asking questions but it was plain enough to them what'd happened. They couldn't get much sense out of Mom because she always forgot her English when she got in a state. They asked me if he had black moods and I said sometimes he did but nothing serious, nothing medical. Then, that same night, after everyone had gone and we were on our own, the phone rang and I answered and this man came on and said, "Rosa, you listen good to me...just tell your mother that Yanis had it easier than he deserved. She'll know what I'm talking about." Then the phone went dead.'

'Did you recognise his voice, the accent?'

'No.'

'What did your mother say when you gave her the message?'

'She turned this deathly colour like she was having a heart attack and I kept asking what it meant but she wouldn't tell me but she said we mustn't say anything to anyone, not even the police, because if we did, they would come back and kill us.'

'Who did she mean, *they*?'

'She never said. Not even on her death bed.'

'But she was terrified of *them* or something *they* might do?'

'Yes, she was. That's true.'

'And you know why, don't you?'

'I've an idea, yes.

In another place, another world, the intense afternoon sun burned back off the tumbling white cottages of Crete. Passengers disembarking from the *Aletha Delyse* at Iraklion's Venetian harbour needed to shield their eyes.

Bea and Evie were among the first ashore after the purser delivered the radio message they had been expecting. It told them to wait on the quayside for a man driving a green Mercedes. Evie, who had experienced cloak – and some dagger – delighted in knowing the frail old lady in the wheelchair had not lost her love of intrigue.

The car arrived and they were driven through the dawdling tourists in the old town's lime washed streets, all blood-splashed by geraniums in pots. They headed up to a private airfield in the scrub beyond where a small private jet floated like a mirage on a long lake of black tarmac. Only when they were climbing above the diamond blue waters of the Sea of Crete did Evie ask where they were going.

'Israel... my love.'

Bea had not needed her pen and pad this time. She'd had years to practice these words.

Rosa Virbalis sat on the end of her bed with McCall. She had a cardboard memory box, too, and held it now across her plump knees.

'I wasn't quite eighteen when Mom died and we had no relatives in Canada so I just had to get on with it... organise things... burial and everything. I wanted never to see Ninth Street again but I had to clear everything out of the house. I wasn't really old enough for all this, you know... still a kid. Most stuff went out as garbage, some stuff to a church, clothes and things. The last room was theirs... Mom and Dad's room... where I'd heard them sometimes... you know, at night. I didn't like being there on my own but I just about got through it."

'Just about?'

'Yeah, just about.'

'You mean something happened?'

'I found some photographs.'

'What of?'

'My Dad.

'Your Dad *how*?'

'In the war.'

'Do you want to show me?'

Rosa Virbalis stood up and gave him an envelope from the box. She had also brought the vodka bottle and topped up their glasses. She was deliberately getting drunk – not laughing or morbid drunk – just drunk, so as not to feel a thing.

The envelope contained yet another copy of Bea's picture of the nine Einsatzgruppen men, button-bright and smart with suitcases packed and guns at the ready. Her father stood with his comrades, men about to do their duty. In no sense was Virbalis the reluctant press-ganged non-entity he had claimed to Canadian immigration. Here stood a proud well-fed Nazi volunteer. And someone had pencilled a cross on his face – just as McCall had seen on Wilhelm Frank in the photograph found in the bones of his hand.

'Where did you get this picture, Rosa?'

'Hidden in Mom's old handbag…wasn't the only one, either.'

She handed him six more, each three inches square and brown like old photographs go. Mementoes for the Virbalis family album. And there is Yanis. Rifle to his shoulder, legs apart for balance. Taking aim at a queue of women. And their babies. Everyone naked at the end of the world. *Bang! Bang! You're dead. Bang! Bang!* Such a noise there would have been. Too loud for the clicks of the camera to be heard. And the pale shapes fall through the air. Nameless and unrecorded. Into the gaping earth. Day after day, pit after pit. There was Virbalis, again. Smiling. A job well done. Virbalis and his friends. Taking a break. Having a smoke. Behind them, their handiwork, already bloating under God's sun. On the back, someone had written *Schutzmann Virbalis.*

'What does that mean, Rosa?'

'A Schutzmann was a sort of policeman.'

McCall thought of the frayed armband in the secret compartment of Bea's bureau… its swastika and that word, *Schutzmann*, sewn in silver thread. How had Bea come by it? Had it belonged to the killer whose daughter now stood so close to him? He could smell the vodka on her breath, the smoke of the joint in her hair. She was holding his arm, supporting herself… becoming tearful, like drunks do.

The last photograph was of Rosa as a small child, laughing in her father's arms. There was love on both their faces as he tickled her under the chin with the very finger he had used to fire his gun.

'You understand, now… don't you, mister?'

'He was killed for revenge, wasn't he?'

'My Mom always feared they'd come for us, too.'

'But *who*?'

'Those Jews, of course. Who else would want him dead?'

The headlights of another car swept the room and Rosa clung to McCall.

'Nothing comes by here this late. Who is it?'

'Maybe someone's lost.'

'Stay with me, mister. Please. I get so afraid.'

She put her arms around McCall's neck and her face to his.

'Can't bear to be on my own… not tonight.'

Then she kissed his mouth. She wanted comfort from the stranger, wanted to be held and desired in the desolate place that had become her life. McCall understood. He knew it, too. They lay together and he didn't think of Helen and chose to forget Evie for if she had come with him, this could never have happened. Then they slept. Then they dreamed.

McCall sees Arie Minsky playing chess with Yanis Virbalis. They sit at a kitchen table. Only a few moves have been made. But there is an end game in sight. A third figure enters, faceless and silent. He creeps up with something in his hand. It is a rope… a rope made into a noose. McCall is somehow in there, hovering above the action but powerless to intervene, to stop what he dreads is about to happen.

Suddenly, the rope is around Virbalis's neck. His eyes bulge and cannot take in what is happening. The table is kicked over. Rooks and pawns are scattered on the floor. Virbalis is dragged from the room like a sack. He kicks and pulls but his struggling does no good. Minsky goads him backwards with a dull-bladed butcher's knife. Virbalis is forced to stand on a gallows made from a beer crate. The rope is secured to a beam above him.

Yanis Virbalis. Nazi collaborator.

No. Only guard.

Liar!

No, guard.

Slaughterman!

Why do you say this?

Because you are the killer of women and children.

But you're my friend –

I spit on you.

171

No, we play chess, you and me.

Then you have lost.

The condemned man cannot control his shaking legs – or anything else. There's a sudden stench of human waste. Virbalis moans with shame and terror. He pisses his overalls and urine begins to run down the wooden crate and forms a little yellow rivulet across the dusty concrete floor.

I was ordered. I had no choice in what I did.

But you have a choice now, Yanis Virbalis.

What choice do I have?

The choice of an easy death or a hard death.

McCall can smell the sour sweat on Virbalis's face. His eyes strain and plead for the mercy he never gave.

I have money –

Keep your money. Rosa will be home soon -

Don't harm her.

Then your wife.

Please, don't hurt them.

I shall cut out their stomachs as you watch, Yanis Virbalis, then you will be next.

No! No! What must I do?

Arie Minsky puts his foot on the beer crate.

Come, Yanis Virbalis… you are a logical man. You know what step to take.

But I am not ready –

Then at least you have something in common with your victims.

At that, Minsky kicks the crate away. Virbalis falls fifteen inches then jerks up on the rope with a crack. The beam shudders and empty beer bottles roll through the dancing man's piss. The executioners melt away.

McCall is left to watch alone. He feels his soul has been stolen, he is desensitised by lawless, vengeful death. There is no satisfaction here, no peace, no justice. There is nothing. Just a dead man twisting on a rope. And the stink of shit.

McCall woke alone in Rosa's bed. He had slept for ten hours. He went downstairs and found her leafing through his research notes and photographs. She looked up and smiled, as if she now had some lien over him and whatever was his – a fair swap for all she had ceded the night before.

'There's juice or coffee if you want.'

McCall saw she'd singled out the pictures of Bea and Minsky on Westminster Bridge and laid them together on the carpet.

'What interests you about those two?'

'Can't you guess?'

'No. Tell me.'

'This is the man who would come to our house to play chess with Dad.'

'And the woman?'

'She was the one who gave the talk at my school. If I hadn't talked to her that night, I'd have stopped him from being murdered.'

McCall left, promising Rosa he would return and explain. He had a vicious migraine starting and Winnipeg seemed a painful long drive away. The snowstorm threatened from the darkened sky began, swirling across the straight gravelled road in countless powdery tornadoes.

He'd gone less than a mile when a black saloon came up quickly in his rear view mirror. He waved it on but the driver didn't overtake. McCall was too preoccupied to care. He now understood why Rosa's mother had blurted out to Ted Cleeve that her husband hadn't tied the knot himself. But how to prove a suicide was murder...

The tailing car's headlights flooded full beam into McCall's mirror, almost blinding him. He accelerated to get clear. Fifty-five, sixty, sixty-five. He knew this was too dangerous for the weather conditions. Still the maniac behind stuck close.

Then McCall felt a violent jolt in his back. The Chrysler was being rammed. His fender flew off with a rip of metal and chrome. Then the lid of the trunk shot up. His attacker smashed into him again and again, trying to flip McCall's car into the fields. The rush of fear within him hadn't time to turn to panic. Even as he struggled to keep control, he saw two points of light reflecting in the blizzard ahead.

McCall braked violently but not soon enough. He went into a skid and slammed into a mesmerised deer. The creature exploded. The white air filled with bloody shrapnel, bits of brain and stomach and tissue spattering the windscreen as the Chrysler careered off the highway and became airborne.

And in that brief eternity, a memory surfaced within McCall – a memory of what had really happened in those missing freeze frames all those years before... the poppies soaking into that sun-filled cornfield, what they were and all that they had meant. His entire life had turned on what he'd blanked out.

Now he realised why.

Chapter Thirty Four

Interrogate memory, McCall. Who were you, once upon a time?
A baby, a toddler, a little boy.
What else?
A witness.
A witness to what?
To what happened.

This is the BBC Light Programme. It's a quarter to two and time for Listen with Mother. Are you sitting comfortably?
He likes this story-teller best – Daphne Oxenford. He's even learnt to say her name. *Daf-en-ee-ox-en-ford.* He repeats it over and over in his head. He used to think she lived in the wireless but he looked inside and she didn't. The wireless is on a shelf by the fireplace. He always sits on a wooden stool to listen. The stool is painted green and the wireless hums and crackles in his ear when it's switched on and the voices come out.

He likes stories. He can read, too. Mummy's taught him. *Ber-lin, Hil-ver-sum, Lux-em-berg.* That's what it says on the dial. People in London are on the wireless. Mummy comes from London. He's been on his own with her today. It's better when they're on their own.

She's washing at the sink. She's wearing an apron over her skirt and a headscarf she calls a turban and puts on when she sweeps the floor. Mummy's always sweeping the floor. It's dirty from the mud outside but it's not their house and the farmer won't make it nice for them. The farm's a long way to walk. They go there to get eggs. Sometimes Mummy cries and he gives her a kiss when her face is wet.

She says she has headaches and they make her cry. When the wireless story finishes, he's going to play outside. He likes playing on his own. He's never really on his own because he makes up stories and there are people in the stories with names and things to do that he's heard on the wireless. It's sunny today. There's a bird's nest in the hedge. He's going to look inside but not so as to scare the bird.

Daddy comes in with his gun. His wellington boots are muddy. Mummy asks him to take them off outside. He shouts at her. He always shouts.

She wants to know where he's been because his food has dried up in the oven. He says he doesn't want any and she says it's because he's been drinking so why does she bother cooking anything. Daddy shouts even louder and says if she didn't shout at him, he would come home. He takes some things from underneath his big jacket and throws them on the table.

There's a rabbit and a beautiful bird with golden red feathers and a long tail. Their eyes are like glass and he looks into them ever so closely and can see himself very small, like someone who could live in the wireless.

Mummy shouts at Daddy again, louder and louder. Sometimes they smack each other and then they both cry. He's seen Daddy cry. He does big cries and his whole body shakes and his face goes red. Then he doesn't do any painting for days and Mummy's always upset then.

He touches the bird's feathers. They're so shiny. The colours all change if you turn his head with your hand. The rabbit's got whiskers and soft patches of white and brown fur with blood on its nose. He doesn't like it when Daddy goes shooting. But he says if he doesn't go shooting, there won't be anything to eat.

His gun's very big and heavy and has two barrels. Daddy's holding it now. Mummy's crying. She says he's no good. But he's just got us something to eat so he must be some good. Daddy says she should have married someone else and Mummy says she wishes she had because he's no use. They're both trying to smack each other again. Daddy's smacked him lots of times. Daddy's boots are making dirty marks on the tiles and Mummy's lost her slippers.

He hides under the table with his hands over his ears because he doesn't like this. He's scared. He can still see them and Mummy's got something in her hand and is trying to scratch Daddy's face with it. He's trying to push her away but she catches him and he squeals and drops the gun.

The gun falls. The gun falls onto the tiles. The gun falls onto the tiles ever so slowly. It hits the tiles stock first. One of the hammers jolts down. A cartridge is fired. The room detonates with noise. The stones in the wall and the glass in the windows shake with fear.

The sound doesn't stop. It has a life of its own. It tunnels into his ears and roars around his skull till he can take no more. Then it all goes quiet.

Daddy picks up his gun and runs from the kitchen. Little particles of plaster are falling from the ceiling.... falling like snow, gently covering the bird and the rabbit and the body of his mother lying on the tiles she tries to keep clean.

He is alone. He kneels by Mummy. She's on her side. One of her hands is stretched out, the other's across her tummy. Her fingers claw at the floor then go still. The back of her dress and her apron are cut up like ribbons. Red ribbons. But it's her skin peeling off where she's been hit by the little lead shots in the cartridge.

That's the end of our story today, children. We'll be here again tomorrow. Until then, goodbye everyone. Goodbye.

There's powdered plaster in Mummy's hair and on her sleepy face. He begs her to wake up. But she doesn't. He'll go and get help, run to the farm, find Daddy. Someone'll know what to do. He kisses Mummy's forehead. His lips feel dusty. He wipes them with the back of his hand then runs into the sunshine. He passes the hedge where the bird's nest is and the tea chest that's his fort and boat but there's no one to be seen.

He's panting for breath and his head still rings with shouts and bangs and all that he doesn't understand. Then he sees Daddy. He calls out but Daddy doesn't hear. Daddy's going to where the farmer keeps his hay for the animals. He calls out but still Daddy doesn't hear so he runs towards him.

The hay bales are stacked on top of each other, higher than a house. Daddy's still got his gun. Something must be wrong with it because he's blowing into the barrels. He's about to shout again when there's another bang – a bang so loud it bounces between the hills and sets all the birds clacking and cawing into the sky.

And there is Daddy on the ground. He's sleeping, too.

Everywhere in the straw above him is covered in new poppies. It's like a field of blood-red poppies, not flat but reared up on its end. And the poppies are all glistening and melting and soaking into the golden hay. Some of the petals fall by his feet and he picks them up. They are warm and wet and discolour his fingers.

Chapter Thirty Five

McCall lay in a field of new corn amid the scatter of offal from the dead deer. Every part of his body hurt and he couldn't move to crawl back inside the shelter of the car. His dim reflection in the silver hubcap slowly became whiter like the figure in his head he had never understood. He thought of soldiers dying in no man's land, calling out for the comfort of their mothers. McCall wanted to cry out for his but the strength was draining from him and the wind would have buried his words in snow if he had.

The moon-driven tides that broke on the black rocks where Herod's palace once stood in Caesarea perpetually shifted the sands that had hidden the evidence of conquest, torture and death since Phoenician times. Man's power ebbs and flows like the constant sea. All his efforts amount to nought in time.

Arie Minsky would walk the beach each day, treading by the drowned remains of the once great city from where Rome had ruled Palestine. He might pick up tiny green-gold coins last used when Jews were being torn apart by tigers to amuse the amphitheatre's mob. More often, it would be perfectly cut tiles from a mosaic – red, ivory, orange and half an inch square, all worn smooth in the silt. Minsky imagined the feet of Herod himself walking on these very fragments when they had been the tiniest parts of some grand and beautiful design, now lost to sight forever. He kept his finds in a shallow olive wood dish on his desk. It was Minsky's unconscious habit to make patterns with them if ever something demanded his unhindered reflection. He was making patterns now, staring through the open window to his garden of bitter aloe trees, troubled by how best to deal with the problem of McCall.

There was a time when Arie Minsky would not have left such a matter to chance.

McCall first dropped acid after a Yardbirds gig in Cambridge in '65 with a philosophy student who stole Jeff Beck's bottle neck from his guitar case but was dead in a year, convinced he could fly from a roof. More such fragments of wild imaginings came to McCall in the moments after his crash. He saw iridescent birds and rainbows of flowers but as he reached out to touch, there was nothing – no colour but white, no movement but wind in that bone-cracking cold where sleep beckoned forever. So the falling snow became the sheets of his bed and he slowly drifted away.

'McCall? McCall? You'll be OK. Do you hear?'

The faintest of sounds found him, like the sonar of a submarine lost deep under the ice. Beep... beep... beep.

Wires. Tubes. Equipment. And above him, a face he didn't know and a hand he'd never held. Or thought he hadn't, anyway.

'You've had an accident. You're in hospital but you're going to be all right.'

Rosa. The dancing man's daughter. Rosa. The woman in the night who cried to be loved. But where was Bea? Where was Francis? Where were the others who meant so much to him?

Far, far away – as they always had been. McCall's eyes closed again.

Beep... beep... beep.

Evie sat in the secure communications room of the British Embassy's ugly box of a building on the sea front in Tel Aviv, waiting for a spook colleague in London to get back in touch.

She had already rung McCall's office at the BBC from Arie Minsky's house in Akko. They said he was still off work sick. No one had heard from him – not even a postcard to Mrs Craven at Garth or to her mother. The only other person Evie guessed McCall might contact was Gerry Gavronski, his lefty magazine chum. Gavronski was a backstairs advisor to the miners' national strike committee. His phone had an ear on it. It had been Evie's job to read the transcripts of Gavronski's private conversations during the strike - *all* of them, even those he'd had with her journo lover…someone her parish officer knew nothing about. That was the way of it in Evie's world. Fathers were not the only ones betrayed.

The embassy cipher clerk handed her the decoded reply from London.

Your target rang G three days ago. Wanted to confirm an "Arie Minsky" was currently in Israel. G duly obliged and called back a number in Elm Creek, Canada listed to a 'Rosa Virbalis'. Target said he would book flight soonest. Target mentioned being in a traffic accident. No further details.

Over supper that night, Evie told Bea and Minsky only that McCall intended to travel to Israel. Minsky did not ask how she had found this out. And, for her part, Evie showed no surprise that he seemed to know the information already.

McCall lay on Rosa's living room couch, face and body still badly bruised, one eye half closed, head stitched up, ribs cracked. It was only McCall who thought himself fit enough to leave hospital.

There was no question of telling her – or the police – what had really happened. Either some homicidal local yahoo had sported with him or someone was giving McCall the gypsy's warning. He knew which was the more likely.

How odd he should owe his life to a Nazi's daughter, passing his wreckage on her way to work. How odd he should research her father's death only to find the truth about his own… and his mother's, too. The forked roads he had travelled since emerging mute and stinking and half out of his head from all he'd seen those years before were gradually coming together.

His anger at Bea and Francis began to abate. They *had* lied – but only to save him from what was locked in his head. Yet that did not get them out of the dock.

Three men – however evil – had died in strange and mysterious circumstances. The fingerprints of Bea, Francis and Arie Minsky were all over the crime scenes. If someone felt threatened by this being exposed and was trying to frighten McCall off, any hack worth a by-line knew this was reason enough to keep buggering on.

He heard Rosa's car then the porch door being unlocked. She came in and saw his obvious discomfort as he carried an armful of logs to the stove.

'You just lay back, McCall. I'll see to it and get us some dinner on.'

Part of him felt indebted to Rosa and wanted to tell her everything – about himself, what happened to his parents, about Bea and Francis and their conspiracy with Minsky.

But he could hear Francis's warning. *Information shared is an advantage lost.* He should leave nothing behind in Canada that might come back and bite him.

Rosa herself never pressed McCall over who the people in his photographs were or what had put him onto them. But on the night before he left she seemed to want him to understand how she'd become reconciled to her father's death.

'I guess there was a kind of terrible rough justice in what happened... him being found and made to pay for his crimes.'

'Yes, but he should've had a trial under the law. Without that, it's mob rule.'

'They never got one... those women and children back then.'

'That's just it, Rosa. What he did was wicked but so was what happened to him.'

'Is it worth all this pain, McCall... raking everything up again to go on TV and say two wrongs don't make a right? How worthwhile is that?'

If Rosa feared what she might suffer after any publicity about how and why her father died, McCall understood more than she could ever realise.

McCall cleared Customs at Ben Gurion Airport, changed dollars into shekels then boarded a bus to that most lucent and holy of cities, Jerusalem. He was immediately enveloped in the foreignness of all around him. Israeli soldiers going home on leave sat with their rifles alongside white-turbaned Bedouin in ankle-length jillabas and excited pilgrims, about to walk Christ's journey to his crucifixion. Through the open windows came the smell of goats and sheep and pine trees blowing from the warm bouldered hills where shot-up army vehicles still rusted with honour from yesterday's wars.

He'd slept fitfully on the long flight from Canada, sustained by pain-killers and Scotch. He ached in body and mind and needed to recover before ever confronting Arie Minsky.

A guest house close to the Jaffa Gate had a third floor room with a bath and a view over the Old City's Armenian Quarter. McCall unpacked and looked down on cowled monks keeping to the shadows of its thick

179

limestone walls. The soft tapping of silversmiths making jewellery came from within houses built before the Crusades.

McCall soaked himself for an hour then put on the jeans and white T-shirt Rosa had washed and walked down through the lobby.

'Excuse, Sir. Mr McCall, Sir?'

He turned to see the smiling Arab receptionist following him outside into the late afternoon sun.

'I have message for you.'

'For me? You can't have.'

'On telephone, Sir. A man says for Mr McCall to go to the American Colony Hotel.'

'But no one knows I'm here. Who was this man?'

'He does not say. He just say Mrs Wrenn will be there at six tonight.'

Bea... in Jerusalem? How the hell did *she* know he was there? McCall was caught off guard. Would Minsky be with her? Why had she quit her cruise? And where was Evie? He looked around. It was easy to feel paranoid here... so many spies and factions, all hating each other.

He disappeared into the sandal-smoothed warrens of the ancient covered market. Traders called from every side – jewellers, artists, potters, trinket merchants, all jostling for his money. He kept moving, breathing in ever-changing aromas – oranges and limes, sandalwood, baking bread, hookahs being smoked by round-bellied men. As he emerged into daylight by the Damascus Gate, he'd decided to go and meet Bea. He was too intrigued not to.

The American Colony was no distance. Its walled inner courtyard was cool, shaded with palms and perfumed by roses. Here sat diplomats, military men and political advisors from every camp, head to head in deniable discussions on this disputed seam between east and west Jerusalem. But of Bea, there was no sign. He checked reception and the restaurant without success.

McCall left after an hour, mightily puzzled. There was a short cut to his hotel through a quiet road between apartment blocks with high-fenced gardens full of trees and bushes. He noticed two youngish men sitting on a stone wall in denim jeans and with red and white shemaghs around their faces. McCall was too preoccupied by thoughts of Bea to notice much else and passed without eye contact. But three paces further on, they stole up behind him.

At that same moment, a small delivery van also started its choreographed approach. McCall half glanced to his left. He'd only time to register the van's sliding door being open. Then his arms were grabbed without warning and forced up his back as he was bundled face down into the van. Someone rammed the door shut. Someone else sat on him. Duct tape was wound round his mouth, eyes and hands. His Canadian injuries went agonisingly live again. The driver was already accelerating away, but gently – no screeching tyres, no dangerous manoeuvres for a witness to recall from the ten seconds it had taken for a man to disappear into the night.

And into McCall's disorientating pain and alarm came a memory out of nowhere... that Arie Minsky's pals kidnapped Adolf Eichmann exactly like this. Then a needle went into McCall's leg and nothing registered any more.

Chapter Thirty Six

The road from Jerusalem to the lowest point on earth cuts through the dimpled brown hills where legend has Moses buried, passes by Bedouin camps all tethered with goats then heads down to the soupy, turquoise waters of the Dead Sea. The mountains of Jordan border the eastern shore, pinkish-purple in the salinated haze and to the west rise the sheer cliffs of the Judean desert, a thousand feet above. They say the ruins of Sodom and Gomorrah are submerged thereabouts, destroyed by a rain of burning sulphur when God judged their peoples wicked. Only stones and rocks remain giving cover to the darting lizards and tiny orange flowers, baking in the *hamsin* winds that roll from the desert like draughts from an oven.

It was near this place that McCall was taken.

'Why are you in Israel?'

'I'm here to see some people.'

'What people will you see?'

'Why do you need to know?'

'Why won't you answer?'

'Because it's none of your damned business and I don't know who you are.'

McCall's cussedness was not without risk. But it owed much to a broken body and the king of all hangovers from whatever drug had knocked him out. His captors wouldn't untape his eyes and hands, either – so he had pissed himself like a child.

'What is your interest in Mr Minsky?'

'Hasn't he told you himself?'

His interrogator sounded young but wasn't Arab or Israeli. He spoke accented English though McCall couldn't work out from where.

'Why are you pursuing him?'

'Let me go and I'll tell you.'

McCall's hands and legs were tied to the wooden chair where he sat. The floor was cement hard. His voice echoed slightly, as if off the inside of a wall. He had to be in a building.

'I have some advice for you, Mr McCall. Leave Israel. Forget all about Mr Minsky.'

'And why should I do that?'

McCall was answered with two punches to the face – quick and hard so his nose bled and his eyes watered and snot ran into his mouth.

"Don't try and be smart. Just do yourself a favour – leave well alone and fuck off while you still can."

Everything went quiet then a car started up and drove away. McCall was alone. Flies began settling on his bloody face. He could not bend low enough to shield himself from them or bear to worsen his migraine by shaking his head. It was another torture. He strained violently against the tapes around his wrists till they bled, too. His screams turned to sobs, his anger to self-pity.

Maybe an hour passed before he heard a vehicle labouring across rough ground towards him. He was terrified of his kidnappers coming back. But he started shouting anyway. Then two car doors slammed shut... footsteps came closer – and the tap, tap, tap of a walking stick.

'Who is it? Who are you?'

No one answered but McCall felt his hands and legs being cut free then a tearing pain as his blindfold was pulled off. The light was sudden and piercingly bright. It took a full minute before McCall could see his rescuers. Two men stood before him. One he had never seen before. The other was Arie Minsky.

Bea waited on the veranda of a cabin at kibbutz Ein Gedi, a few miles further south but still overlooking the Dead Sea. They grew peppers and avocados there, made the desert bloom with exotic flowers. It was Bea's vision of paradise yet she dreaded the coming hour.

The kibbutz paramedic drove up in his little open truck. Arie was crouched in the back where McCall was stretched out on a bundle of sacks. The two men laid him down indoors like a corpse from a cross for Bea to undress then bathe as only a mother might.

She could have wept at how he looked – eyes swollen, face bruised yellow and caked with blood, body bent with hunger and all the re-disturbed injuries of his car crash. They gave him water and tablets to make him sleep. Bea stayed with him all day and all night. She never left his side.

Minsky returned to Akko. McCall was best left alone with Bea for the present. He rested for much of each day. Bea brought his meals to where he sat in the garden outside – yoghurt, fruit, cold meats, cheese – and smiled her crooked smiles as his strength slowly returned.

She said Evie was back in London but knew she would want to send love. McCall didn't respond. Bea's speech was becoming less jumbled but McCall didn't really want to talk, not until three nights after he had arrived. They were sitting beneath uncountable millions of stars, each a reminder of the smallness of human existence, of how little we know, still less understand.

'Why didn't you tell me the truth about my parents, Bea?'

'Couldn't... so hard.'

'But I've remembered, you see.'

'Wanted to... Mac, believe please.'

'Then why didn't you?'

'Moment passed... older you were, truth more pain for you.'

'So it was better I lived a lie?'

'Did our best, Mac... believe, please.'

He did... up to a point. Yet part of him would always feel tricked, as if something beyond value been taken from him. He had it back now – but only at a price. Yet if the coin he'd paid had the heads of Elizabeth and Edward McCall on one side, stamped on the other were the faces of three dead Nazis. Bea still had questions to answer about them.

'Who kidnapped me, Bea? Who kidnapped me and why did they do it?'

'Not know, Mac.'

'Tell me the truth this time. It was Arie, wasn't it?'

'Cannot say. Please, cannot.'

'I know about Arie and those Nazis who died.'

No, no, no –'

'And all about you... cheating on Francis.'

'No, no, no.'

Bea stood up with both hands to her ears like a child not wanting to listen anymore. Then she locked herself in the bedroom. It was what Helen would have done if he had ever been given chance to confront her, too.

Arie Minsky returned to Ein Gedi next morning. On one level, McCall owed Minsky for freeing him. But how could he have known where McCall would be if he hadn't put him there in the first place? Minsky had survived behind Nazi lines, taken years to hunt down his enemies and get away with murder. He had motives aplenty to throw a scare into McCall. But for now, both were locked in an uneasy stand off.

'Feeling any better, Mac?'

'A bit, yes. Thank you.'

'I remember you in short pants... skinny little kid, always playing cowboys and Indians in Garth Woods.'

Minsky smiled fondly to himself.

'And now you're the sheriff, after me for murder.'

McCall's stomach tightened. He was not ready for this, physically or any other way. Minsky looked a good two decades younger than his eighty odd years, lean and toned and tempered in fires that those who'd seen would never forget.

'We have much to discuss, Mac.'

Minsky walked with him to a table beyond the kibbutz's dining hall where the aerial roots of a Banyan tree formed a stockade against the fierce sun. Black and white wheatears dipped and drank in water spilling from a fountain of Egyptian porphyry. Here there was peace. Minsky brought them omelettes, orange juice, baklava. He was a fastidious eater. No crumb was allowed to settle on his white shirt, no flake of pastry on his chin.

'Whatever you think of me, Mac, you must go easy on Bea.'

'In what way must I?'

'You must never forget that most bereaved kids are good at convincing adults they're fine because that's what the adults want to hear.'

'You mean it makes it easier for them?'

'In a way, yes. But for Bea and Francis, where was the wisdom in making you retrieve something so terrible that your subconscious had already buried it deep?'

The sound of the water fountain reminded McCall of the stream in Garth Woods, of Francis so burdened and betrayed, of innocence lost.

'How could such a thing happen... my mother and father to die like that?'

Arie Minsky hesitated, but only for a moment.

'The newspapers said it was murder and then suicide.'

'Half wrong – as usual.'

'Well, only one person could ever say for sure what happened that day, Mac...'

'Yeah... I know that now. I know it was an accident. The gun just fell on the floor while they were having a row. My father didn't mean to kill her. He wasn't a murderer... he didn't have to kill himself.'

Minsky nodded in agreement. But he was grimly aware that McCall needed to be confronted by a second painful truth if he was to understand the one which had just been so grievously revealed to him by accident. Minsky began to tell him how Edward McCall cracked up on a bombing mission with Francis and was then unjustly convicted of cowardice.

'He'd been a hero till that raid, Mac... a hero to be broken on the wheel of war and humiliation as a warning to others. His life fell apart after that... he couldn't take it.'

Debts mounted, despite help from Francis, so Edward and Elizabeth left Somerset and took their son to Devon. That was where the shooting tragedy happened. Francis's fake newspaper article was an attempt to lay a false trail should his stepson ever set out in search of his parents.

'Never, ever forget, Mac – Bea and Francis acted in good faith, in your best interest as they saw it.'

McCall listened to this new evidence as a juror might hear the family context of an appalling crime. Yet he knew nothing anyone could say anymore would fill the emptiness he still felt inside... the void where his mother should have been.

Chapter Thirty Seven

'Come on, Mac, let's take a trip into the desert... you and me.'

'Without your goons this time?'

'I haven't got any *goons*.'

'So who kidnapped me and how did you know where'd I'd be?'

'Israel's a small country. Not much happens here without certain people finding out.'

'Then you'll know who my kidnappers were?'

'The question isn't simply *who*, Mac... it's *why* that's more interesting.'

They drove to Masada, a mountain fortress towering above the Dead Sea. Soldiers of Rome's Tenth Legion laid siege to a band of Jewish fighters at Masada soon after the time of Christ. Faced by slavery or death, the rebels chose to put themselves to their own swords and Masada came to symbolise sacrifice and resistance against an oppressor.

A steep path zig-zagged up through sheer falls of scree and rock to the incandescent summit, fourteen hundred feet above. McCall should never have set out on such a climb. He was too weak, the heat too fierce. It took nearly two hours to reach the top. McCall was all in – and was about to be tested further in such a place as the devil challenged Jesus to turn stone into bread.

'So, Mac – let's hear it, tell me about the evidence you've got against me.'

McCall felt cornered... put up or shut up. He had no choice but to spell out what he'd discovered of the suspicious deaths of the three Nazis in Bea's photograph – Rösler, Frank and Virbalis – and the conspiracy he alleged she, Francis and Minsky were in.

'Is that it, Mac? Is that all you've got?'

'So it's not true? It's all a coincidence?'

'Whether it is or it isn't, you must know you'll never fly that by a libel lawyer.'

A group of off duty Israeli soldiers passed by with a guide, about to learn that survival never came without a butcher's bill.

'All right, I've heard you out now do you want to hear my side?'

'Sure, Arie. I'd hate to think someone wanted me dead for no reason.'

Minsky's eyes hardened against him.

'You need to listen and learn, my friend. Rösler died in a freak road accident. That's not me saying it – the German police say it. They also say that Wilhelm Frank got lost in those underground tunnels and starved to death. And here's something you might not know but Yanis Virbalis committed suicide because he knew the Soviet authorities were making moves to extradite him from Canada to stand trial for war crimes in Lithuania.'

'So why did Francis film each of these men?'

'He's dead. We can't ask him. But he took his camera everywhere. You know that.'

'But why do you appear in the footage of Rösler and Frank?'

'My passport from then will show I was never in Germany, or Canada, either.'

'But Bea and Francis were, at the relevant times.'

'Yes, on diplomatic postings or one sort or another – so what?'

'But you worked with Virbalis, on the railways. You lodged across the street from him with old Miss Deware –'

'A woman who's been blind from birth. What a persuasive witness she will make.'

'How do you know she's been blind from birth?'

'That's my business.'

'I bet it is. OK, why was Bea giving a talk at the school that Virbalis's daughter attended on the very night he supposedly committed suicide?'

'Mac, Mac – first a blind witness, now an alcoholic... or had she sobered up by the time you got her into bed?'

Even in the desert, Minsky wasn't breaking sweat to outbox him.

'Mac, whatever you *think* you've got, it's going nowhere... is it?'

Minsky's whole manner changed then. He pushed back his curling, silver hair and placed a protective arm around McCall's shoulder.

'Let us not fall out about this. Come, let me show you the world from on top of Masada so you might see a few things about history that really matter.'

They walked in silence through the roofless buildings where the rebels against Rome had lived and prayed, kept amphorae of wine, taken ritual baths and finally slaughtered themselves. The remains of a man and boy were found intact beside that of a young woman, hair still in braids, dainty leather sandals at her feet, all preserved for two thousand years in the hot, dry air. Nearby were pyramids of huge stone balls, still waiting to be heaved down on an enemy long since gone to dust – just as those he had sought to conquer.

'That's all they had back then, Mac... rocks. Rocks against a Roman legion.'

Minsky leaned over the casemated walls and looked down on black, fan-tailed ravens wheeling over the wilderness that shimmered into the Negev desert.

"You can't report this on the BBC but we're making nuclear bombs over there... a place called Dimona. We never admit it but those who would push us into the sea know about it... and I'm glad they do for we'll not die like we did, without price, ever again."

Between Masada and Dimona had come the blood and ashes of the Holocaust. McCall still believed the three old Nazis died in revenge for some collective sin from that time – however hard Minsky tried to convince him otherwise.

And if McCall now understood how and why his first father came to be called a murderer, it followed that he felt compelled to discover what had driven the second to actually become one. McCall would stick close to Minsky, whatever the risk to his health.

Chapter Thirty Eight

The cries of peacocks echoed back from the bare mountain escarpment beyond the kibbutz garden where Bea and McCall walked arm in arm through an aisle of palm trees to a bench in the shade.

'Angry with me, aren't you?'

'No Bea, not about my parents... not anymore.'

'Then about Francis and Arie?'

'Yes, I am a little... you know I am.'

They found a place to sit and Bea took McCall's hand as she had on their first walk, far away and long ago in the woods of Garth Hall. Time was a luxury she no longer had and not all her secrets should be buried with her.

'We couldn't child get, Mac... Francis, me.'

'I know. It must have been so upsetting for you both.'

'Like you and Helen.'

'Except Helen *did* have a baby.'

'Not yours, though.'

'No, that's true... it probably wasn't mine.'

'Same as me.'

'But you didn't have a baby.'

'Not baby from Francis, no. Arie baby.'

McCall withdrew his hand.

'Minsky? You mean you had a baby with Minsky?'

'Yes, Arie baby.'

McCall stood up so he could look down upon her.

'God, Bea. You did *that* to Francis as well?'

He turned to leave but she pulled him back.

'Listen me, Mac... please.'

She began a disjointed account of how she had met Minsky in Prague then escaped from the Nazis only to miscarry their child and never be able to conceive again.

'Price of sin, Mac... I paid much.'

Bea met and married Francis later but in those less enlightened times, she could not risk disgrace by confessing why she was barren – or that her love for Arie hadn't died.

Then Francis and Minsky became friends. Francis accepted his rival's part in Bea's life for he worshipped her unconditionally and just as she was – imperfectly adorable.

'Francis didn't judge me, Mac.'

Maybe he didn't. But McCall could not forget those childhood memories of Francis being too bereft to explain why Bea was missing from both their lives nor his last days when he had called her a witch. But there was nothing more to be said or done that would make a jot of difference any more.

Bea now intended to stay in Israel for whatever span remained to her. She wanted nothing of England anymore. All that she had was Mac's. He thought about trying to comb her out some more about the dead Nazis but Minsky arrived before he could. Neither man had concluded his business with the other.

They drove away in Minsky's Volvo. McCall watched Bea in the wing mirror, waving, and getting smaller every moment.

Little was said in the hour or so it took to reach the hotel in Jerusalem where McCall should have stayed on the night he was abducted. He paid the overdue bill and retrieved his travel bag then joined Minsky for mint tea in a café by the Street of Sorrows.

Minsky, open blue shirt, pale linen suit, had a foreign correspondent's knack for knowing where best to get watered. McCall unzipped his bag. He could now even the score and produce his research – the notes, documents, pictures linking the suspicious deaths that Minsky so mockingly derided. He caught Minsky smiling.

'Don't waste your time, my friend. What you are looking for will not be there.'

McCall tried not to panic. All the clothes and clutter from his empty bag lay on the table between them. But Minsky was right. The research file was missing.

'OK, Arie. Where is it? Who's got it?'

'If you'd have played this game as long as me, Mac, you wouldn't even have to ask.'

'Look, I've been kidnapped and beaten up and now my stuff's been stolen –'

'Keep calm, Mac.'

'How the hell can I when you're having me over like this?'

McCall raged inside, not just at Minsky but at his own stupidity. He should have had copies made of everything and put somewhere safe.

'What's missing is proof of nothing, Mac. It's neither here nor there that it's gone.'

'But Francis set me on all this. Francis left me the clues.'

'Dear, dear Francis. He killed thousands of Germans, you know… bombed them to hell, innocent or guilty. His mind must have got so mixed up in the end.'

'By what, Arie?'

'Oh, the usual… love, grief, remorse. All the regrets that keep the old from their sleep. Come, McCall. Let me show you what keeps me from mine.'

They drove towards the coast in silence, to a museum of the nearly indescribable. It was closed but Minsky knew how to have any door opened. Inside was cool and dimly lit for what was on show was alien to the light of day.

Huge photographs were suspended on boards from the ceiling, blow-ups of people and places to guide the visitor through a brief moment in time, from the ghettoes to the gas chambers.

Lodz, Bialystok, Warsaw, Vilna…Auschwitz, Mauthausen, Treblinka, Chelmno.

So it went on… snapshots from the world's end. A child might hold a doll, a woman a fur coat or an elderly man a string bag with all his life inside it. In their faces could be fear or hope. But naked at the edge of the pit, they would all look the same. They would all burn. Minsky stood in front of a cast iron door salvaged from a death camp furnace. He put the outstretched fingers of his right hand to its rough blackness, as if to commune for a moment with all those whose lives it had shut out. Alongside was a large map showing areas the Nazis had made *Juden frei* by 1944. A slab of metal, a piece of paper. Nothing connected to everything.

The only sounds were their footsteps, Minsky's walking stick, the distant air-con. No clock was needed here. Time was on hold forever. A hill of shoes confronted them – men's, women's, children's. All sizes, all colours, lace-ups, button-sided, slip-ons, sandal-strapped.

Here were artefacts from a world as archeologically lost as Masada and its skeletons. Minsky turned one over in his hand… a tiny, calf leather bootee, white going yellow and as soft as the skin of the baby who would have worn it.

McCall stared across at Minsky, suddenly grown very old.

'That's the infinite cruelty for visitors to this place, McCall – never knowing if it was your child or your wife or your parents who wore this or touched that… '

Minsky closed his eyes and put the little shoe to his face to breathe in all that it was, all that it meant, for he had nothing else to hold onto.

'Try to imagine, McCall… all that anger and hatred in your head, eating away at you like a cancer. How would you deal with it?'

'I can start to understand someone's desire to have revenge for a great wrong, but then to scheme and plan for it over several years and to kill in cold blood… well, that's a rare form of hatred.'

'Though not unknown.'

'Maybe not but if a Jew murdered some old Nazi this way, it'd be wrong but people might understand why. What's harder to figure out would be a non-Jew's motivation.'

'Well, hypothetically, let us say such a person, a woman for instance, lost a child and blamed the Nazis for her loss and so strongly did she psychologically identify with the suffering of Jewish mothers that there was nothing she wouldn't do to hold those responsible to account.'

'But Arie, what if this fictional woman needed her non Jewish husband to help her? Why would he act outside the law and take such a risk?'

'Because love between people is a complex and inexplicably powerful force, McCall.'

They left the museum's bleak, necrotic imagery and drove up the Mediterranean road to Akko. It was into the sea off Israel that the ashes of Adolf Eichmann were dumped after he was hanged and the ghosts they had just left could rejoice. McCall said he had been told Minsky played a part in Eichmann's capture.

'No, that's just gossip. I was never there.'

'No? Ah, well... but if nothing else, Eichmann proves it's better to put someone on public trial than to bump them off in some dark corner.'

'In the case of Eichmann, I agree. To see him in his glass cage before the Jewish people and Jewish judges was hugely symbolic. It proved the Nazis had failed to destroy us. But not all the cases were like Eichmann's.'

They walked the length of Akko's defensive sea walls in virtual silence, by the groin-vaulted passageways of the old town where Venetians, Pisans and Genoese quartered themselves with Jews and Arabs long before the violent coming of the Templars and the Teutonic Knights of the Crusades. Old blood, bad blood. It had lustrated the very stones they trod. McCall detected Minsky becoming increasingly preoccupied, oblivious to their surroundings. Then he stopped and faced McCall and made what could have been a plea of mitigation to a court before details of the crime itself had been heard.

'You must believe one thing, Mac... I was not born to be a killer. Parts of my life I regret most bitterly but I had no choice. I was caught up in the war, in events without precedent and these made me the man I became in a world where it was barely possible to remain human when everything around us had become so *inhuman.*'

McCall said nothing. He wasn't required to. Minsky began to tell the story of what had happened to his wife and children and sister amid the trees and picnic places of Ponar. His source was a neighbour from Vilna who'd survived against all the odds, someone who knew his family – and who also found out the identity of a man in the SS killing squad which had exterminated everyone Minsky loved.

'That man's name, McCall... it grew like a tumour in my gut until it consumed everything I was. I had to find him and I didn't care how long it took or what methods must be employed. I would find that man and I would bring him to *my* justice.'

'And did you?'

'Eventually, many years later, yes.'

'That can't have been an easy or a simple task.'

'No...I needed the help of some good people.'

'But you eventually confronted this SS man?'

'In his home, yes.'

'What in God's name did you say to him?'

'He was given a choice. He had all the addresses of his former comrades and we had some petrol and a lighter.'

'*We*?'

'You'll get no details from me, McCall... it is enough to say the SS man understood the terms of the deal he was being offered and we got what we wanted.'

'Without burning him alive?'

'That came later.'

'You mean - ?'

'Cars can be dangerous things, Mac, especially if something goes wrong with them.'

'Christ, Arie. This was Rösler, wasn't it? Jakob Rösler – '

'Who is to say, McCall... though such a man with that same name was at Ponar and such a man took lots of photographs of his brave comrades going about their daily work.'

'And such a man died in a car crash, didn't he?'

'I cannot say, I wasn't there.'

'And were Wilhelm Frank and Yanis Virbalis in that same SS squad, too?'

Minsky just shrugged. He would make no more admissions, however oblique. McCall continued to play the priest.

'Arie, did any of these hard deaths ease your own pain?'

'No.'

'Or bring back a single one of the six million who died.'

'No... they didn't.'

'So it was all pointless... the most Pyrrhic of victories.'

'If you say so.'

'Then why are you telling me any of this now?'

'Because you deserve something Mac... and maybe I need something, too.'

'To confess, you mean?'

'But not on television, my friend. I'm giving you no corroboration for anything.'

'So nothing you've said is evidence of anything?'

'That's right. I could be making it all up.'

'And I'm not going to get my research file back, am I?'

'They'll ask me to become Pope before that happens.'

McCall knew he had been out-flanked by an infinitely wilier opponent.

'But I've still got all the footage Francis shot if I wanted to use it.'

'Really? Then I must give you my address in Rome.'

'You mean that's been stolen, too?'

'Not by *me*, Mac. Get that into your head.'

'Then who?'

'You won't want to know this but there's something at my house you must see before I answer that.'

Chapter Thirty Nine

The basement in Minsky's house doubled as a bomb shelter in case of rocket attack from Lebanon or Syria or an enemy who thought Hitler's work unfinished. In his heart, Minsky wearied of war. He wished only to die in peace, far from the saps and trenches of the front line wherein all his days had been spent. That was possible now – but on Bea's terms. She said McCall had been through enough and was owed the truth... or as much of it as Minsky felt able to impart. So the two men sat in a windowless room of books on military conflict and politics and pictures of Minsky meeting army generals or alongside tanks or with pilots who had just ruined somebody's day. It was an old man's domain, full of memories but no plans.

'As soldiers, we were always taught to obey orders –'

It was enough now for McCall to sit quiet and sip the iced water he'd been given.

'– But I'd always the poet in me... thinking for myself. Not really a team player. I was in the Jewish underground in the thirties then the war came and I fought with the British. Afterwards, we wanted those Jews who'd escaped the Holocaust to come to Palestine but the British wouldn't allow it and the man we came to blame for this was your Foreign Secretary back then, Ernest Bevin. You've heard of him?'

'Of course.'

'Well, I was sent to London to kill Bevin.'

The headline brevity of Minsky's admission was meant to shock. And it did.

'But Bevin didn't get assassinated.'

'No. I thought my orders were bad politics so I sabotaged the plan.'

'How could you do that?'

'By then I knew Francis and we came to an arrangement. I gave him Bevin's life.'

'You did what?'

'I gave him Bevin's life.'

'In return for what?'

'First, we Jews avoided creating a whole lot more enemies which is what would've happened if I'd assassinated a big European politician. Then Francis agreed to give me a bit of unofficial help on something else.'

'I don't follow. What could he help you with?'

'A bit of rat catching.'

Everyone had gained. Francis edged up Whitehall's greasy pole, Minsky's family was avenged, Bevin kept breathing. The cost – a few worthless snuffed-out lives. The arithmetic didn't remotely upset men whose generation counted deaths in millions.

'So you're saying Francis *was* implicated... and by inference, Bea, too?'

'I'm saying nothing that can be proved or quoted, Mac. But if you want to know who's stolen your material then look no further than the mourners at Francis's funeral.'

'Don't be ridiculous. They were just old men.'

'They are *now*. But once they were Francis's closest friends and colleagues... and who amongst us wants their secret past exposing on television?'

McCall thought immediately of steely Mr Fewtrell who'd heard the evil of Nuremberg and of some of the other pensioners at the graveside, tied till death in the black life of Intelligence.

'So you're saying *these* people knew?'

'Of course they did. Francis needed his unofficial back covering.'

'But why would he film everything and leave evidence to implicate you all?'

194

'We needed positive identities. Just imagine if we'd got it wrong.'

'But Francis kept the footage – '

'It was a bit of insurance on me, Mac. I'd have done the same in his position.'

Minsky went to a cupboard and took out a video cassette.

'Anyway, it's all academic now, Mac. When you get home, the chances are someone will have done a little housekeeping in the dacha...'

McCall's head went into his hands.

'...So I'm afraid you're always going to be stuck between what you know and what you can show."

Minsky slotted the tape into his recorder and dimmed the lights.

'This won't help you much but Francis sent it to me when his crisis of conscience began to affect him and we started to worry what he'd do next.'

> *We all conk out some time, Arie, and I find myself doing a bit of cleaning up after myself and the mess I've made of things in my life, not just the war, though God knows how I'll explain myself at the Pearly Gates... no, it's afterwards that's bothering me. I'm ashamed, shouldn't have done what I did... gone along with it for as long but the truth was whatever Bea wanted, Bea got. I wouldn't have denied her the moon on a stick if she'd asked for it but I want you to take care of her when the time comes. She loved you more... I've always known that. I want you to look out for young Mac, too. I'm leaving him a few clues about what's nagging at me but there are still people around who'll not want him to succeed. He'll come to you for guidance in due course so please don't turn him away. He is my son and you must treat him as such for all this has cost me my peace of mind. I think that's everything I need say so mark my words my friend and find a god to pray to for forgiveness.*

Francis stared hard into the camera then moved out of shot. Minsky removed the tape.

'You'll not need me to tell you this, Mac, but Francis was the most ethical and moral of men. It was Francis who put a stop to what had been going on.'

'How did he do that?'

'After Canada, he felt it was all wrong and like you, he said it wasn't bringing a single victim back to life. I've told you already. Men like Francis and me, we weren't born to be killers. We were made to become so.'

'Did Bea agree to call a halt?'

'Not immediately but what Francis was saying got to us. The emptiness of it all... the brutality. I knew the scales would never balance, even if I drowned in the blood of all those I held responsible. That's the truth of it... and that's the price I'll pay till the day I die.'

A pair of jet fighters spun over Minsky's house towards the border with Lebanon, drowning out the cooing collared doves in his aloe trees. McCall was alone in the garden trying to unpick Francis's motives, to make sense at last of why he had willed him his incoherent story.

Francis could have been exacting revenge on a faithless wife or using McCall as an instrument of jealously to harm the real tenant of Bea's heart from beyond the grave. But that ran counter to everything McCall knew about a man he had loved. Francis was trying to atone. McCall felt sure of it.

And in his gathering dementia, he'd conflated one guilt with another – that for incinerating all those unseen German civilians with the greater burden of conspiring with Bea and Minsky to bring about the deaths of three men without the justification of war and thereby keep her affections. In the end, what did it amount to but murder? What else but madness was its reward?

Minsky suggested a drink in a bar on the waterfront. The setting sun gilded the ocean and lit the little triangles of canvas bending home toward port. Sea birds fell from the warm, evening sky and came among the honey-stoned houses of Akko's old town. A church bell rang the hour and children were called indoors. Cats fought, dogs barked and the sea sucked at the rocks below.

Insofar as McCall knew his story now, he was becoming reconciled to never telling it. Any public interest was far outweighed by personal harm. Rosa Virbalis had been right. So had the old cop in Oberammergau.

Minsky carried a dish of olives and bread and two glasses of beer to their table. They toasted each other – not as friends but as combatants coming to a truce.

'Arie, you must tell Bea not to worry. Your story isn't going to come out. I'll only mention it to Evie and her job's keeping secrets so it'll go no further.'

Minsky set his glass down on the metal table between them.

'I wouldn't bother doing that, McCall.'

'Why? Bea's told her, has she?'

'You really are still concussed, aren't you?'

'Sorry, I don't follow.'

Minsky leaned forward and took McCall's hands in his own.

'It was Evie who traded you in, my friend.'

'*Evie...?*'

'Yes... how else could the mourners have got into you?'

196

'No, no, you're wrong, Arie. She wouldn't do that.'

'I'm afraid Evie's got other loyalties.'

'Look, Evie's coming to live with me... in Garth. That's the plan. Honestly. We're setting up home together directly I get back.'

'Listen, Mac. Evie's got a husband... he's called Phillip, he teaches history at University College.'

'No, she's had boyfriends, but –'

'Honestly, Mac. Evie's moved out of Highgate, gone back to Phillip in Clapham. Her flat's already been re-let.'

McCall stared back at him. He suddenly felt Evie's kiss on his cheek. Then a great sadness and a sickness for home swept over him. He wanted to be away and out of this foreign place, to be far from its lies and to be beneath the trees of an ancient wood where the wind blew and the water ran and the spirits of childhood might return him to all those secret places he had lost. Arie Minsky, the childless man, understood this and held McCall as a father might, close and tender, for he more than anyone else knew that neither of them would ever find their way back there again.

THE END

Lightning Source UK Ltd.
Milton Keynes UK
UKOW01f1032121017

310861UK00011B/613/P